THE PATRIOT

This is the translation by Robert Scott-Buccleuch of the novel by Lima Barreto — *Triste Fim de Policarpo Quaresma*, first published in Rio de Janeiro in 1911.

THE PATRIOT

LIMA BARRETO

TRANSLATED BY
ROBERT SCOTT-BUCCLEUCH

REX COLLINGS • LONDON • 1978
In association with *SEL EDITORA: RIO DE JANEIRO*

First published in Great Britain by Rex Collings Ltd
69 Marylebone High Street, London W1

ISBN 0 86 036060 1

Typesetting by Malvern Typesetting Services
Printed in Great Britain by Biddles Limited, Guildford, Surrey

Contents

A Brazilian Don Quixote

'A Brazilian Don Quixote': this was how, in 1916, the essayist and critic Oliveira Lima hailed the novel *Triste Fim de Policarpo Quaresma* ('The Sad End of Policarpo Quaresma') now published in English under the title of *The Patriot*. Its author, Lima Barreto (1881–1922), a Mulatto from Rio de Janeiro, belonged to the lower middle-class of the Brazilian Second Empire, being born seven years before the abolition of slavery in the country, and eight years before the Republic.

His father had been a printer — working at the same time at the Rio newspaper *Tribuna Liberal* and at the National Press — who, held as being pro-Emperor, lost both jobs when the Republic was proclaimed in 1889. The son, Afonso Henriques de Lima Barreto, to use his full name, wanted to be an engineer, went through primary and secondary schools, and was approved at the Polytechnic College's entrance examination, but the illness of his father, who became insane in 1902, prevented him from going on with his studies. He then started to write for newspapers and became what could at the time be called in Brazil a professional journalist.

Lima Barreto's first novel, *Recordações do Escrivão Isaias Caminha*, was published in 1909. *The Patriot* was written two years later especially to be serialized in the Rio newspaper *O Jornal do Comercio* where it ran from 11 August to 19 October 1911. Published in book form in 1915, it was not unanimously well received as Oliveira Lima's comparison with Don Quixote seems to indicate. By the standards of previous Brazilian literature the book was written in such a new narrative language that to some critics it had no meaning. However, many of his fellow-writers saw immediately that that poor Negro, who was then also a civil servant at the Ministry of War, had something to add to the literature of his country.

By calling it *The Patriot*, the English translator of the novel, Mr Scott-Buccleuch, shows the heart of the matter. What Policarpo Quaresma insists on being—as well as what Lima Barreto himself was—can only be explained by this perhaps old-fashioned word 'patriot'. Policarpo sees his country as the best possible place in the world to live in, and the rivers of Brazil are the widest, the longest, the most beautiful of all rivers, and the land is the most fertile, and he tops his patriotic ideology by proclaiming that the Tupí language—the old *lingua franca* of the Brazilian Indians—should be officially adopted by the country to replace the colonial language, the European Portuguese.

My generation was deeply influenced by Lima Barreto's, or Policarpo's ideas. We were all very nationalistic. When I was writing my very first poems and short stories, I and a group of young men in Rio decided to learn Tupí and to write our poems and stories in Tupí. We used to meet in a café at the Saens Peña Square in the borough of Tijuca, to discuss our ideas and to show each other how far we had gone with our Tupí writings. This was at the end of the thirties. In the Second World War Brazil was the only Latin American country to send soldiers to fight, under a British commander in Italy, and my generation accepted, perhaps a little reluctantly, the idea of also being part of a European cultural heritage.

In the novel Policarpo is, as Lima Barreto himself might have been, appalled by the contrast between the country—or his ideas on the country—and the establishment, or the people who, being the Government, were the symbols of the establishment. The strong man of the Brazilian Republic, Marshall Floriano Peixoto, is still today a controversial character, and Lima Barreto sees and depicts him with all the ideas of the Brazilian liberals of the last decade of the nineteenth century. In so doing he writes a political novel, in a different way from how Stendhal understood the expression, and he shows the Brazilian scene in a period of turmoil and change. Mainly on account of *The Patriot* Lima Barreto must be seen not only as the novelist of his time in Brazil but also as its historian.

His style, in writing his stories, is different from that of another Brazilian writer, Machado de Assis (1839–1908), also a mulatto from Rio de Janeiro, held by many as the best stylist in Portuguese prose in the last two centuries. Machado had a kind of Lawrence Sterne style, with an irony that made him the possessor of a literary excellence rare in the Americas. Lima Barreto, on the other hand, was more serious-minded, saying exactly what he meant to say, but the irony is also there, perhaps a bitter irony in which the weaknesses and strengths of the middle class parade before you.

The Patriot is also a novel of Rio de Janeiro. It shows the then capital-city of Brazil in its moment of change, when it started to transform its old colonial aspect into a new New World city. The novelist lived in the suburbs of Rio, and these suburbs were a new facet of the city he knew so well. He spent his whole life in Rio de Janeiro or its surroundings, having very rarely been far from it (one year before he died he went to the State of São Paulo, 200 miles from Rio de Janeiro). In his private life Lima Barreto's drinking habits made him a lonely man whose company was not sought after by many of his contemporaries. More than once he had to enter an asylum for treatment.

As an artist he belived in literature as firmly as in a religion. He believed man can be saved by the strength and the power of a literary mysticism. In his own words: '. . . through Art man is not dependent on the biases and prejudices of his time, his birth, his country, his race: he goes beyond all that to reach the total life of the Universe . . .'

ANTONIO OLINTO
London, July 1977

Introduction

There is a much quoted phrase of Alexandre Herculano: 'A língua portuguesa é o túmulo do pensamento,' which may be loosely interpreted as meaning that literature written in the Portuguese language is doomed to remain unknown by the non-Portuguese speaking world, that is by the overwhelming majority of educated men and women. Innumerable examples could be cited to support the truth of this, but perhaps none is so striking as that afforded by the figure of the Brazilian writer Lima Barreto.

Generally acknowledged as one of Brazil's leading novelists, Lima Barreto immediately invites comparison with the father of the Brazil novel himself, Machado de Assis: both were mulattos, both lived in and wrote about Rio de Janeiro, and the work of both is deeply rooted in the European tradition. But whereas the works of Machado de Assis have been laboriously dissected by departments of Luso-Brazilian studies in Europe and the United States, and in translation made known to a wide reading public, Lima Barreto remains almost entirely unknown outside his own country and Portugal.

There are various reasons, which will be suggested later, for this neglect. Fortunately, however, there are signs of a revival of interest in Lima Barreto both in Brazil and abroad. In 1952 he was the subject of one of the finest biographies written in Brazil—*A Vida de Lima Barreto* by Francisco de Assis Barbosa, to whom I am indebted not only for the biographical sketch which follows, but also for his encouragement when I first proposed undertaking the translation of the present work.

Furthermore, important studies of his works are proceeding in the United States, the U.S.S.R. and Czechoslovakia. These will no doubt help to make Lima Barreto's name better known in academic circles, but they will not introduce him to the vast reading public. Here we must acknowledge the force of Alexandre Herculano's half-truth, recognizing that writers such as Lima Barreto can be rescued from semi-oblivion only by the translator.

Afonso Henriques de Lima Barreto was born on 13 May, 1881 and died on 1 November, 1922. His short life-time saw a complete transformation of life in Brazil; this was due not only to those events and influences that affected the world at large, but also to profound changes taking place within Brazil itself. He had childhood memories of such far-reaching events as the Liberation of the Slaves in 1888, and the Proclamation of the Republic in 1889. He was a lad of twelve when the rebellion against President Floriano Peixoto broke out in 1893. This episode forms the background to Part 3 of *The Patriot*, and surely such a delightful account of Rio under bombardment could only come from an eye-witness. As a man he saw the transformation of his beloved native city, which lost its old colonial and imperial appearance, into the Rio de Janeiro that is familiar to the modern tourist. Perhaps most important of all, he became bitterly aware of the growing American economic domination of his country.

Both his parents were mulattos, and both appear to have been people of considerable strength of character. His father, João Henriques, was a master typesetter, highly respected in his profession, while his mother, after her marriage, founded and ran a small school for girls. The marriage was a happy one, but unfortunately short-lived: João Henriques was left a widower when Afonso was only seven years old, and there were three younger children to be provided for as well. The early loss of a mother's affection, and the subsequent periods of schooling away from home had an important effect on the formation of an intelligent but abnormally sensitive child.

The boy's intelligence was noted with satisfaction by his father, who determined that Afonso should have the finest education available; his ambition was to make him an engineer. From 1890 to 1894 Afonso attended the Liceu Popular, one of the best schools in the city, whose founder and director was a Mr William Henry Cunditt, a Scotsman and former British Consul in Rio. Three more years were spent in other boarding schools and in studying privately for admission to the Polytechnic School, where he was finally matriculated in 1897. But the engineering course was little to his liking; he was following it merely out of respect to his father. He barely kept abreast of his studies, preferring to spend his time devouring Kant, Spencer, Comte, Condillon, Condorcet and Le Bon.

It was during these Polytechnic years that he began to feel more acutely the double barrier that separated him from the rest of his companions: his poverty and his colour. His wealthy fellow students enjoyed a social life that was denied to him, whilst at the same time the influence of their parents smoothed out any obstacle in the way of their academic progress. It is probable that Lima Barreto bore his poverty cheerfully, but the slights and insults occasioned by his colour caused him the acutest suffering. Every one of his novels bears strong autobiographical influences, and his first published novel, *Recordações do Escrivão Isaías Caminha*, gives vivid instances of the humiliations to which he was subjected.

Being but little interested in his scientific studies Lima Barreto plodded slowly through his Polytechnic course, frequently held up by examination hurdles that his wealthy colleagues easily surmounted. But he was destined not to complete his studies. In 1902 a second tragedy befell the family when the father, João Henriques, went mad. This meant that the responsibility of maintaining the family fell upon the shoulders of the young Afonso. He left school, and with much difficulty, in 1903, obtained a miserably paid post as clerk in the Ministry of War. His father remained a burden to him for the remainder of his life: in fact he outlived his dedicated son by a mere forty-eight hours.

In the years that followed Lima Barreto was obliged to accustom himself to the boring, monotonous work of a humble civil servant; the salary was poor but it was guaranteed, and together with his father's pension kept the family above starvation level. His observations on the deadening nature and the futility of the work in these government offices are to be found in his novel, *Vida e Morte de J. M. Gonzaga de Sá*.

To escape from the depressing atmosphere of his home and the dullness of his work Lima Barreto threw himself into the bohemian life of the city, frequenting cafés, bookshops and libraries, and mixing with artists, journalists, poets and young outspoken thinkers. His great ambition was to be a writer: he wrote articles for newspapers, tried unsuccessfully to become a professional journalist and sketched plans of future novels. The driving force behind this ambition was not a disinterested love of letters; rather it was an urge to expose and if possible rectify the social injustices that, in a land of plenty, condemned so many to life of poverty and misery. There is an implacable social purpose behind almost everything he wrote, and it is this that distinguishes him from Machado de Assis and links him to the great writers of the North-East that were to follow.

In 1907 he founded a literary periodical, *Floreat*. This died an early death the following year, but not before the first chapters of his novel, *Isaías Caminha*, which he published in it, had attracted favourable comment from the eminent critic José Veríssimo. This novel was eventually published in Lisbon in 1909, much to the delight of the aspiring author. But it was very coolly received in Rio, where the bitterness of the satire and the invective against easily recognizable figures in the journalistic world brought about a conspiracy of silence on the part of many newspapers and reviewers.

The publication of his novel did not, as he had hoped, establish him as a writer. Though it was gratifying to the aggrieved mulatto, the ambitious Civil Service clerk, to see his work in print, what he had done was to make powerful enemies and arouse hostility that was to make his already difficult life no easier or happier. In fact the combined effect of the tragic circumstances of his home life, the dull drudgery of his work and the hostility of the literary world he strove to enter drove him deeper and deeper into a life of bohemian abandon. He took to drink, little by little becoming a hopeless

xiii

alcoholic. He became a familiar figure staggering round the streets and bars of the city, eventually becoming the victim of hallucinations as terrible as those that afflicted his poor mad father. In 1914 and again in 1918 he was forcibly confined in asylums, where the doctors diagnosed his complaint as neurasthenia. Each time he was released after a few months, but the cure effected was only temporary; his continued drinking ruined his health, aged him prematurely and was responsible for his death at the early age of forty-one.

One of the many extraordinary things about Lima Barreto is that despite his addiction to alcohol, and its tragic consequences, his mind remained lucid and alert, and he went on writing almost to the day of his death. He even made good use of his personal experience of madness and asylums in several of his works, among them *The Patriot*. Admittedly, by 1911 his best work was behind him — *Isaías Caminha, Gonzaga de Sá*, and his masterpiece, *Triste Fim de Policarpo Quaresma*, to which I have given the title, *The Patriot*. This last established his reputation as an author, and to such an extent that his work was frequently compared, not always unfavourably, with that of Machado de Assis. A number of other novels followed terminating, in the last year of his life, with *Clara dos Anjos*, written in two months, and based on a rough plan he had sketched out eighteen years earlier. These were in addition to a continuous stream of articles on political and literary themes, and a large number of excellent short stories.

For Lima Barreto writing was his whole life; as has already been said, literature was the means by which he expressed his revolt against the social conditions of his time. He vented his fury on the mediocre, complacent established writers, the press lords, the venal politicians, the self-seeking professional men, the industrialists, the Americans, his hatred of Americans being exacerbated by his sympathy for the American Negro, whose humiliation he felt in his own skin. Finally despairing of achieving anything by argument he even advocated violence in order to overthrow the system which condemned the great majority of the people to a life of poverty, serfdom and hopelessness. It is doubtful, though, how seriously he held this view. In practice his ideas were probably closer to those expressed in *The Patriot*—the pessimistic acceptance of the futility of all action, and of violence in particular. But his theories, as well as his art, contain much that will appeal to the modern reader, and not only in Brazil.

Why then was Lima Barreto allowed to sink into relative obscurity at home and oblivion abroad? I suggest there are two main reasons for this. In the first place this served the interests of the Brazilian establishment, who did not relish the home truths flung at them with so much vigour. Not many institutions escaped his attention, and in a country where by tradition the seamier aspects of public life must always be decently concealed behind a transparent cloak of exaggerated politeness, Lima Barreto's direct attacks were, to say the least, in very bad taste. But far more important is the fact that Lima Barreto lived and wrote during a transitional period of Brazilian life and literature. He grew up in the shadow of Machado de Assis, and within a few years of his death the literary centre of gravity had shifted away from Rio to the North-East—to Bahia, Pernambuco and Alagoas. Consequently the interest of students and readers has tended to skip from the dominating figure of Machado de Assis straight on to the colourful and exciting work of such writers as Graciliano Ramos, José Lins do Rego and Jorge Amado, to name but a few. Small wonder then that Lima Barreto has been overlooked, even though his work is a definite link between the two, combining as it does the European ties of Machado de Assis with the profound social consciousness of the North-Eastern writers. That such neglect is undeserved and unjust I hope the present work, which is offered in English translation for the first time, will do something to prove. Moreover, it is my convinced opinion that no student of Brazil can afford to ignore the works of Lima Barreto, and no lover of literature should be denied the opportunity of making acquaintance with such a character as Policarpo Quaresma.

The Patriot is unquestionably Lima Barreto's greatest work. It is so not merely because of the unforgettable (I am tempted to write immortal) character he has created, but because it is written with a restraint and good-humoured tolerance that is scarcely to be found in any of his other novels. He has disciplined the passionate outbursts, curbed the bitterness of his satire and avoided personal attacks on individuals, unless we so qualify his masterly portrait of the national hero, Floriano Peixoto. It certainly offended the supporters of the former president, as well it might, but Lima Barreto's assessment of him has a definite ring of truth about it. Not that this is likely to influence the history books.

The novel embraces a great deal of Brazilian life, a great deal that is typically Brazilian; and be it noted that the word must be Brazilian: the expression Latin-American is meaningless in this context. To many readers some characters and incidents will appear grotesque and exaggerated, but to those who are so fortunate as to have had some contact with this great and essentially loveable people they can only bring a delighted smile of recognition. I refer to such incidents as the civilian bystander being allowed to fire a gun at the enemy (where else in the world could that possibly happen?); to Caldas trying to find his ship; to Quaresma's petition to Congress, and to others. Unfortuntely I also refer to such men as the man from Itamarati, showing the awful, paradoxical capacity for cruelty of a gentle, kind-hearted people. Whoever knows Brazil today knows that this is Brazil. Whoever knows Brazil today knows that Doctor Campos, General Albernaz, Ricardo Coração dos Outros, Armado Borges, Genelício, and all the others in this rich gallery are as alive today as they were half a century ago. And I am glad to think too that Policarpo Quaresma himself is by no means extinct.

But it is not my intention here even to begin a critical assessment of Lima Barreto's work, or of The Patriot; this must be left to others far better qualified than myself. My aim is merely to introduce the writer and his novel to the English reading public and to let the work speak for itself.

ROBERT SCOTT-BUCCLEUCH   Rio de Janeiro, October 1976.

PART ONE

I

The Guitar Lesson

Policarpo Quaresma, better known as Major Quaresma, arrived home at quarter past four in the afternoon as was his custom. For more than twenty years it had always been the same. Leaving the War Ministry Arsenal, where he was under-secretary, he would pick up some fruit in the shops, occasionally buy a cheese, and never fail to get the bread from the French bakery.

This would take him less than an hour so that at twenty to four, or thereabouts, he would catch the tram and be at the threshold of his house in the distant São Januário suburbs at quarter past four to the minute, as exact as the appearance of a star, an eclipse or some such phenomenon which can be mathematically calculated and predicted.

His habits were well known in the neighbourhood; so much so that in Captain Claudio's, where it was the custom to dine at about half past four, as soon as they saw him pass, the lady of the house would call to the maid, 'Alice, it's dinner time; Major Quaresma's just gone by.'

And so it had been every day for almost thirty years. Living in his own house and enjoying a private income over and above his salary, Major Quaresma was able to maintain a standard of living superior to what the latter would normally permit; a fact which won him the consideration and respect of his neighbours, as a man of substance.

He lived in monastic isolation, never receiving anyone,

1

though he was polite with his neighbours, who found him odd and misanthropic. If he had no friends in the district he had no enemies either, and the only hostility he had ever aroused was that of Dr Segadas, a well-known local consultant, who would not admit that Quaresma had his own library of books: 'What for, if he had no university education? Mere pedantry!'

The under-secretary showed his books to no one, but it happened that whenever the windows of his library were opened, the shelves, laden from top to bottom, remained in full view of the road.

Such were his habits; lately, however, there had been certain changes which had provoked comment in the district. Until then the only persons who used to visit him were his goddaughter and her father; but lately a small, thin, pale man with a guitar in a leather case had been seen entering his house regularly three times a week. The curiosity of the neighbourhood was instantly aroused. A guitar in such a respectable house. What could it mean?

That same afternoon one of the most beautiful of the Major's neighbours took a walk with a friend, and together they spent their time strolling up and down, stretching their necks whenever they passed in front of the peculiar under-secretary's window. Their curiosity was not unrewarded. The major was seated on the sofa holding the instrument as if to play and listening attentively to his companion beside him. 'Look, like this, major.' And the strings gently sounded as the note was plucked. Then the teacher explained, 'That's D, you understand?'

No further explanation was needed: the neighbours immediately concluded that the major was learning to play the guitar. But really! A serious man like him engaged in such frivolities!

At about four o'clock one hot afternoon, under the fierce, pitiless March sun, the windows on both sides of a deserted São Januário street were rapidly, almost instantaneously filled. Even in the general's house young ladies flocked to the window. What could it be? A parade? A fire? Nothing of the sort: coming up the road with bent head and taking short steps

2

like a yoked ox was Major Quaresma. Under his arm was a shameless guitar.

It is true that the guitar was decently clad in paper, but its covering scarcely concealed its shape. The scandal reduced somewhat the consideration and respect which Major Policarpo Quaresma enjoyed in the neighbourhood. They said he was out of his mind, mad. But he took no notice and went serenely on with his studies.

Quaresma was a small, thin man and wore pince-nez. His eyes were always downcast, but when he fixed them on someone or something they assumed a sharp brilliance, behind their lenses, as if he wished to penetrate to the very soul of the person or object before him. They were, however, always lowered as if he guided himself by the tip of the goatee which adorned his chin.

He always wore a striped morning coat. The colour might be black, blue or grey, but it had to be a morning coat. And rarely was he to be seen without a tall, narrow-brimmed top hat of an old-fashioned design dear to him.

When he arrived home that day his sister opened the door for him and asked:

'Do you want dinner right away?'

'Not just yet. Wait a little, Ricardo's coming for dinner with us today.'

'Policarpo, have a little more sense. It isn't right for a respectable man of your age and position to be going around with that good for nothing singer.'

The major put down his parasol — an old parasol with a wooden shaft and a curved handle encrusted with small lozenges of mother-of-pearl.

'I'm afraid, sister, that you're greatly mistaken,' he replied. 'It is prejudice to suppose that every man who plays the guitar is a social outcast. The modinha is the truest expression of our national poetry and the instrument most adapted to it is the guitar. It is we who have abandoned the form; but in Lisbon in the last century with Father Caldas, who had an audience of ladies of the aristocracy, it was much in vogue. Beckford, a prominent Englishman, holds it in high esteem.'

3

'But that was long ago; nowadays . . .'

'What difference does that make, Adelaide? We ought not to allow our traditions, our truly national customs to die . . .'

'Very well, Policarpo, I don't wish to contradict you, carry on with your fads if you want to.'

The major went into an adjacent room while his sister disappeared into the house. Quaresma undressed, washed, put on some comfortable clothes and went into the library where he sat down to rest in a rocking chair.

It was a large room with windows looking on to a side street, all lined with book-cases. There were about ten of these, with four shelves, without counting the small ones for the larger volumes. A careful inspection of that immense collection of books left one amazed at the idea behind its organization.

In fiction there were only national authors or those considered as such: Bento Teixeira's *Prosopopéia*; Gregório de Matos, Basílio da Gama, Santa Rita Durão, José de Alencar (complete), Macedo, Gonçalves Dias (complete) as well as many others. For sure there was not a single national or naturalized author from the eighties until then missing from the major's shelves.

There was a rich collection on Brazilian History: The chroniclers, Gabriel Soares, Gandavo; and Rocha Pita, Frei Vicente do Salvador, Armitage, Aires do Casal, Pereira da Silva, Handelmann (*Geschichte von Brasilien*), Melo Morais, Capistrano de Abreu, Southey, Varnhagen, as well as others rarer and less well known. And as regards travel and exploration what wealth there was! There were Hans Staden, Jean de Léry, Saint-Hilaire, Martius, Prince de Neuwied, John Mawe, von Eschwege, Agassiz, Couto de Magalhães, and if such names as Darwin, Freycinet, Cook, Bougainville and even the famous Pigafetta, chronicler of Magalhães' journey, were also included, the reason is that these last named travellers, for a shorter or greater length of time, visited Brazil.

In addition there was an assortment of other books, dictionaries, encyclopedias, compendiums, manuals etc. in various languages. This showed that his preference for the

4

poetry of Pôrto Alegre and Magalhães did not spring from an incurable ignorance of the literary languages of Europe; on the contrary the major had a good working knowledge of French, English and German, and if he didn't speak these languages he read and translated them with ease. The reason was to be found in the peculiar nature of his mind and the powerful feelings that had directed his life. Policarpo was a patriot. Ever since he was a young man of twenty he had been utterly possessed by love of his country. It was no common, idle, empty love; it was serious, all absorbing, and sincere. It excluded ambition in politics or the administration; what Quaresma envisaged, or rather what his patriotism led him to envisage, was an all-embracing knowledge of Brazil leading to an examination of its resources which would later enable him to propose reforms and progressive measures with a full understanding of the problems involved.

No one knows for sure where he was born, but it was certainly not in São Paulo, or Rio Grande do Sul, or Pará. One looked in vain for any sign of regionalism; Quaresma was first and foremost a Brazilian. He had no special preference for this or that part of his country, so much so that what stirred his feelings was not the plains of the south with their herds, nor the coffee of São Paulo, nor the gold and diamonds of Minas, nor the beauty of Guanabara, nor the height of the Paulo Afonso falls, nor the imagination of Gonçalves Dias, nor the dynamism of Andrade Neves—but all this fused together into one harmonious whole under the banner of the Cross and Stars.

As soon as he was eighteen he wanted to be a soldier, but the medical board turned him down. He suffered bitter disappointment but did not reproach his country. The government was liberal; he turned conservative and continued more than ever to love the 'land that bore him'. Since the colours of the army were denied to him he sought the administration, and of its different branches he chose the military.

There he was at home. Each day, surrounded by soldiers, cannon, veterans, and documents filled with accounts of so

5

many kilos of gunpowder, names of rifles, and technical terms of ballistics, he lived in an atmosphere of war with its courage, victories and triumphs which together have forged the spirit of the nation.

His leisure hours he devoted to an intense study of the country: its natural resources, its history, its geography, its literature and its politics. Quaresma knew the species of minerals, vegetables and animals to be found in Brazil; he was familiar with the value of the gold and diamonds exported by Minas, the Dutch wars, the Paraguayan campaigns, the sources and the course of every river. Vehemently and passionately he would maintain the pre-eminence of the Amazon over every other river in the world. In this respect he even went so far as to commit the crime of amputating a few kilometers from the Nile, the rival to 'his' river to which he most objected. Heaven help whoever cited this example to his face! Normally calm and polite, the major became excited and rude whenever the comparative lengths of the Amazon and the Nile were under discussion.

For more than a year he had been applying himself to a study of Tupí-guaraní. Every morning, before 'Aurora, with her rosy fingers prepared the way for fair Phoebus,' until lunch, he grappled with Montoya's *Arte y diccionario de la lengua guaraní ó más bien tupí*, studying the caboclo language passionately and assiduously. At the office, when the junior employees, clerks and writers, learned of his studies of Tupí, for some unknown reason they took to calling him Ubirajara. On one occasion when the clerk Azevedo was signing in, he didn't notice who was beside him, and remarked absentmindedly in a playful tone, 'Have you noticed that Ubirajara is late today?'

Quaresma was well thought of in the Arsenal: his age, his learning, and the modesty and honesty of his behaviour earned him the respect of all. Sensing that the nickname was meant for him he did not lose his dignity and burst out with insults and imprecations. He drew himself up, straightened his pince-nez and raised his forefinger in the air.

'Don't be so frivolous, Senhor Azevedo,' he said. 'I beg you not to ridicule those who are working silently for the glory and emancipation of our native country.'

That day the major conversed little. During the coffee break, when the employees had left their benches, it was his custom to pass on to his companions the fruits of his investigations, being the discoveries of national resources that he made in his study at home. One day it was oil that he had read somewhere was being found in Bahia; another time it was a new species of rubber tree that was growing by the river Pardo in Mato Grosso, or else a famous intellectual whose great-grandmother was Brazilian; and when he had no discovery to announce he would break into chorography, and describe the course of rivers, their navigable limits, the insignificant improvements needed to transform them into waterways from mouth to source. He was passionately fond of rivers; mountains held no appeal for him. Too small perhaps . . .

His colleagues listened to him respectfully, and to his face no one, apart from young Azevedo, would dare to contradict him or make a joke or a wisecrack. Behind his back, though, they took revenge for his tediousness by making fun of him: 'That Quaresma! What a bore! What the deuce . . . he thinks we're school kids. He doesn't talk about anything else.'

And so life went by, the major spending his days half at the office where nobody understood him, and the other half at home where nobody understood him either.

On the day they called him Ubirajara, Quaresma became silent, reserved and taciturn, and was only moved to speech because, when they were washing their hands in the washroom next to the office, ready to leave, someone sighed and said, 'Oh Lord, when shall I be able to go to Europe.' That was too much for the major: he looked up, straightened his pince-nez, and in a friendly persuasive manner said, 'How ungrateful you are. You have such a beautiful, rich country of your own and yet you want to visit other people's. If it were possible one day I should travel my own country from end to end.'

The other retorted that here there were only mosquitoes and fever; the major countered with statistics and even, in his exuberance, proved that Amazonas had one of the best climates in the world. Its climate had been maligned by sick wretches who had come from there . . .

Such was Major Policarpo Quaresma, who had just arrived at his house, as he did every afternoon except Sundays, at quarter past four to the minute, as exact as the appearance of a star or an eclipse. For the rest, he was a man like any other, excepting those with political or financial ambitions, of which he himself had absolutely none.

Sitting in the rocking chair right in the middle of his library, the major opened a book and began to read it while he waited for his guest. It was old Rocha Pita, the enraptured, euphuistic Rocha Pita of the *History of Portuguese America*. Quaresma was reading that famous passage: 'Nowhere else is the sky so limpid or so resplendent the dawn; in no other hemisphere does the golden sun shine so . . .' but was unable to finish it. There was a knock at the door. He went to open it himself.

'Am I late, major?' asked the visitor.

'No. You're just on time.'

Into Major Quaresma's house there stepped Senhor Ricardo Coração dos Outros, famous for his talent at singing modinhas and playing the guitar. At first his fame was limited to a small suburb of the city, where at the parties he and his guitar were what Paganini and his fiddle were to the fiestas of the nobility. But gradually, as time passed, it spread throughout all the suburbs, establishing itself so completely that it came to be identified with them. Do not think, however, that Ricardo was any mere singer of modinhas, a vagabond minstrel. No; Ricardo Coração dos Outros was an artist, a frequent and honoured guest of the best families of Méier, Piedade and Riachuelo. There were few nights when he was without an invitation. Whether it was at Lieutenant Marques' house, or Doctor Bulhões' or Senhor Castro's, his presence was always earnestly solicited and appreciated. Doctor Bulhões regarded him with special admiration, reverence and awe, and whenever he sang would fall into an ecstasy. 'I am very fond of singing,' the doctor said once on the train, 'but only two

8

people measure up to my standards: Tamagno and Ricardo.' The doctor had a great reputation in the suburbs, but not as a medical man (for he had never so much as prescribed castor oil) but as an expert on telegraphic legislation being, as he was, head of a division of the Telegraph Department.

And so it was that Ricardo Coração dos Outros enjoyed the universal esteem of suburban high society. This is a rather special high society, being high only in the suburbs. Generally speaking it is composed of civil servants, small business men, doctors with a modest practice, lieutenants of various regiments — an élite that holds firmer sway over the pot-holed roads and the parties and balls of those distant regions than does the bourgeoisie in Petrópolis and Botafogo. But it is only there, in the parties, balls and roads. For there, if one of its representatives happens to meet a lesser being, he scrutinizes him slowly from head to toe as much as to say, 'Go to my back door and I'll give you a plate of food'. The suburban aristocracy prides itself on having lunch and dinner every day, with plenty of beans, dried meat and stew. For this, in its view, is the touchstone of nobility, distinction and good breeding.

But outside the suburbs, in the Rua do Ouvidor, in the theatres and the important gatherings in the centre of town, these people shrink, fade away and disappear. Their wives and daughters no longer display the beauty with which, almost daily, they dazzle the handsome gentlemen at the interminable balls of their own regions.

Ricardo, after being the poet and singer of this curious aristocracy, went further and attached himself to the city proper. His fame had already reached São Cristóvão, and soon (so he hoped) Botafogo would invite him, for his name had already appeared in the newspapers, where they discussed the merits of his compositions and his poetry . . .

But what was he doing there in the house of a high minded person of such austere habits? It is not difficult to discover. Naturally he was not there to assist the major in his studies of Brazilian geology, poetry, mineralogy and history. As the neighbours rightly surmised, Coração dos Outros had come simply to teach the major to sing modinhas and to play the guitar. Nothing more than that.

In accordance with his ruling passion Quaresma had for long been considering what was the poetico-musical form most characteristic of the national spirit. After consulting historians, chroniclers and philosophers, he became convinced that it was the modinha accompanied by the guitar. Once assured of this truth he did not hesitate: he set out to learn the Brazilian instrument par excellence, and initiate himself into the secrets of the modinha. He was a complete novice in the matter, but he decided to find out who was the foremost instrumentalist and singer in the city, and took lessons with him. His aim was to discipline the modinha and develop from it a great new art form.

Ricardo had come to give him his lesson, but before this, at his pupil's special invitation, he was to share his dinner. It was for this reason that the famous singer had arrived early at the under-secretary's house.

'Can you play D sharp, major?' asked Ricardo as soon as he sat down.

'Yes.'

'Let's see.'

So saying he was about to take out the hallowed guitar, but there was not time. Dona Adelaide, Quaresma's sister, entered and ushered them into dinner as the soup was on the table getting cold.

'Please excuse the simplicity of the meal, Senhor Ricardo,' said the old lady. 'I wanted to make you a chicken with petits-pois, but Policarpo wouldn't let me. He said that petits-pois is foreign and that I should use pigeon peas instead. Whoever heard of chicken with pigeon peas?'

Coração dos Outros suggested that it might be good: it would be a novelty and there was no harm in experimenting.

'It's a fad of his, Senhor Ricardo, this wanting only national products. The rubbish we have to swallow! Uhh!'

'Now you're being prejudiced, Adelaide. Our country, which has every variety of climate in the world, is capable of producing all that is necessary for even the most exacting stomach. It's you who are unreasonable.'

10

'What about the butter which goes rancid so quickly?'

'That's because it's made of milk. If it was like that foreign stuff, made of grease from the drains, perhaps it wouldn't go bad . . . You see, Ricardo, they don't want anything that our own country produces . . .'

'That's usually the case,' said Ricardo.

'But they're wrong . . . They don't protect our national industries . . . I'm not like that: if it's produced here I never buy the imported article. I use national cloth for my clothes, the boots I wear are made here, and so on.'

They sat down at the table. Quaresma picked up a small crystal decanter and poured out two glasses of Parati rum.

'That's part of the national plan too,' remarked his sister, with a smile.

'Of course, and it makes a delicious aperitif. Not like those disgusting vermouths. This is pure wholesome alcohol from the sugar-cane, not from potatoes or corn . . .'

Taking his glass Ricardo carefully and respectfully raised it to his lips, as if with his whole being he were to imbibe the national liqueur.

'It's good, isn't it?' said the major.

'Delicious,' said Ricardo, smacking his lips.

'It's from Angra. And now you're going to see what wonderful wines we have from Rio Grande. Pooh to your Burgundy and your Bordeaux! We have much better in the south!'

And the dinner went on in this vein: Quaresma praising the national products, fat, bacon and rice, while his sister raised small objections and Ricardo said, 'Yes, yes, there's no doubt,' rolling his small eyes in their sockets, wrinkling his narrow forehead which vanished into a crisp shock of hair, and trying to force his tiny, harsh features into a sincere expression of satisfaction and appreciation.

After dinner they went to see the garden. It was unique— not a single flower. The wretched garden balsam, gladioli, muddy spider-flowers, dreary manacás and other fine specimens of our meadows and fields were far from worthy of the name. In gardening, as in everything else, the major was essentially nationalistic. Roses, chrysanthemums, magnolias — those exotic flowers — were not for him: our country had others more beautiful and expressive, more aromatic, like those he had there.

Once again Ricardo was in full agreement, and the two returned to the living room while the dusk fell very slowly and lingeringly, as if the sun were taking a long, reluctant farewell of the earth, gilding everything with the liquid melancholy of its poetry.

As soon as the gas was lit the maestro took hold of the guitar, tightened the stops, and ran up and down the scale, bending over the instrument as if wanting to kiss it. He played one or two chords to test it and then turned to his pupil who was ready with his in position:

'Let's see. Play the scale, major.'

Quaresma prepared his fingers and ran them over the instrument, but in his execution there was neither the assurance nor the grace as when the master performed the same operation.

'Look major, like this.'

And he showed the position of the instrument as it lay across his lap in his outstretched left arm, held lightly by the right; then he added:

'Major, the guitar is the instrument of love. It needs passion to be able to speak . . . It must be caressed, but caressed gently and affectionately as if it were your beloved, your betrothed, so that it may utter what we ourselves feel . . .'

Guitar in hand, Ricardo became effusive, eloquent, his whole being trembled with passion for the much slighted instrument.

The lesson lasted for fifty minutes, after which the major felt tired and asked the maestro to sing. It was the first time Quaresma had asked him to do so, and although flattered, professional vanity demanded that he should at first refuse.

'Oh, I've no new composition of my own.'

'Sing one by somebody else,' said Dona Adelaide humbly.

'Good heavens, madam, I only sing my own. Bilac — do you know him? — wanted to write a modinha for me but I didn't accept. "Senhor Bilac, you know nothing about the guitar," I said. It's not a question of writing correctly some verses which say pretty things; the essential thing is to find the words that are suited to the guitar. For example, if I said as I at first intended in "Her foot", one of my modinhas: "your foot is a leaf of clover"—it wouldn't go with the guitar. Listen.'

Accompanied by the instrument he sang softly: 'Your— foot—is—a—leaf—of—clo—ver.'

'You can see,' he went on, 'how it doesn't go. Now listen: your—foot—is—a—love—ly—rose. It's quite different, don't you agree?'

'Undoubtedly,' said Quaresma's sister.

'Sing that one,' suggested the major.

'No, it's too old,' said Ricardo. 'I'll sing "The Promise", do you know it?'

'No,' they both replied.

'Oh, it's going around, just like Raimundo's "Doves".'

'Do sing it, Senhor Ricardo,' begged Dona Adelaide.

At last Ricardo Coração dos Outros once more tuned his guitar and began softly:

> 'I promise by the Holy Sacraments
> That I will be your love. . .'

'Notice the imagery,' he said during a pause. 'Notice how much imagery there is.'

And he went on with his song. The windows were open. Girls and youths began to gather on the pavement to listen to the minstrel. Sensing the interest in the street, Coração dos Outros modulated his voice, assuming a fierce tone, supposed to express tenderness and enthusiasm. When he finished the applause resounded outside, and a girl came in looking for Dona Adelaide.

'Sit down, Ismênia,' she said.

'It will only take a moment.'

Drawing himself up in his chair, Ricardo glanced at the girl and continued to hold forth on the modinha. Quaresma's sister, taking advantage of a pause, asked the girl:

'Well, when are you getting married?'

13

It was a question she was always being asked. Then she would bend to the right her sad little head, crowned with magnificent chestnut hair tinged with gold, and reply:

'I don't know . . . Cavalcânti graduates at the end of the year and then we'll fix the date.'

This was said slowly, with a notable drawl.

The girl, the daughter of the general, one of Quaresma's neighbours, wasn't bad looking. She was, in fact, quite attractive with her delicate, irregular features and air of good nature.

That engagement of hers had already lasted years. Cavalcânti, her fiancé, was studying to be a dentist, a two years' course which he had dragged out to four, so that Ismênia had always to answer the inevitable question, 'Well, when are you getting married?' — 'I don't know . . . Cavalcânti graduates this year and . . .'

Deep down she was not greatly concerned. For her there was only one important thing in life, which was to get married. But there was no hurry; nothing in her demanded haste. She had already got herself a man; the rest was a question of time.

After answering Dona Adelaide's question she explained the reason for her visit. She had come, on behalf of her father, to invite Ricardo Coração dos Outros to sing at their house.

'Father loves modinhas,' said Dona Ismênia. 'He's from the north, and as you know, Dona Adelaide, people from the north are very fond of them. Why don't you come?'

So off they went.

II
Radical Reforms

Major Quaresma had not left the house for about ten days. In his cosy, quiet São Cristóvão house he occupied his days in the manner most useful and agreeable to a man of his spirit and temperament. After his morning *toilette* and coffee he would sit on the divan in the main room and read the newspapers. He read several, always in the hope of finding in one or the other some curious item of news or hint of an idea that would be useful to his beloved country. His bureaucratic habits obliged him to lunch early, and rather than break them, although he was on holiday he continued to have his first sitting-down meal at half-past nine in the morning.

After lunch he would take a stroll round the orchard, an orchard in which national fruit trees predominated: the pitanga and cambuim receiving the same meticulous treatment recommended by pomiculture as if they were cherries or figs.

It was a leisurely, philosophical stroll. Whilst talking about old times to Anastácio, the negro who had served him for thirty years, — about the marriage of the princesses, the Souto affair and other matters — the major kept his mind fixed on the problems that had been worrying him lately. After an hour or so he would return to the library and bury himself in the publications of the Historical Institute, in Fernão Cardim, Nóbrega's letters, the annals of the Library, or von den Stein, taking copious notes, which he kept in a small briefcase by his side. He was studying the Indians, though it is not quite correct to say he was studying them since he had already done so long ago, not merely their language, which he was almost able to speak, but also from the point of view of ethnology and anthropology. He was revising (that is a better way of putting it); refreshing his memory on certain points of his earlier studies, because he was engaged in organizing a system of ceremonies and feasts, based on the customs of our forest dwellers, and affecting the whole range of social relationships.

In order to understand his motives it must not be forgotten that the major, after thirty years of patriotic meditation, study and reflection, was now arriving at his period of fructification. His undying belief that Brazil was the foremost country in the world, and his intense love for his native land, were now actively urging him on to great undertakings. He felt within him an overwhelming impulse to take positive action and put his ideas into practice. They were small reforms, mere touches, because (in his opinion) the great fatherland of the Cross required nothing more than time in order to surpass England.

Experiencing every climate, it possessed every fruit, every useful animal and mineral, the finest cultivable land and the bravest, gentlest, most hospitable and most intelligent people in the world — what more could it want? Time and a little originality. He no longer entertained any doubts about this, but as regards originality of habits and customs, his doubts were not so much dissipated as transformed into certainty after he took part in the 'Tangolomango' revels at a party given in the general's house.

It happened that the visit of Ricardo and his guitar to the gallant soldier awakened in the general and his family a taste for the songs, celebrations and customs that were what is called genuinely national. They all conceived the desire to feel, dream and write poetry in the popular manner of the old days. Albernaz remembered having seen such ceremonies when he was a child: Dona Maricota, his wife, even remembered some Christmas-tide verses; and their children, five girls and a boy, seeing in all this a pretext for parties, consequently applauded their parents' enthusiasm. The modinha was not enough: their lively spirits demanded something more plebeian, more characteristic and extravagant.

Quaresma was delighted when Albernaz spoke of organizing a traditional festival, in the true northern style, to celebrate the anniversary of his enlistment. In the general's house it was the custom that every anniversary had its celebration, so that in a year there were never less than thirty, not counting Sundays and holidays, when there was dancing too.

16

Until then the major had given little thought to such things as parties and traditional dances, but he soon saw the deeply patriotic significance of the scheme. He gave his approval and encouragement to his neighbour. But who was to produce it and provide the verses and the music? Then someone remembered old mother Maria Rita, a negress and former washerwoman of the Albernaz family, who lived in Benfica. So, without delay, off went the two of them cheerfully, General Albernaz and Major Quaresma, on a fresh, clear April afternoon.

There was nothing martial about the general, not even the uniform, which possibly he did not so much as own. During the whole of his military career he had not seen a single battle, held a command, or done anything related to his profession and his artilleryman's course. He had always been an adjutant, an assistant, responsible for this or that, a clerk or store-keeper, and when he was made general he was secretary to the Supreme Military Council. His manner was that of a good head of department, and his intelligence was not much different. He knew nothing of wars, strategy, tactics or military history; his knowledge of this was limited to the battles of the Paraguayan war, to him the greatest and most notable war of all time.

The imposing title of general, calling to mind the superhuman feats of such as Caesar, Turenne and Gustavus Adolphus, ill fitted that placid, mediocre, simple man, whose only concern was to marry off his five daughters and pull strings to get his son through the Military College examinations. It was not in his interests, however, that anyone should doubt his military capacity. He himself, aware of his very civilian mien, would from time to time recount some wartime incident or anecdote of service life. 'It was at Lomas Valentinas,' he would say . . . And if anyone asked, 'Were you there at the battle?' he would immediately answer, 'No, I missed it. I fell sick and returned to Brazil just before. But I heard from Camisão and Venâncio that it was a grim affair.'

The tram which took them to old Maria Rita's house passed through one of the most interesting parts of the town. It went through Pedregulho, one of the old ports of the city and former terminal of a road to Minas which branched off to São Paulo and opened communications with Curato de Santa Cruz. Along this road beasts of burden used to bring to Rio the gold and diamonds of Minas, and of late the so-called products of the country. It is less than a hundred years since the wagon-trains of King Dom João VI used to pass by like heavily laden ships, swaying over their four widely spaced wheels, on their way to far-off Santa Cruz. Not that one may believe this to have been a particularly impressive sight; the court was hard up for money and the king dissolute. Despite the tattered soldiers, sorrily mounted on spiritless nags, the procession must have had its grandeur, not in itself but in the humiliating marks of respect that all had to show to his pathetic majesty.

With us everything is inconsistent, temporary and transitory. There was nothing there to recall the past. The old houses with their huge, squarish windows with small-framed casements had not been there for long; less than fifty years.

There were no reminiscences as Quaresma and Albernaz passed by all this and went on to the end of the line. Before reaching it they contemplated the racecourse district, a small area of the city crowded with stables and stud farms for race-horses, where one could see enormous horseshoes, sets of whips, horses' heads and other emblems of the sport on the gate-posts, panels of the doors, and everywhere where such decorations look well and attract attention.

The old negress' house was beyond the terminus close to the Leopoldina railway station. They set off in that direction and passed by the station. In an immense yard, black with coal dust, were amassed piles of wood and immense deposits of sacks and charcoal. Further on was a locomotive yard with engines shunting and whistling.

Finally they reached the path where Maria Rita's house was. As the weather had been dry they were able to walk along it. Beyond the path a vast area of marshy flats, desolate and forbidding, stretches down to the interior of the bay, and on the horizon loses itself in the foothills of the blue mountains of

18

Petrópolis. They arrived at the old woman's house. It was low, whitewashed and roofed with heavy Portuguese tiles. It stood a little back from the road. On the right was a rubbish heap: kitchen scraps, rags, sea-shells, broken china—a hoard to delight the heart of some archaeologist of the distant future; on the left there was a papaya tree, and on the same side, near the fence, some rue. They knocked. A little black girl appeared at the open window.

'What do you want?'

Drawing closer they explained what they wanted. The girl called into the interior of the house:

'Grannie, there are two men want to speak to you. Please come in,' she added, turning to the general and his companion.

The room was small and had no ceiling. Cluttering the walls to about two thirds of their height there were coloured lithographs from calendars, miniatures of saints and illustrations from newspapers. Next to Our Lady of Penha there was a picture of Victor Emmanuel with his enormous moustaches in disarray; a sentimental drawing from a calendar—the head of a dreaming woman—seemed to be looking at St John the Baptist alongside. By the door that led to the interior of the house a lamp on a corner shelf was blackening a china figure of Our Lady of the Immaculate Conception.

It was not long before the old woman appeared. She wore a lace blouse which showed her thin chest, and a double string of beads round her neck. She limped with one foot, and seemed to want to help herself along by putting her left hand on her leg.

'Good afternoon, Maria Rita,' said the general.

She answered, but gave no signs of having recognised whom she was talking to. The general interrupted her:

'Don't you know me any more? I'm the general, Colonel Albernaz.'

'Ah, it's the colonel . . . It's been so long. How is Dona Maricota?'

'She's well. Listen, we want you to teach us some ballads.'

19

'Who, me, senhor?'

'Come now, Maria Rita . . . you don't forget anything . . don't you know "Bumba-meu-Boi"?'

'Oh senhor, I forget.'

'And "Boi Espácio"?'

'That very old, when we slaves—what for senhor colonel want know that?'

She spoke slurring her syllables, with a gentle smile and a vague look.

'It's for a party . . . What one do you know?'

Her grandchild, who until then had listened to the conversation without speaking a word, roused herself to say something, disclosing for an instant a dazzling row of perfect teeth:

'Grannie doesn't remember.'

The general, whom the old woman referred to as colonel, having known him in that rank, paid no attention to the girl's remark, and insisted:

'You can't have forgotten. Surely you remember something, don't you?'

'I only know "The Bogeyman",' said the old woman.

'Sing it, then.'

'But you know it. Don't you? Course you know it.'

'No I don't; sing it. If I knew it I wouldn't have come here. You can ask my friend here, Major Policarpo, whether I know it or not.'

Quaresma nodded his head and the old negress, perhaps with fond memories of the time when she was a slave and wet-nurse on some rich well-provided estate, lifted up her head as if to assist her memory, and sang:

> 'Here comes the bogeyman
> From behind the hill,
> To eat the little master
> With a mouthful of meal.'

'But that's just an old children's lullaby,' exclaimed the general in disgust. Don't you know anything else?'

'No senhor. I forget.'

The two left the house, crestfallen. Quaresma was despondent. How was it that the people did not retain the traditions of thirty years ago? How quickly their songs and games slipped from their memory. It was surely a mark of weakness, a sign of inferiority compared with those stubborn peoples who kept them for century after century. Something had to be done to promote the cult of traditions, to keep them always fresh in our memories and our customs . . .

Albernaz was vexed. He had counted on arranging a good number for the party he was giving, and the opportunity was being lost. It was almost a chance of marriage for one of his four daughters that was slipping away; his four daughters, for one of them was provided for, thank God.

Dusk was falling, and they arrived home full of the gloom of the moment.

Their disappointment, however, lasted only a matter of days. Cavalcânti, Ismênia's fiancé, informed them that nearby there lived a man of letters who was a persevering collector of popular Brazilian tales and songs. They sought him out. He was an old poet who had been famous in the seventies or thereabouts, a simple, inoffensive man who had allowed himself to fall into oblivion as a poet, and now occupied himself publishing collections of tales, songs, adages and popular sayings that nobody read.

He was overjoyed when he learned of the purpose of the two gentlemen's visit. Quaresma was enthusiastic and spoke warmly; so did Albernaz, for he saw in his party with a folklore presentation a means of drawing attention to his house, attracting people and . . . marrying his daughters.

They were received in a spacious room, but it was so full of tables, shelves crammed with books, folders and tin boxes that one could scarcely move in it. On one box was written, 'Santa Ana dos Tocos'; and on one folder, 'São Bonifácio do Cabresto'.

'You have no idea,' said the old poet, 'of the wealth of our popular poetry; what surprises it has in store for us . . . Only the other day I received a letter from Urubu-de-Baixo with a beautiful song. Would you like to see it?'

21

The collector rummaged amongst some folders and finally unearthed a paper from which he read:

> 'If God cared for a poor man,
> Like this I would not be,
> He'd find within her tender heart
> A little place for me.
>
> For the deep love I bear her,
> Now from my breast must fly,
> And straightway from my eyes it leaps
> Up to the clouds on high.'

'Charming isn't it? . . . Quite delightful. Oh but if you only knew the simian cycle, the collection of stories the people have about the monkey? . . . It's a genuine mock epic.'

Quaresma gazed at the old poet with the gratified astonishment of one who has come across a fellow being in the desert; and Albernaz, temporarily carried away by the folklorist's enthusiasm, revealed greater intelligence in the look which he cast at him.

The old poet put the Urubu-de-Baixo song in a folder, then took another from which he drew several sheets of paper. He rejoined his two visitors and said,

'I am going to read you a short story about the monkey, one of many told by our people . . . I alone have almost forty, and I intend to publish them under the title of "Stories of Brer Monkey".'

And without asking their leave or whether they were disposed to listen, he began:

'The monkey and the judge. A band of monkeys were playing, jumping gleefully from tree to tree at the edge of a grotto. Then suddenly one of them noticed at the bottom of it a jaguar that had fallen in. Moved by sympathy the monkeys decided to rescue it. So they tore down creepers, bound them firmly together, and tying the rope, so made, round their waists, they threw one of the ends to the jaguar. By their united efforts they succeeded in hauling him up, and untying themselves quickly, fled to safety. One of them, however, was not quick enough, and the jaguar promptly seized him.

22

' "Be patient, Comrade Monkey," he said. "I am hungry and you must be good enough to let me eat you."

'The monkey begged, pleaded and wept, but the jaguar appeared inflexible. Then the monkey reminded him that the question should be resolved by the judge. They went to him, the monkey held securely all the time by the jaguar. Amongst the animals it is the turtle who is judge, and he holds his court by the riverside, standing on a stone. The two arrived and the monkey stated his case.

'The turtle listened to him, and at the end commanded:

'"Clap your hands."

Although secured by the jaguar the monkey was able to clap his hands. It was now the turn of the jaguar, who also stated his case, giving his reasons. As before the judge gave his command:

'"Clap your hands."

'The jaguar had no alternative but to release the monkey, who made his escape, as did the judge, who threw himself into the water."'

When he finished reading the old man turned to them:

'Don't you find that interesting? Most interesting! Our people have so much inventiveness, such creative spirit — the essential material for interesting fabliaux . . . The day some literary genius appears to fix this in an imperishable form . . . Ah! Then!'

As he said this a lingering smile of satisfaction lit up his face and two tears glistened in his eyes.

'Now,' he said, once the emotion had passed, 'let's consider what is best for our purpose. The "Boi Espácio" or the "Bumba-meu-Boi" is a bit too difficult for you yet . . . It's best to go slowly and begin with the easiest . . . Here we have the "Tangolomango", do you know it?'

'No,' said the other two.

'It's most amusing. Have ready ten children, a mask of an old man's face, a fancy dress for one of the gentlemen, and I'll put it on.'

The great day arrived. The general's house was full. Cavalcânti had come, and he and his fiancée, standing apart in a window recess, appeared to be the only ones not interested in the performance. He was talking a lot and pulling faces; she was more reserved, looking at him from time to time with an expression of gratitude.

Quaresma played the part of 'Tangolomango'. Wearing an ancient overcoat of the general's and a huge old man's mask, and grasping a curved stick in the shape of a crosier, he entered the room. The ten children sang in chorus:

'Once a mother had ten children,
Kept in a cauldron all the time:
Along came old man Tangolomango,
Took one away and then there were nine.'

At this the major advanced, beating the ground with his stick and shouting, 'Ho! ho! ho!' The children fled, until finally seizing one he carried it off to another room. This was repeated, to the great amusement of the spectators, until at the fifth verse he ran out of breath, his eyes clouded over and he fell to the ground. They took off his mask, patted him, and Quaresma regained consciousness.

The accident, however, did nothing to diminish his enthusiasm for folklore. He bought books and read all the publications on the subject. But disillusionment came at the end of several weeks of study: almost all the traditions and songs were foreign, including even the 'Tangolomango'.

It was therefore necessary to find something original of our own, something created by the airs of our own native country. This idea led him to study the customs of the Tupinambá Indians; and as one idea leads to another he widened his aims and set about preparing a code of relationships, greetings, domestic ceremonies and entertainments based upon Tupí custom.

He had devoted himself to this arduous task for ten days when, one Sunday, his work was interrupted by a knock at the door. He opened, but did not shake hands. He broke out weeping, howling and tearing his hair as if he had lost a wife or a child. His sister and Anastácio both came running while his friend and his god-daughter, for it was they who had

24

knocked, remained aghast in the doorway.

'What's the matter, my old friend?'

'What is it, Policarpo?'

'Godfather, what . . .'

He went on weeping a little longer. Then he dried his tears and explained in the most natural tone of voice:

'You see! You haven't the slightest notion of what is Brazilian. You wanted me to shake your hand. That's not our way. Our greeting is to cry when we meet friends, which is what the Tupinambás used to do.'

His friend Vicente, the daughter and Dona Adelaide looked at each other without knowing what to say. Was the man going out of his mind? The absurdity of it!

'But Senhor Policarpo,' said his friend, 'it may well be very Brazilian, but it's also very distressing.'

'Of course it is, godfather,' added the girl quickly. 'It's ominous in fact . . .'

This friend of his was Italian by birth, and the story of their relationship is worth recounting. Twenty odd years ago, as an itinerant greengrocer, he had been supplier to Quaresma's household. Quaresma already had his patriotic ideas but was not too proud to talk to the greengrocer, and even took pleasure in seeing him sweaty and bent under the weight of his baskets, and two red spots burning on the white cheeks of the recently arrived European. But one fine day when Quaresma was wandering in the Largo do Paço, deep in meditation on the wonders of the Mestre Valentim fountain, he happened to meet the greengrocer. He spoke to him with that simplicity of manner which is peculiarly his, and was aware that the young fellow was seriously worried about something. Not only did he make exclamations from time to time quite unconnected with the matter in hand, but he compressed his lips, ground his teeth, and clenched his fists in rage. On questioning him the major learnt that he and an associate had had a difference about money, and the Italian was intending to kill him, as with the loss of his good name he would soon be reduced to misery. He recounted this with such vehemence and ferocity that it required all the major's calm and tact to dissuade him

25

from his purpose. And not stopping there, he also lent him money. Vicente Coleoni set up a greengrocer's shop, made a profit, went into the construction business, married and had that daughter of whom his benefactor was the godfather. It would be idle to point out that Quaresma was unaware of the contradiction between his actions and his patriotic ideas.

The truth is that these ideas were not yet firmly established, but were already floating around in his head, working on his consciousness in the form of vague desires, the whims of a lad of little more than twenty years old, whims which would not be long in gathering strength and only wanted the passage of years to blossom forth into deeds.

It was therefore his friend Vicente and his god-daughter Olga whom he received according to the legitimate ceremonial of the Tupinambás; and if he was not wearing the traditional dress of this interesting people, the reason was not that he did not possess it. It was ready to hand, but he did not have the time to undress.

'Are you doing a lot of reading, godfather?' asked the girl, gazing at him with her bright eyes.

The two were much attached to each other. Quaresma was inclined to be reserved, and the embarrassment he felt about showing his feelings made him sparing in demonstrations of affection. One could guess, though, that she occupied the place in his heart of the children he never had, and never would have. This lively girl, accustomed to speak her mind freely, did not conceal her love, the more so because of her indistinct recognition in him of something superior: his quest of an ideal, his tenacity in pursuing a dream, an idea, in short his venturing into the uppermost regions of the spirit, something which she observed in no one else of her acquaintance. This admiration was not the result of her education, which had been the usual for girls of her class. It came from a natural inclination of her own, perhaps from her European blood, which made her a little different from our young women.

It was with a bright, searching look that she had asked the question:

'Well godfather, are you doing a lot of reading?'

'Yes, a great deal, my child. You know I am planning great works, a reform, the emancipation of a people.'

Vicente had gone into the house with Dona Adelaide and the two remained alone in the library talking. The girl noticed that Quaresma was different. He talked now with so much assurance, he who was formerly so modest, even hesitant in his speech—what the deuce! No, no it wasn't possible . . . But, who knows? And what an unusual joy there was in his eyes—the joy of a mathematician who has solved a problem, or a successful inventor.

'Don't get yourself mixed up in some conspiracy,' said the girl, joking.

'You needn't worry about that. This is coming naturally, violence won't be necessary . . .'

At that moment Ricardo Coração dos Outros came in wearing his long, trailing serge morning coat, and with his guitar in its leather case. The major introduced them.

'I already know you by name, Senhor Ricardo,' said Olga.

Coração dos Outros was filled with gratification and pleasure. His small features expanded into a satisfied smile, the skin, normally the colour of old marble, becoming smooth and youthful. That girl, who seemed rich, and who was certainly well-bred and pretty, knew him; how flattering! He, who was always clumsy and tongue-tied in the presence of girls, whatever their station in life, took courage, found his voice, and spoke agreeably and eloquently.

'Then you have read my verses, madam?'

'I haven't had that pleasure, but some months ago I read an appreciation of one of your works.'

'In the "Tempo", wasn't it?'

'That's right.'

'It was most unfair,' added Ricardo. 'The critics just can't get away from the question of metre. They say that my verses aren't verses . . . But they are: they're verses for the guitar. You, sir, know that verses for music are different from ordinary verses, don't you agree? It is not surprising then that my verses, made for the guitar, are in another metre and

27

follow a different system, don't you think?'

'Naturally,' said the girl. 'But it seems to me that you make the verses for the music and not the music for the verses.'

And she gave a slow, enigmatic smile as she gazed brightly at him, while Ricardo, with his sharp little mouse-like eyes, uneasily tried to guess what she meant.

Quaresma, who until then had remained silent, broke in: 'Ricardo is an artist, Olga. He works and strives to dignify the guitar.'

'I know, godfather, I know . . .'

'Here in Brazil, madam,' said Coração dos Outros, 'these patriotic aims are not taken very seriously, but in Europe they command respect and everyone helps. Major, what is the name of that poet who writes in colloquial French?'

'Mistral,' replied Quaresma, 'but it's not French, it's Provençal, a language in its own right.'

'Yes, that's right,' agreed Ricardo. 'And isn't Mistral highly considered and respected? I am doing exactly the same thing with the guitar.'

He looked triumphantly from one to the other.

'Do continue in your attempt, Senhor Ricardo,' said Olga, 'it is most praiseworthy.'

'Thank you. You may be sure, madam, that the guitar is a fine instrument, and one of the most difficult too. For example . . .'

'What's that,' put in Quaresma abruptly. 'There are others more difficult.'

'The piano?' asked Ricardo.

'The piano my foot. The maracá, the inúbia.'

'I've never heard of them.'

'Never heard of them? That's the limit. The most Brazilian instruments possible: the only ones that are really and truly so. The instruments of our forebears, that gallant race that strove and are still striving to win possession of this beautiful land. The caboclos!'

'A caboclo instrument, come, come,' said Ricardo.

'Caboclo. What difference does that make? Léry says that they are very harmonious and pleasing to the ear . . . If it is

28

just for being caboclo, then the guitar is no good—it's a braggadocio's instrument.'

'Braggadocio, major. You shouldn't have said that . . .'

And the two plunged into a heated discussion in front of the surprised, alarmed girl, who was unable to account for the unexpected change in the temperament of her godfather, until then so easy-going and calm.

III
Genelício's News

'Well, when are you getting married, Dona Ismênia?'

'In March. Cavalcânti has graduated now and . . .'

At last the general's daughter was able to give a definite answer to the question they had been asking her for almost five years. Her fiancé had finally reached the end of his dentist's course and had fixed the wedding for three months hence. Great was the joy of the family; and as in such a case rejoicing could not be celebrated without a dance, a party was announced for the following Saturday as custom demanded.

The bride's sisters, Quinota, Zizi, Lalá and Vivi, were more pleased than she was. It was as if she was leaving the way free for them, and it had been she who, until then, had prevented them from getting married.

Having been engaged for nearly five years Ismênia already felt herself half married. This feeling, and the feebleness of her character, made it impossible for her to feel much happier. Nothing changed. For her, getting married was not a matter of love, nor had it anything to do with sentiments or feelings: it was an idea, purely an idea. Her rudimentary little intelligence made a distinction between the idea of getting married and love, the pleasures of the senses, a certain amount of freedom, motherhood, even the husband himself. Since she was a child she had heard her mother say, 'Learn how to do this, because when you get married . . .' or else, 'You must know how to sew buttons on, because when you are married . . .' Every moment, every hour there was this, 'because when you get married . . .' so that the girl became convinced that marriage is the sole aim of our existence. Education, personal satisfaction, happiness, all this was useless; life was summed up in one idea: getting married.

Nor was it just within her family that she came up against this preoccupation. At school, in the street, in friends' houses, they only talked about marriage. 'You know, Dona Maricota, Lili has got married; she didn't do all that well for herself as her husband is nothing in particular or else, 'Zezé is crazy to get married, but my goodness, she's so plain . . .'

Life, the world, the wide variety of feelings and ideas, our own right to happiness, became mere trifles to that tiny brain. To her, getting married assumed such an importance, a kind of duty, that not to marry, to remain a spinster, an 'aunt', appeared to her criminal and shameful. Being of feeble character, incapable of feeling anything deeply and intensely, with no emotional capacity for love or passion, the idea of 'getting married' had fixed itself in her mind like an obsession.

She was not bad-looking: dark, with delicate features, a badly shaped but elegant nose, neither very small nor very thin, and with her appearance of passive good nature and laziness of body, mind and feelings—she was that type of girl whom boyfriends call 'a pretty little thing.' Her crowning beauty, however, was her hair: thick, silky, chestnut locks, tinged with gold.

She took up with Cavalcânti when she was nineteen, and in view of her weak will and her fear of not finding a husband it is not surprising that the future dentist made an easy conquest.

Her father pulled a long face. He kept close watch over his daughters' love affairs. 'Always tell me who they are,

Maricota,' he used to say. 'Keep a sharp eye open . . . It's better to forestall than to remedy . . . He may be a good-for-nothing and . . .' Learning that Ismênia's young man was a dentist he was not very pleased. What is a dentist? he asked himself. A semi-literate type, a kind of barber. He would have preferred an officer with his widow's fund and half salary pension; but his wife convinced him that dentists earn a lot, so he gave his consent. Thereupon Cavalcânti began to frequent the house as the accepted fiancé, but not having formally proposed it was not yet 'official'.

At the end of the first year, when the general learned of the difficulties his future son-in-law was facing to finish his studies, he came generously to his assistance. He paid his matriculation fees, books and other things. Not a few times Dona Maricota, after a long talk with her daughter, would approach her husband and say, 'Chico, let me have twenty milreis; Cavalcânti needs to buy a Manual of Anatomy.'

The general was good-hearted, kind and generous; apart from his soldier-like pretensions there was no flaw in his character. Furthermore, the necessity of marrying off his daughters made him even better when their interests were at stake.

He would listen to his wife, scratch his head, and give the money; and to save his future son-in-law expenses he invited him to dinner every day. And so the courtship had continued until then.

'At last,' said Albernaz to his wife when they were retired to bed after the proposal, 'we're going to see the end of it.' And Dona Maricota replied, 'Yes, luckily everything is going to turn out well.'

The general's resigned satisfaction was, however, false: in point of fact he was jubilant. Whenever he met a friend in the street, at the first opportune moment he would say, 'Life is hell! Do you know, Castro, that on top of everything I have a daughter getting married.'

At which Castro would say, 'Which one?'

'Ismênia, the second one,' replied Albernaz, and adding 'You're the lucky one, you had only sons.'

31

'Ah, my friend,' said the other slyly, 'I learned the formula. Why didn't you do the same?'

Taking his leave, old Albernaz went round the stores and the china shops buying more plates and dishes and a centre-piece for the table, for the party had to have an air of riches and plenty that would express the full measure of his satisfaction.

On the morning of the day of the party to celebrate the engagement Dona Maricota got out of bed singing. This was unusual, but on especially happy occasions she would warble an old aria of the days of her girlhood, and her daughters, recognizing in this a sure sign of good humour, would run to her asking for this or that. She was very active and hard-working: no housewife could be more economical or sparing, or make her husband's money and the work of the servants go further than she did. As soon as she was up she set everyone, maids and daughters, to work. Vivi and Quinota saw to the cakes; Lalá and Zizi helped the girls arranging the rooms and the bedrooms, while she and Ismênia were to set the table, preparing it tastefully: à magnificent sight. It was to remain thus adorned from early morning.

Dona Maricota was overjoyed; she could not understand how a woman could live without being married. It was not just the dangers to which she was exposed and the lack of security; it seemed to her wrong and dishonourable to the family. Her satisfaction was not due merely to things turning out well, as she said. It was deeper, coming from a mother's family instincts.

She was preparing the table, nervous and happy; her daughter was cold and indifferent. 'But my dear,' she said, 'it doesn't seem as if it is you who are going to be married. What a long face! You look like one of the Seven Sleepers!'

'Mother, what do you want me to do?'

'It's not nice to laugh too much and prance about like a coquette, but neither do you have to be as you are. I never saw a bride like that.'

For an hour the girl strove to appear more cheerful, but soon the poverty of her nature, incapable of any stirring feelings, made itself felt; her natural temperament got the better of her and she sank into her customary morbid lethargy.

Many people came. Besides the girls and their respective mothers the general's invitation brought Rear Admiral Caldas, Doctor Florêncio, the water engineer, Major (honorary) Inocêncio Bustamente, Senhor Bastos, an accountant and relation of Dona Maricota, and other important persons. Ricardo had not been invited as the general was afraid of what people might think about his presence at a serious party; Quaresma had been but had not come, and Cavalcânti had dined with his future in-laws.

At six o'clock the house was already crowded. The girls surrounded Ismênia, complimenting her, not without a touch of envy in their eyes.

Irene, a tall, fair girl said, 'If I were you I'd buy everything at the Park.'

They were talking about the trousseau. All of them, though they were single, were giving advice: they knew the cheap shops, the items which were important and those which could be dispensed with. They were up-to-date.

Armanda, with a wicked gleam in her eyes, said, 'Yesterday in the Rua da Constituição I saw a lovely double bedroom suite. Why don't you go and see it, Ismênia, it isn't expensive?'

Ismênia was the least enthusiastic, hardly replying to the questions, or if she did, answering with monosyllables. There was a moment when she almost relaxed and smiled happily. Dr Estefânia, who was wearing a ring with as many stones as a jeweller's shop, suddenly put her full lips to the bride's ear and whispered something. When she finished whispering, as if wishing to confirm what had been said, she opened wide her mischievous, sparkling eyes and said aloud, 'That's all I want to see . . . They all say they won't . . . I know . . .' She was alluding to the reply to her whispered remarks that Ismênia had grudgingly given: 'Not likely!'

While talking, all the girls had their eyes fixed on the piano. The young men and some of the older ones were gathered round Cavalcânti, who looked very solemn in a large black morning coat.

'Well, doctor, you made it, hey?' said one as a form of compliment.

'That's right. I worked for it. You have no idea of the blunders and the difficulties . . . it was heroic . . .'

'Do you know Chavantes?' asked another.

'Yes, he's an old-timer, a gay lad . . .'

'Was he your class-mate?'

'Yes, that is he was doing medicine. We matriculated the same year.'

Cavalcânti had no time to attend to one before he was obliged to listen to another.

'It's a great thing to be graduated. If I had listened to my father I wouldn't now be sweating over debit and credit columns. If I cut my arm there's no blood to flow.'

'My dear sir, nowadays it doesn't mean a thing,' said Cavalcânti modestly. 'With these private Academies . . . Do you know they are already talking about a private School of Dentistry. That's too much. A difficult, expensive course that requires corpses, apparatus and good teachers, how can a private concern maintain it? If the government does it badly . . .'

'Well doctor,' said another, 'my congratulations. I say to you what I said to my nephew when he graduated: "Drill away!" '

'Ah, your nephew is graduated then?' Cavalcânti enquired politely.

'Yes, in engineering. He's in Maranhão, on the Caxias road.'

'A fine career.'

During the intervals between the conversation they all looked at the new dentist as if he were some supernatural being. For all those people Cavalcânti was no longer a mere man; he was a man and something more, something sacred and of a superior nature. But they did not superimpose on his present image the things he perhaps might know or might have learnt. This did not enter into it at all. For some he continued to be ordinary and common in appearance, but changed in substance, different from them, anointed with some extra-terrestrial, almost divine essence.

Around Cavalcânti, who was in the reception room, were gathered the least important. The general had remained in the dining room smoking, surrounded by the higher ranking and the oldest. With him were Rear Admiral Caldas, Major Inocêncio, Doctor Florêncio and Captain Sigismundo of the Fire Brigade.

Inocêncio took advantage of the opportunity to consult Caldas on a point of military legislation. The Rear Admiral was most interesting. In the Navy he was almost exactly what Albernaz was in the Army. He had never been at sea, except during the Paraguayan war, and even then for only a very short time. The fault, however, was not his. As soon as he became a First Lieutenant he withdrew little by little into himself, abandoning his circle of acquaintances, so that with no protection or friends in high places they forgot about him and never gave him a sea-going commission. It is a curious thing about military administration: commissions are awarded on merit, but only to one's protégés.

On one occasion, as a Lieutenant-Commander, he was given a ship in Mato Grosso. He was put in command of the battleship *Lima Barros*. Off he went, but when he reported to Flotilla Commander he was informed that no such ship existed on the river Paraguay. He enquired here and there and someone ventured the opinion that the *Lima Barros* might be attached to the upper Uruguay squadron. He consulted the Commander.

'In your place,' said his superior, 'I would leave immediately for the Rio Grande Flotilla.'

So he packed his bags for the upper Uruguay, where he finally arrived after an arduous, tiring journey. But there, too, the *Lima Barros* was not to be found. Where could it be? He wanted to telegraph to Rio de Janeiro but was afraid of being reprimanded, particularly as he was not in very high favour just then. So he remained a month in Itaqui, vacillating, receiving no salary and not knowing which way to turn. Then one day it occurred to him that the ship might be in Amazonas. He embarked with the intention of going to the extreme north, and as he passed through Rio he reported to Naval authorities as was the custom. He was arrested and sent before a court martial.

The *Lima Barros* had been sunk during the Paraguayan war.

Although acquitted, he never more found favour with the ministers and their generals. They all thought of him as a blockhead, a musical comedy commander who chased after his ship round the four points of the compass. They left him 'laid up', as they say in service slang, and it took him almost forty years to rise from midshipman to commander. When, as chief officer, he was retired from active service with a further promotion in rank, all his bitterness towards the Navy was directed to the tedious job of studying the laws, decrees, warrants, notices and consultations dealing with the promotion of officers. He bought catalogues of legislation, compiled collections of laws and reports, and filled the house with all this boring, wearisome administrative literature. He showered the Navy ministers with petitions requesting a reconsideration of his retirement. These circulated for months round the chain of departments, and after the Naval Council or the Supreme Military Tribunal had been consulted, were always rejected. Lately he had appointed a lawyer to work in the federal court, and there he passed from one public notary to the next, rubbing shoulders with bailiffs, clerks, judges and lawyers—that coarse rabble of the courts who seem to have contracted all the ills with which they come in contact.

Inocêncio Bustamente had the same mania for going to law. Stubborn and pig-headed, he was also submissive and servile. A former volunteer, and holding the honorary rank of major, not a day passed without him going to headquarters to check on the progress of his various petitions. In one he requested a place in the Home for the Disabled; in another the rank of lieutenant-colonel; in another such and such a medal; and when he hadn't one of his own he checked on those of other people. He was not above concerning himself with the petition of some nitwit who, because he was an honorary lieutenant of the National Guard, requested promotion to the rank of major on the grounds that two stripes plus two more make four—that is, a major.

Knowing the meticulous studies the admiral had made, Bustamente put his question to him.

'I can't say off-hand. The Army isn't my speciality but I'll see what I can do. That's in a mess too.' And after replying he would scratch one of his white sideboards, which gave him the appearance of a 'commodore' or a Portuguese farmer, for he had strong traces of the Lusitanian.

'Ah, in my time,' put in Albernaz, 'talk about order; talk about discipline!'

'You don't get them like that nowadays,' said Bustamente.

At that, Sigismundo ventured his opinion, saying, 'I'm not a soldier, but . . .'

'What do you mean you're not a soldier?' said Albernaz vehemently. 'It is you who are the true ones. You are always in the face of the enemy, don't you agree, Caldas?'

'Of course, of course,' said the admiral, stroking his sideboards.

'As I was saying,' went on Sigismundo, 'although I'm not a soldier I would venture the opinion that our forces are in a bad way. Where is there a Pôrto Alegre or a Caxias?'

'They don't exist any more, old man,' said Doctor Florêncio in a soft voice.

'I don't know why not if everything is planned so scientifically nowadays.'

It was Caldas who spoke, trying to be ironical. Albernaz was indignant and retorted with warmth, 'I'd like to see these playboys, with their 'x's and 'y's, at Curupaiti, hey Caldas? Hey Inocêncio?'

Doctor Florêncio was the only civilian in the group. An engineer and civil servant, with the tranquillity of his existence and the passage of years he had lost all the knowledge which he might have possessed on leaving school. He was more a drainpipe keeper than an engineer. Living near to Albernaz, he rarely failed to come and spend the afternoon playing solo with the general.

'You were there, weren't you, general? asked Doctor Florêncio.

Without hesitating, becoming confused or stammering, the general replied in the most natural manner, 'No, I wasn't. I fell sick and returned to Brazil just before. But a lot of my friends were there: Camisão, Venâncio . . .'

There was silence, and all looked at the night which was closing in. From the window of the room where they were not a single mountain could be seen. The horizon stretched no further than the bottom of the yards of the neighbouring houses with their washing-lines, their chimneys and the cheeping of chickens. A leafless tamarind tree sadly called to mind the open air and the wide, boundless vistas. The sun had already sunk behind the horizon, and the pale glow of the household lanterns and gas lights began to appear behind the window panes.

Bustamente broke the silence: 'This country is going to the dogs. Just think of it, my petition requesting promotion to lieutenant-colonel has been six months in the Ministry.'

'It's a disgrace,' they all exclaimed.

It was night. Dona Maricota came to where they were, active and bustling, her face shining with happiness.

'Are you saying your prayers?' she said. And then added, 'Do you mind if I have a word with Chico?'

Albernaz left the circle of his friends and went to a corner of the room where his wife whispered something to him. He listened to her, then returned to the group, and halfway said out loud, 'If they aren't dancing it's because they don't want to. Is it my fault?'

Dona Maricota went up to her husband's friends and explained: 'You know if you don't encourage them, no one picks a partner, no one plays. There are so many girls and boys there, it's such a shame.'

'Alright, I'll go,' said Albernaz.

He left his friends and went to the reception room to start off the dance.

'Come on girls. What's all this? Zizi, a waltz.' And he went round himself pairing them off. 'No, general, I've already got a partner,' said one girl. 'It doesn't matter,' he replied, 'dance with Raimundinho, the other one can wait.'

After starting off the dance he returned to the group of friends, sweating, but pleased with himself. 'Being a family man is no joke. You feel such a fool,' he said. 'You are the clever one, Caldas, not getting married.'

'But I have more children than you: eight nephews and nieces, and then there are the cousins.'

'What about a game of solo,' suggested Albernaz.

'How can we, we're five?' said Florêncio.

'No, I don't play,' said Bustamente.

'Then we'll play four, with one dropping out,' said Albernaz.

The cards were brought together with a small, three-legged table. The partners sat down and cut for deal. Florêncio won, and they began. Albernaz had an attentive air when he played: his head fell down over his shoulders and his eyes took on an expression of concentration. Caldas sat up straight in his chair, playing with the serenity of a lord high admiral at a rubber of whist. Sigismundo played carefully with a cigarette in the corner of his mouth and his head to one side to escape the smoke. Bustamente went to watch the dancing.

The game had begun when Dona Quinota, one of the general's daughters, crossed the room and went to drink some water. Caldas, stroking one of his sideboards, asked the girl, 'Well, Dona Quinota, what's happened to Genelício?'

The girl turned round with a coquettish look, and clicking her tongue, said with feigned ill temper, 'How should I know? Do I go chasing him?'

'You don't have to get angry, Dona Quinota, I was only asking,' said Caldas.

The general, who was examining his hand attentively, interrupted the conversation with a grave voice, 'I pass.'

Dona Quinota withdrew. This Genelício was her young man. A relative of Caldas, his marriage into the family was taken for granted, and his candidature approved by all. Dona Maricota and her husband overwhelmed him with parties. He was a young man of under thirty who worked in the Treasury, and already, in the middle of his career, threatened to have a brilliant future. No one could be more cringing and servile than he was. He had no sense of propriety or shame. He plied his chiefs and superiors with all the incense he could. On leaving the office, he would loiter about, washing his hands three or four times, so as to be able to catch the director at the door. He would accompany him, talking about the work, giving ideas and opinions, criticizing this or that colleague, and leave him at the tram if the man was going home. Whenever a minister came in he would get himself chosen as spokesman for his companions and make a speech; for birthdays it would be a sonnet which always began, 'Hail,' and ended with, 'Hail, thrice Hail.' The model was the same. He just changed the name of the minister and put the date. The following day the newspapers would mention his name and publish the sonnet.

He had been promoted twice in four years, and was now working for a higher post in the Audit Office about to be created.

For fawning and manoeuvering his way up he had a veritable genius. Not limiting himself to sonnets and speeches, he sought other ways and means. One of these was by publications in the daily newspapers. With the aim of impressing the ministers and directors with his superior learning, he would churn out lengthy newspaper articles on public accountancy. They were nothing more than collections of musty decrees, spiced here and there with quotations from French or Portuguese authors.

The interesting thing is that his companions looked up to him, holding his knowledge in high esteem, and in his section he was respected as a genius, a genius of documents and information. Add to this that in addition to his secure administrative position Genelício was finishing a course at law school, so many titles together could not fail to make a favourable impression on the Albernaz' matrimonial ambitions.

Outside the department he had a haughty manner, made comic by his poor physique; but he was strengthened and sustained by the conviction of the immense services he was rendering to the State. He was a model employee.

40

The game continued in silence and the night drew on. At the end of the hands there would be a brief comment or other, and at the beginning would be heard only the sacramental calls of the game: 'solo, kitty, double, pass.' Once made, they played on in silence; from the reception room, however, came the gay sounds of dancing and conversation.

'Look who's here.'

'Genelício,' said Caldas. 'Where have you been, lad?'

He placed his hat and walking stick on a chair and greeted them. Small, already with a slight stoop, thin faced and with blue-tinted pince-nez, all about him betrayed his profession, his tastes and his habits. He was a clerk.

'There's nothing wrong, my friends. I was just seeing to some business of mine.'

'Going well?' asked Florêncio.

'Almost guaranteed. The minister promised . . . No trouble at all, I'm well in.'

'I'm very pleased,' said the general.

'Thank you. Do you know something, general?'

'What?'

'Quaresma has gone mad.'

'But . . . what? Who told you?'

'That guitar player. He's already in the asylum . . .'

'I guessed as much,' said Albernaz. 'That petition could only come from a lunatic.'

'But that's not all, general,' added Genelício. 'He wrote out an official letter in Tupí and sent it to the minister.'

'That's what I was saying,' said Albernaz.

'Who is he?' asked Florêncio.

'A neighbour; he works in the arsenal. Don't you know him?'

'A little fellow with pince-nez?'

'That's the one.'

'You couldn't expect anything else,' said Doctor Florêncio. 'Those books, that mania for reading . . .'

'Why did he read so much?' asked Caldas.

'A screw loose, somewhere,' said Florêncio.

Genelício interrupted authoritatively: 'He wasn't graduated, what did he want books for?'

41

'Very true,' said Florêncio.

'Books are all very well for the educated, for doctors,' put in Sigismundo.

'It ought to be forbidden,' said Genelício, 'for anyone without a university degree to own books. That way we should avoid such tragedies. Don't you agree?'

'Of course,' said Albernaz.

'Of course,' said Caldas.

'Of course,' added Sigismundo.

They were silent for a moment, and their attention turned again to the game.

'Are all the trumps out?'

'You should have counted, my friend.'

Albernaz lost, and there in the reception room there was silence. Cavalcânti was going to recite. He walked triumphantly across the room, a broad smile on his face, and took up his position beside the piano. Zizi accompanied him. He coughed, and in his harsh voice, giving much emphasis to the final 's'es, he began:

> 'Life is a comedy without sense,
> A story of blood and dust,
> A sunless desert . . .'

And the piano rattled away.

IV
Disastrous Consequences of a Petition

The events referred to by the grave personages gathered round the solo table on that memorable evening of Ismênia's engagement party had occurred with breath-taking rapidity. The force of Quaresma's ideas and feelings had made itself felt in an unexpected burst of whirlwind activity. The first move caused surprise, but there came others and yet others, so that what at first seemed an oddity or mild aberration soon assumed the appearance of downright lunacy.

It happened that some weeks before the engagement, at the opening of the session of the House of Representatives, the secretary was obliged to proceed to the reading of an unusual petition, one fated to enjoy more publicity and excite more comment than is usual with documents of such nature.

The clamour and disorder, characteristic of the meditation which is so indispensable to the dignified task of legislating, prevented the deputies from hearing it; the journalists, however, who were near the table did so, and broke out into peals of laughter ill suited to the dignity of the place. Laughter is contagious: the secretary, in the middle of the reading was laughing discreetly; by the end the president was laughing, the recorder was laughing, the attendant was laughing, the whole table and the people around it were laughing uproariously at the petition, trying to contain themselves, but some with the tears rolling down their cheeks.

Whoever was aware of the labour, effort, and disinterested, noble-minded thought represented by that sheet of paper, could not but feel the acutest grief at hearing the inoffensive laughter with which it was greeted. That document that reached the table of the House merited anger, hatred, an enemy's jeers perhaps, but not that hilarious reception, that innocent, artless hilarity as if one were laughing at some tomfoolery, a kind of circus or the contortions of a clown.

Those who laughed, however, did not know the motive, and only saw in it an object of honest, well-meaning merriment.

43

The session that day had been dreary, and for this reason, next day, the political columns of the newspapers published the following petition and commented on it at great length.

The petition read as follows:

'Policarpo Quaresma, Brazilian citizen and civil servant — convinced that the Portuguese language is not native to Brazil; that for this reason the spoken and written language in general, but especially in the field of literature, is placed in the humiliating position of suffering continual hostile criticism from the proprietors of the language; aware, too, that within our country authors and writers, particularly grammarians, do not agree on what constitutes grammatical correctness, witness the bitter polemics daily taking place between the most erudite students of our language — invoking the right conferred on him by the Constitution, does hereby request that the National Congress shall decree Tupí-guaraní the official and national language of the Brazilian people.

'The petitioner, leaving aside the historical arguments which support his ideas, begs leave to remember that language is the noblest manifestation of a people's intelligence, its most original and expressive creation, and that therefore the political emancipation of a country requires its linguistic emancipation as a necessary complement and consequence.

'Furthermore, Honourable Members of Congress, Tupí-guaraní, a unique language, agglutinative it is true, but afforded much varied richness by reason of its polysynthesis, is the only one capable of expressing our beauties, of putting us in close contact with our nature, and of adapting itself perfectly to our vocal and cerebral organs by reason of it being the creation of peoples who have lived and still live here, the possessors of a physiological and psychological structure towards which we are inclining; thus may we avoid the sterile grammatical controversies resulting from the difficult adaptation of a language from another region to our cerebral structure and vocal apparatus — controversies which so much impede the progress of our literary, scientific and philosophic culture.

'This petition is submitted for consideration in the confidence that the wisdom of our legislators will find the means to implement the measures proposed, and that the House and Senate will duly ponder their importance and utility.'

The major's petition was duly signed and stamped, and for days was the subject matter of every speech. It was published in every newspaper with facetious comments, and there was no one who failed to make a joke about it or who did not sharpen his wit at the expense of Quaresma's admonition. They did not stop at that: mischievous curiosity went further. They wanted to know who he was, what he did, was he married or single. An illustrated weekly published a caricature of him, and he was pointed out in the street.

As for the small, humorous papers, those gay, witty weeklies, they really murdered the poor major. With a frequency which indicated the editors' joy at finding an easy subject, the columns were full of, 'Major Quaresma said this', or, 'Major Quaresma did that'.

One of them, in addition to other references, dedicated a whole page to the subject of the week. The illustration was entitled, 'The Santa Cruz Slaughterhouse, according to Major Quaresma,' and the picture showed a queue of men and women marching towards a sacrificial tree seen on the left. Another referred to the case with a drawing of a butcher's shop. 'P. Quaresma — Butcher'; underneath a cook was asking the butcher, 'Have you any cow's liver?' To which the butcher replied, 'No, we only have virgin's. Do you want some?'

The comments, of greater or less degree of wit, poured forth uninterruptedly, and as a result of Quaresma's complete lack of friends in journalistic circles, with an unusual persistence. The under-secretary's name was juggled with for a fortnight.

Quaresma was deeply upset by all this. Having lived for thirty years, almost alone, without coming into conflict with the world, he had acquired a keen sensibility which was liable to cause him intense suffering at the slightest thing. He had never sought publicity or suffered criticism, but lived immersed in that dream of his which was nursed and kept alive by the warmth of his books. Apart from these he knew no one,

45

and with the few people he spoke to he merely exchanged banalities of everyday conversation, things remote from his innermost feelings. Not even his god-daughter, whom he respected above all others, was able to break down this reserve.

This withdrawal into himself gave him a peculiar aloofness to everything, disputes and ambitions; for all those things that make for enmity and quarrels were foreign to his temperament. Unconcerned about money, fame or status, living in his dream world, he had acquired the simple-mindedness and purity of soul one finds in dedicated men, the great scholars, sages and inventors, men who are more tender, ingenuous and innocent than the damsels of the poetry of by-gone ages. Such men are rare, but they exist, and when one finds them, even though they reveal traces of madness, one feels greater sympathy towards one's fellows, more pride in the human race, and more faith in the well-being of mankind.

The continued mockery of the newspapers and the manner in which people looked at him in the street exasperated him, and his ideas became more firmly rooted within him. The more jokes and witticisms he was submitted to, the more he reflected on his petition, weighing every aspect of it, examining it meticulously, comparing it with others and recalling the authors and authorities; and the more he did so, the more convinced he became of the futility of the criticism and the superficiality of the wit. The idea grew on him, dominated him, absorbing him more and more.

If the press had greeted the petition with a levity which was at heart inoffensive and without malice, Quaresma's department was furious. In bureaucratic circles superiority which derives from without, which is made and fashioned of materials other than official correspondence, knowledge of regulations and good handwriting, is received with the hostility of petty jealousy. It was as if they saw in the possessor of this superiority a traitor to mediocrity, to paper-pushing anonymity. It is not merely a question of promotion or financial interest; there is the question of self-respect, of wounded feelings, when they see their colleague, a slave like themselves, subject like them to the regulations, the whims of

46

the directors and the superior glances of the ministers, enjoying a greater claim to consideration, and some right to infringe the rules and instructions. He is regarded with the dissimulated hatred which the plebeian murderer has for his noble counterpart who has killed his wife and her lover. Both are murderers, but even in prison the aristocrat and the bourgeois bring with them the flavour of their world, a little of their fastidiousness, their inconformity, which wound their humble companion in distress.

And so it is that, in an office, when someone appears who does not make clear the whys and wherefores of his appointment, out come the pettinesses, the whispered slanders, the gossip, the whole arsenal of jealousy of a woman who is persuaded that her neighbour is better dressed than she is.

They get on better, or rather they are more easily accepted, those who earn recognition by their reports, their manner of writing or their dedication to their work, even doctors and graduates, than those who have reputation and fame. Office workers in general are totally incapable of recognizing the work or merit of a colleague, and none can be persuaded that that fellow, that clerk like themselves, can do anything to be of interest to strangers and make a stir in the whole city.

Quaresma's sudden popularity, his success and ephemeral renown, annoyed his colleagues and superiors. 'Just imagine it,' said the secretary. 'That fool writing to Congress and proposing something or other. The audacity of it.' The director, on passing through the office, looked at him through the corner of his eyes, regretting that the regulations did not cover the case, and so permit a severe reprimand. The least censorious was the filing clerk, and he called him an idiot.

The major felt only too keenly the falseness of the atmosphere, and the allusions made, and this increased his anger and the stubbornness with which he clung to his ideas. He did not understand why his petition should have aroused such a storm and such general ill will: it was a perfectly innocent, patriotic admonition which deserved, and ought to have had, the consent of everyone. He returned to the idea, pondered it and examined it with greater attention.

47

The extensive publicity given to the matter reached the ears of his friend Coleoni in his mansion, 'Real Grandeza'. A widower, and rich with the profits of his building contracts, the former greengrocer had retired from business and lived quietly in the spacious house which he himself had built, and which had the architectural features to which he was addicted: ornamented cornices, an immense monogram over the front door, two china dogs on the pillars of the front entrance, and other details of a similar nature.

In the centre of the grounds was the house, standing on a high basement. In front and alongside was a reasonable garden decorated with multicoloured globes; there was also a verandah and an aviary where, in the hot season, the wretched birds would die. It was a bourgeois establishment in the national taste: ostentatious, expensive, ill-suited to the climate and comfortless.

Within, extravagance was the rule, everything obeying a baroque fantasy, a hopeless eclecticism. The pieces of furniture were crowded on top of each other, carpets, pelmets, and bibelots, and his daughter's disorderly, undisciplined imagination brought even more confusion to that collection of expensive objects.

He had been a widower for some years, and had an elderly sister-in-law to look after his house and his daughter, and to supervise his parties and entertaining. Coleoni willingly accepted this gentle tyranny. He wanted to marry his daughter well, and after her own inclination, so he put no obstacle in her path.

At first he thought of giving her to his assistant or overseer, a kind of architect who did not draw the design, but planned houses and large buildings. He began by sounding out his daughter. He found no resistance, but neither did he find any acceptance. He decided that Olga's dreamy nature, reminiscent of a heroine, and her intelligence and imagination would not combine well with the rustic ignorance and simplicity of his assistant.

She wants a doctor — he thought — we'll see to it. Naturally he won't have a penny to his name, but I have, so things can be arranged.

He had become accustomed to see in the Brazilian doctor the marquis or baron of his native land. Each country has its own nobility: there it is the viscount, here it is the doctor, graduate or dentist, and Coleoni thought it quite reasonable to buy the satisfaction of ennobling his daughter with a few thousand milreis.

There were times when he became rather tired of the demands of his daughter. Fond of retiring early, he was obliged to spend night after night at the dances in the Lírico; enjoying sitting down with his slippers on, smoking a pipe, he had to walk the streets for hours on end after his daughter, skipping in and out of fashion shops, to have bought, at the end of the day, half a metre of ribbon, some pins, and a bottle of scent.

It was amusing to see him at the milliner's with the self-satisfied look of a father trying to ennoble his child, giving his opinion about materials, finding this one prettier, comparing that one with another, with a lack of feeling for these things that was apparent even when he paid for them. But he insisted on going, taking his time, striving to acquire the secret, to enter the mystery, with a genuine fatherly frankness and obstinacy.

So far, so good; he was able to master his annoyance. But what really irritated him were the visits of Olga's friends, their mothers and sisters, with their airs of false nobility and their dissimulated contempt, showing the old contractor what a difference there was socially between him and his daughter's friends and colleagues.

At heart, however, he did not mind very much: this was what he wanted and had worked for, and he had to accept it. Nearly always, during such visits, Coleoni would withdraw into the house. But this was not always possible: his presence was required at the larger parties and receptions, and it was then that he felt the thinly veiled disdain of the gentry who frequented his house. He had always been a contractor, with few ideas outside his job so that, unable to pretend, he had no taste for the gossip about weddings, dances, parties and expensive excursions.

49

Occasionally, one politer than the others would suggest a game of poker; he accepted and always lost. He went so far as to form a circle at home, of which the famous lawyer Pacheco was a member. He lost heavily, but that was not the reason he gave up. What did he lose? A few thousand: —peanuts! The fact was, however, that Pacheco played with six cards. The first time Coleoni noticed this he attributed it to nothing more than mere distraction on the part of the distinguished journalist. An honest man would not do that. The second time, could it also be? And the third?

So much distraction was not possible. Assured that he was being cheated, he kept quiet, restraining himself with a dignity hardly to be expected in a former contractor, and waited. When they next played, and the trick was practised again, Vicente lit a cigar, and in a perfectly calm voice said:

'Do you know that in Europe they now have a new way of playing poker?'

'What is it?' someone asked.

'There isn't much difference: you play with six cards, or rather one of the players does.'

Pacheco pretended it was a mistake, went on playing and winning, said goodnight at midnight very politely, made a few remarks about the game, and never returned.

As was his morning custom Coleoni was reading the papers, with the slow deliberation of the man who is little accustomed to reading, when he came upon the petition of his friend of the arsenal. He did not fully understand it, but the newspapers made such a joke of it, really going to town over the matter, that he imagined that his former benefactor was implicated in some criminal plot, and had inadvertently committed some grave error.

He had always thought of him as the most honest man in the world, and still did; but you never know . . . Wasn't it the last time they visited him that he had behaved so strangely? It could have been a joke . . .

Although he was now wealthy, Coleoni had a high regard for his obscure friend. This was not merely the gratitude of the peasant who has received a great favour, but a double respect

50

for the major for his being both a civil servant and an educated man. He was a European, of humble, rustic origin, so that deep down he still retained that awe with which peasants regard those who have received the investiture of the State. And as, despite many years in Brazil, he had not yet learned to distinguish between learning and titles, he held his friend's erudition in the highest esteem.

It is, therefore, not surprising that he was dismayed to see Quaresma's name involved in matters that were condemned by the newspapers. He read the petition again but did not understand what it meant. He called his daughter.

'Olga.'

He pronounced the girl's name almost without an accent; but when speaking Portuguese the words had a peculiar huskiness, and his sentences were interspersed with Italian exclamations and expressions.

'Olga, what does this mean? *No capisco* . . .'

Taking the newspaper, the girl sat down near him and read the petition and the commentaries.

'*Che*. Well?'

'Godfather wants to substitute the Tupí language for Portuguese. Do you follow?'

'What!'

'We speak Portuguese now, don't we? Well, from now on he wants us to speak Tupí.'

'*Tutti?*'

'All Brazilians, everyone.'

'*Ma che cosa!* Is it possible?'

'Perhaps. The Czechs have their own language and were obliged to speak German after the Austrian conquest; the inhabitants of Lorraine, the French . . .'

'*Per la madonna!* German is a language, but that Hottentot, *ecco*.'

'Hottentot is African, father; Tupí is Brazilian.'

'*Per Bacco!* It's all the same . . . He's mad.'

'But he's not mad at all, father.'

'What? Is this the idea of someone, bene?'

'Perhaps not wise, but not mad either.'

51

'*No capisco.*'

'It's an idea, father, a plan which is perhaps absurd at first sight, ·out of the ordinary, but not altogether mad. It's outrageous perhaps, but . . .'

However much she tried she could not see her godfather's act in the same light as her father. In him spoke the voice of common sense; in her, the love of great deeds, adventure and daring enterprises. She remembered what Quaresma had said to her about emancipation; and if she felt anything other than admiration for the major's boldness, it was certainly not disapproval or pity; it was sympathy and compassion at seeing so misunderstood the gesture of the man whom she had watched for so many years, in isolation and obscurity, obstinately pursuing his dream.

'This means trouble for him,' said Coleoni.

And he was right. The filing clerk's verdict was accepted in the discussions in the corridors, and the suspicions that Quaresma was mad were hardening into a certainty. At first the under-secretary weathered the storm well, but he grew annoyed when he suspected that they believed him ignorant of Tupí, and was filled with a silent rage which he could with difficulty suppress. How blind they were! He, who had made a close study of Brazil for thirty years, and as a result of these studies had been forced to learn that guttural German—he, not to know Tupí, the Brazilian language, the only one that was so—what a contemptible idea!

Let them think him mad if they wish. But to doubt the sincerity of his affirmations, no, not that! And studying ways and means of justifying himself, he became absent-minded, even while writing and doing his regular work. He lived two distinct lives: one devoted to his day to day obligations, the other to the problem of proving that he knew Tupí.

It happened that one day the secretary was away and the major took his place. There was a lot of work, and he himself drafted out and copied a part of it. He had begun to copy a document about some business in Mato Grosso in which Aquidauana and Ponta-Porã were mentioned, when at the bottom of the room Carmo said with a sneer:

'You know, Homero, talking is one thing, knowing is another.'

Quaresma did not so much as raise his eyes from the paper. Whether it was the Tupí words on the minute or Carmo's remark, the fact is that he insensibly began to translate the official document into the Indian language.

His absent-mindedness returned when he had finished it, but soon other employees came along for him to check the work they had done. Other matters drove it out of his mind, and completely forgotten about, the document in Tupí was borne away with the others. The director signed it without noticing, and the Tupinambá letter passed on to the ministry.

There it caused indescribable confusion. What language was it? Dr Rocha, the ablest man in the office, was consulted on the matter. He wiped his pince-nez, seized the paper, put it back to front, turned it upside down and concluded that it was Greek because of the 'y's.

In the office Dr Rocha enjoyed a great reputation for learning on account of his being a graduate in law and never speaking a word.

'But,' said his chief, 'are official communications permitted in a foreign language? I seem to remember there's an instruction of '84 . . . Check on it, Dr Rocha.'

They consulted all the regulations and indexes of legislation; they went from desk to desk to ask if anyone remembered, but nothing dealing with the matter could be found. At last, after three days of meditation, Dr Rocha went to the chief and announced confidently and emphatically:

'The '84 instruction deals with spelling.'

The director gazed at his subordinate with admiration and with an even higher opinion of the employee's intelligence, dedication and diligence. He was informed that there was no legislation dealing with the language in which official documents should be written, but that, nevertheless, the use of a language other than that of the country would appear to be irregular.

On the strength of this information and of other consultations made, the minister sent back the document to the arsenal with a reprimand.

What a morning that was in the arsenal! The buzzers sounded furiously, the office boys bustled about in terror, and the secretary, who was late in arriving, was asked for every minute.

Reprimanded! said the director to himself. There went his general's stars. So many years spent dreaming of those stars, and to see them slip through his fingers like that, perhaps because of a prank by some clerk. Things might change though. What a hope!

The secretary arrived and went to the director's office. When he knew what it was all about, he examined the document, and saw by the handwriting that it was Quaresma who had written it. The colonel ordered him to be sent for. Quaresma came thinking about some Tupí verses that he had read that morning.

'So, you have taken to playing jokes on me, have you?'

'What?' said Quaresma in surprise.

'Who wrote this?'

The major did not require to examine the paper. He saw the handwriting, remembered his fit of absent-mindedness, and admitted without hesitation, 'I did.'

'So you confess?'

'Of course. But sir, you don't know . . .'

'What's that you say? I don't know!'

The director rose to his feet, white lipped, his hand raised to his head. He had been offended three times: in his personal honour, the honour of his class, and that of the educational establishment he had attended, the Praia Vermelha school, the foremost scientific establishment in the world. More than this, he had written a short story, 'Homesickness', for the college magazine, *Pritaneu*, a work that had been highly praised by his colleagues. And so, having passed all his examinations with 'good' or 'distinction', he wore on his brow the double crown of scholar and artist. So many weighty titles, rarely found in one person, even in a Descartes or a Shakespeare, transformed that —'you don't know'—from a clerk, into a serious offence, an insult.

54

'Don't know! How dare you say that to me! Have you by any chance taken the Benjamin Constant course? Do you know Mathematics, Astronomy, Physics, Chemistry, Sociology, and Moral Philosophy? How dare you then? Do you think that because you have read a few novels, and picked up a bit of French, that you are in the same class as one who got 90% in Calculus, 100 in Mechanics, 80 in Astronomy, 100 in Hydraulics, 90 in Descriptive Analysis? Do you?'

The man shook his hand in rage, looking furiously at Quaresma who already imagined himself before the firing squad.

'But colonel . . .'

'There's nothing more to be said. Consider yourself suspended until further orders.'

Quaresma was gentle, good-natured and modest. It had never been his intention to doubt the wisdom of his director. He made no claims to be a scholar, and had used the words as preface to his apology; but when he was confronted with that torrent of knowledge and titles rushing in such fury, he lost the thread of his argument, his voice, his ideas, and remained utterly speechless.

The vanquished Quaresma slunk out of the office like a criminal, while the colonel glared at him furiously, indignantly, as one who has been wounded in the very depths of his being. He left. Arriving in the main office he said nothing: he took his hat and his walking stick and rushed out of the door, staggering like a drunken man. After walking a little, he went to the bookshop to fetch some books. Just as he was going to take the tram he met Ricardo Coração dos Outros.

'Early isn't it, major?'

'Yes, it is.'

They said no more, and there was a strained silence between them. Ricardo spoke again:

'You look as though you have something on your mind today, major. Some very important idea.'

'I have, my boy, but not just today. I've had it a long time.'

'It's good to think. It's a consolation to have a dream.'

'Perhaps it is; but it also makes us different from others, and creates barriers between men.'

And the two went their ways. The major caught his tram, and the carefree Ricardo walked with his awkward gait down the Rua do Ouvidor, his trousers turned up over his ankles, and his guitar, in its leather case, tucked under his arm.

V
The Statuette

It was not the first time she had been there. More than a dozen times she had climbed the wide stone staircase with its marble statuary from Lisbon on either side, 'Charity' and 'Our Lady of Mercy'; had passed between the Doric columns of the main entrance, crossed the tiled courtyard where, to the left and to the right, Pinel and Esquirel meditated on the distressful mystery of madness; had climbed the other carefully polished stairway, and met her godfather at the top, heavyhearted, absorbed in his dreams and ambitions. Her father occasionally brought her on Sundays when, in compassionate fulfilment of a friend's duty, he came to visit Quaresma. How long had he been there? She did not remember for certain; three or four months, if that much.

The name alone inspired fear. The asylum. It is like an entombment while still alive, a half burial, the burial of the spirit, of our guiding reason whose absence rarely affects the body itself. Health does not depend on it, and there are many who even appear to take a firmer hold on life, prolonging their existence, when it departs mysteriously from the body.

With what terror, a kind of fear of the supernatural or horror of an invisible, omnipresent enemy, did the poor people refer to that institution at Praia das Saudades! Better a quick death, they said.

At first sight it was difficult to understand this fear, this dread of the people for that huge, grim, forbidding house, half hospital, half prison, with its high railings and barred windows, stretching for several hundred metres, and overlooking the green immensity of the sea, there at the entrance of the bay, at Praia das Saudades. One entered and saw calm, pensive, contemplative men, like monks in retreat at prayer. Then, with that quiet, undisturbed, dignified entrance, one soon lost the popular idea of madness: uproar, wild antics, raving, and howling stupidity everywhere.

There was nothing like this: all was perfectly calm, quiet and orderly. But when eventually, in the visiting room, one examined more closely the bewildered appearance of the inmates, their contorted faces, some idiotic and expressionless, others distracted, submerged in some endless dream of their own, and saw, too, the agitation of some, contrasting sharply with the apathy of others, then it was that one truly felt the horror of madness, with its painful mystery of the flight of the spirit from what it supposes to be real, to seize and cling to the appearance of things and mere shadows.

Whoever has once beheld this indecipherable enigma of our very nature is struck with terror at the thought that the seed is planted in each one of us, and that the slightest thing may cause it to grow, binding us, crushing us with an absurd, chaotically distorted view of ourselves, our fellow men and the world. Every madman carries his own world within himself, and for him fellow beings do not exist: what he was before his madness is different, very different, from what he later becomes.

And this change does not begin, or rather its beginning is not felt, and it almost never ends. How had it been with her godfather? First of all, that petition . . . But what was that? A whim, a fancy, something unimportant, an old man's idea of no consequence whatever. And then the document. It was not

57

important; mere absent-mindedness, something that happens all the time . . . And finally? Downright madness; grim, ironical madness, that removes our soul and replaces it with another that debases us . . . That final downright madness, the exaltation of the self, the mania of refusing to go out, declaring himself persecuted and seeing enemies in his closest friends. How heartrending that had been, that first phase of his delirium when, in his irritable restlessness, he spoke incoherently, his words unrelated to what went on around him or to past events, so that one could not trace their origin or discover what prompted them. And the fear that took hold of the gentle Quaresma! It was the fear of one who has seen a cataclysm, making him tremble all over, from head to foot, and rendering him indifferent to all but his own delirium.

The house, his books and his money matters were all set at nought. For him nothing of this counted, it did not exist, had no importance. Such things were shadows, appearances: what was real were his enemies, those fearful enemies whom, in his delirium, he never succeeded in naming. His old sister, stunned and bewildered, with no one to fall back on, was utterly at a loss. Having been brought up at home always with a man beside her, first her father, then her brother, she was unable to fend for herself or deal with business, authorities and influential people. At the same time her inexperience and her sister's tenderness made her hesitate between the belief that all this was really true, and her suspicion that it was madness, pure and simple.

Had it not been for the intervention of her father (and for this Olga loved her rough, simple father all the more) who took charge of the family's affairs, and succeeded in converting Quaresma's imminent dismissal into retirement, what would have become of him? How easily our life can fall to pieces about our ears. That sensible, honest, methodical man with a secure job looked unshakeable; yet it needed but one little grain of folly . . .

Her godfather had been some months in the asylum, and his sister was unable to visit him. The shock to her nerves had been so great, and so much was she affected by seeing him in his wretched condition, shut up in that semi-prison, that an attack had been inevitable.

Olga and her father, sometimes just her father, came to see him. These, and occasionally Ricardo, were the only ones to do so.

That Sunday was particularly lovely, especially in Botafogo, close to the sea, with the high mountains outlined against a silken sky. The air was soft, and the sun shone gently on the paved streets. During the journey her father read the newspapers while she, deep in thought, glanced at the illustrated magazines she was taking to please and amuse her godfather.

He was a private patient, but even so, at first she had felt a certain embarrassment at mixing with the other visitors. It seemed to her that her fortune placed her above the necessity of witnessing wretchedness; but she suppressed this selfish thought, and her pride of class, and was now able to walk in normally, thus enhancing her own natural grace. She loved these sacrifices and self-denials, and being convinced of their importance, she felt pleased with herself.

There were other visitors on the tram, who promptly got off at the gates of the asylum. As at the gates of all our social infernoes, there were people of different social position, birth and fortune. Death is not the only leveller: madness, crime and sickness pass their levelling influence over the distinctions that we invent. The well-dressed and the ragged, the elegant and the poor, the handsome and the ugly, the intelligent and the ignorant—all entered serious and respectful, with a glint of fear in their eyes, as if they were entering another world.

They went up to their relatives and the parcels were unwrapped: there were sweets, tobacco, socks, slippers, sometimes books and newspapers. Some of the patients conversed with their relatives, others did not, maintaining a stubborn, inexplicable silence, while others remained indifferent. And such was the varied character of these meetings, and so much did its manifestations differ in the one and the other, that one tended to forget the affliction from which all those wretches suffered, thinking more in terms of personal caprice, with each one following the dictates of his own free will.

She reflected on the variety of life, how the sadder aspects outnumber the joyful ones, and how sorrow is more varied than joy, being the very moving force of life itself. This observation gave her a kind of satisfaction, for her curious, intelligent nature found pleasure in the simplest discoveries of her mind.

Quaresma was better. The frenzy had passed, and the delirium seemed about to disappear completely. The shock of finding himself in those surroundings had produced a reaction that was both necessary and salutary. He was mad, for if they put him there . . .

There was even a satisfied smile lurking beneath his greying moustache when he came to greet his god-daughter and her father. He was a little thinner and his black hair a little whiter, but his general appearance was the same. He had not altogether lost the meekness and gentleness of his manner of speaking, but when excited he became bitter and suspicious. On seeing them, he said warmly:

'So you came after all . . . I was waiting for you . . .'

They exchanged greetings, and he gave an affectionate hug to his god-daughter.

'How is Adelaide?'

'She's well. She sends her love, but she didn't come because . . .' said Coleoni.

'Poor thing,' he said, hanging his head as if to drive away an unpleasant memory. Then he asked, 'And Ricardo?'

Full of eagerness and joy at seeing him already safe from the near-death of insanity, his god-daughter was quick to answer. 'He's well, godfather. He came to see daddy a few days ago and said that your pension is almost through.'

Coleoni and Quaresma had both sat down, but the girl remained standing, the better to look at her godfather with her bright eyes and steady gaze. House guards and doctors passed in and out with professional indifference. The visitors avoided meeting each other's eyes as if not wishing to be recognized in the street. Outside the day was beautiful; the air was soft, the sea boundless and sombre, the mountains outlined against a silken sky—nature's beauty majestic and unfathomable. Coleoni, though a regular visitor, now noted the improvement in his friend with a satisfaction which showed itself in a slight smile that played over his features. At one point he said:

'You're much better now, major, do you want to go home?'

Quaresma did not answer immediately. He thought a little and then replied slowly and firmly:

'It's better to wait a while. I'm better . . . I'm sorry to give you so much trouble, but you have been so good to me you must put it down just to goodness itself. If you have enemies you need to have good friends too . . .'

Father and daughter glanced at each other. The major looked up and seemed to be on the verge of tears. The girl put in quickly:

'You know, godfather, I'm getting married.'

'It's true,' added her father. 'Olga is going to get married and we came to bring you the news.'

'Who is your fiancé?' asked Quaresma.

'He's a young man . . .'

'Of course,' interrupted her godfather with a smile.

The two laughed with him, unaffectedly and happily. It was a good sign.

'His name is Armando Borges and he is graduating as a doctor. Are you pleased, godfather?' said Olga politely.

'So it will be early in the new year.'

'That's what we are hoping,' said the Italian.

'Are you very much in love?' asked Quaresma.

She did not know how to answer. She would have liked to feel she was in love but she was not. So why was she marrying? She did not know . . . It was some impulse from without, something not of her—she did not know. Did she love another? Again the answer was no. None of the boys she knew was sufficiently distinguished to strike her; none had that indefinable quality of feeling and intelligence that would fascinate and captivate her. She could not define it, nor had she yet analysed her feelings to discover what quality she would

61

prefer to see dominant in a man. It was the heroic, the unusual, the enthusiasm for great things; but in the mental confusion of our early years, when our ideas and desires are jumbled together and mixed up, Olga was unable to recognize and grasp this aspiration, or to conceive this manner of loving a man.

And she was right to marry without following her ideal, for it is so difficult to discern this clearly in a man of twenty to thirty, and she was quite likely to take a goose for a swan. She was marrying because it was the custom in society to do so, and partly out of curiosity, to widen her horizons and sharpen her sensibility. All this passed through her mind in a flash, and she answered her godfather, but without conviction:

'Yes, very much.'

The visit was not prolonged much further. It was better that it should be rapid so as not to tire the patient. As they left, the two did not trouble to conceal that they were pleased and hopeful.

There were already some visitors at the gates, waiting for the tram. As this was not at the stop they began to walk towards it along the front of the asylum. Halfway there they passed an old negress leaning against the railings and crying. The good-hearted Coleoni went up to her:

'Well old lady, what's the matter?'

The poor woman looked up at him through her tears, with a gentle gaze that was full of inconsolable grief, and replied:

'Ah, sir . . . It's a terrible thing . . . Poor lad, he was such a good son.'

And she went on crying. Coleoni was moved; his daughter looked at the woman with interest, and then asked:

'Is he dead?'

'It would be better if he was, miss.'

And through her tears and sobs she told how her son no longer recognized her or answered her questions: he was like a stranger. She wiped her tears and said finally:

'It was the "evil eye".'

The two walked sorrowfully away, carrying in their hearts a fraction of that humble grief.

The day was cool, and the breeze which began to blow ruffled the surface of the sea to form little white waves. The Sugar-Loaf rose up black, solemn and erect from the breakers, as if casting a shadow over the brilliance of the day.

In the Institute for the Blind a violin was playing, and the plaintive, drawn-out sounds of the instrument seemed to be inspired by all the sadness and solemnity around them.

The tram was late, but it finally arrived and they took it. They got off in the Largo da Carioca. It is good to see the city on a Sunday, with its shops closed and its narrow streets deserted, where footsteps echo as in silent cloisters. The city is like a skeleton: it lacks its flesh, which is the movement and activity of carriages, carts and people. At the door of one shop or another the shopkeeper's children ride their bicycles or play with balls, so that one feels even more forcibly the difference of the city from the day before.

The habit of visiting nearby beauty spots was not yet popular, and the only people to be seen were the occasional couple hurrying to pay a call as they were now doing. The Largo de São Francisco was quiet, and the statue which stood in the middle of whàt was once a small garden, now disappeared, seemed merely an ornament. The trams arrived lazily, carrying few passengers. Coleoni and his daughter caught one which took them to Quaresma's house. They went there. Evening was closing in, and already Sunday-best clothes could be seen through the windows: negroes in light-coloured clothes and smoking long cigars or cigarettes; groups of sales clerks with gaudy buttonholes; girls in starched muslin; antediluvian top-hats side by side with heavy, black satin dresses adorning the ample bodies of sedentary matrons; and in this manner was Sunday embellished by the simplicity of the humble, the wealth of the poor, and the ostentation of fools.

Dona Adelaide was not alone: Ricardo had come to visit her, and they were talking. When Coleoni knocked on the door he was telling the old lady about his latest success:

'I don't know what to do, Dona Adelaide. It's such a nuisance, I don't write down my music.'

It was a case that would put any author on the spot. Senhor

63

Paysandón, who was a well known composer in the Argentine city of Córdoba, had written to him asking for some examples of his music and songs. This put Ricardo in a predicament. He had the lyrics written out, but not the music. It is true that he knew it all by heart, but to write it down from one hour to the next was a task beyond his powers.

'It's the very devil,' he said. 'Not so much for me, but to lose this chance of making Brazil better known abroad!'

Quaresma's old sister was not very interested in the guitar. Her upbringing, seeing the instrument in the hands of slaves and such like, precluded its being given serious attention by people of a certain class. But she politely put up with Ricardo's obsession, for she was beginning to feel a measure of esteem for the famous troubadour of the suburbs, an esteem which arose from his dedication to the family during their recent drama. Ricardo had taken upon himself all the small jobs and duties, running errands here and there, discharging them willingly and expeditiously.

It was he, in fact, who was dealing with his former pupil's retirement. It was an arduous task, that of 'liquidating' a retirement, as it is called in bureaucratic jargon. A solemn decree may authorize some poor fellow's retirement, but there is the red-tape of a dozen departments and officials to go through before the matter is concluded. Nothing surpasses the gravity with which the employee informs us that he is still making the calculations. And the thing drags on for a month, even more, as if it were a case of celestial mechanics.

Coleoni was acting as the major's agent, but not being well versed in official matters he had handed over that part of his authority to Coração dos Outros. The latter, thanks to his popularity and affability, had overcome the resistance of the bureaucratic machine, so that the whole affair was expected to be wound up very soon. It was this that he announced to Coleoni when he came in, followed by his daughter. Both he and Dona Adelaide asked after their friend and brother.

The sister had never understood her brother very well, and now understood him no better as a result of this crisis. But with the simple affection of a sister, she had suffered deeply, and was desperately anxious for his recovery.

Ricardo Coração dos Outros was fond of the major, and had found in him that moral and intellectual support that he needed. The others liked to hear him sing, but their enjoyment was that of mere dilettantes; only the major appreciated the full significance of his efforts, and recognized the patriotic importance of his work. And now he had his own private troubles — his fame, the reward of years of slow, uninterrupted work, was threatened. A creole singer of modinhas had appeared who was beginning to make a name for himself, and whose name was already being mentioned together with his. His rival annoyed him for two reasons: first because he was black; secondly, because of his ideas.

It was not that he had any particular aversion towards negroes. What he saw in the fact of a famous negro playing the guitar was that this would lower even more the prestige of the instrument. If his rival played the piano and became famous for that, there would be nothing wrong. On the contrary, the lad's genius would dignify his person through the medium of the highly respected instrument. But playing the guitar, the opposite was true: the prejudice against his person served to disparage the mysterious guitar which he, Ricardo, so much prized. And furthermore, there were those ideas of his! Really! To expect the modinha to say something and to have regular versification! What stupidity!

And Ricardo began to think of this unexpected rival who had thus appeared before him as an unforeseen obstacle in his own wonderful path to glory. It was necessary to get rid of him, crush him, prove his own unquestionable superiority. But how?

Mere publicity was not enough; his rival used it too. If he could find some famous person, an outstanding man of letters, who would write an article about him and his work, victory was assured. He thought of a periodical, *The Guitar*, in which he would defy his rival, and crush him in the ensuing polemics.

This was what he wanted, and his hopes lay with Quaresma, who was at present in the asylum, but fortunately on the way

65

to recovery. Consequently his joy was great when he knew that his friend was better.

'I couldn't go today,' he said, 'but I'll go on Sunday. Is he any fatter?'

'Just a little,' said the girl.

'He was able to talk well,' added Coleoni. 'He even looked pleased when he learned that Olga is going to get married.'

'Are you getting married, Dona Olga? Congratulations.'

'Thank you,' she said.

'When will it be, Olga?' asked Dona Adelaide.

'Not till the end of the year . . . There's plenty of time yet . . .'

This immediately produced a storm of questions about her fiancé and speculation about the wedding. Olga was vexed: she considered both the questions and the speculation presumptuous and annoying. She tried to turn the conversation, but they always returned to the same subject, not only Ricardo but Adelaide too, more talkative and curious than usual. This torture, which was repeated during every visit she made, almost made her regret her engagement. At last she found a subterfuge by asking:

'How is the general?'

'I haven't seen him, but his daughter always calls here. He is well, I expect; it is Ismênia who's the sad one—she's broken-hearted, poor thing.'

Dona Adelaide then recounted the drama that had shaken the general's daughter's little soul. Cavalcânti, that Jacob of five years' standing, had left for the interior three or four months ago and had sent neither letter nor card. The girl considered their engagement broken, and being incapable of stronger sentiments or any more serious application of her mental and physical energies, took it very badly, seeing it as something beyond hope, something that absorbed all her attention.

For Ismênia it was as if all the marriageable young men had ceased to exist. To find another would be an insoluble problem, a task beyond her powers to perform. It was too difficult. To flirt, write letters, make eyes, dance, go for walks—she couldn't go through that again. It was obvious that she was fated not to marry, to be an aunt, to endure throughout her life the terrifying condition of spinsterhood. She scarcely remembered what her fiancé looked like, with his staring eyes and strong, bony nose; but quite unconnected with his memory there always came to her mind, every morning when the postman failed to hand her a letter, this other idea: not to be married. It was a punishment . . . Quinota was going to be married, Genelício was already seeing to the papers. And she, who had waited so long and been the first to get engaged, was to be cursed, humiliated before them all. It even seemed that they were both pleased at Cavalcânti's inexplicable flight. How they had laughed during Carnival! How they had thrown her premature widowhood in her face during the merrymaking! The zest they had put into the confetti throwing and perfume squirting showed only too clearly their happiness on the wonderful, coveted path towards matrimony, in the face of their forsaken sister.

She managed to hide the feelings produced by their happiness, which seemed to her unfriendly and offensive. But her sister's raillery when she was constantly telling her, 'Have fun, Ismênia. He's a long way away so enjoy yourself,' made her furious, with the terrible fury of the weak, which eats away slowly, inside, because it cannot burst out in any other way.

So in order to drive away unwelcome thoughts she took to observing the childish spectacle in the streets, the multicoloured bunting and the brilliant streamers hanging from the balconies; but what had the best effect on her poor, repressed nature were the lines of dancers, and the noise of the tom-toms, timbrels, drums and cymbals. And so those thoughts slumbered, drowned in the uproar, and like the idea that had pursued her for so long, were prevented from entering her head.

Besides this, the extravagant Indian costumes, the ornaments of a frankly savage mythology—alligators, snakes, turtles, all so much alive—these brought to her feeble imagination glowing pictures of limpid streams, boundless forests, regions of calm and purity which comforted her.

And the Carnival songs too, bawled out with a remorseless rhythm and almost entire lack of melody, served to repress the pain within her which, stifled, restricted and held back, clamoured for release in screams which she no longer had sufficient strength to utter.

Cavalcânti had left a month before Carnival, and after this great Carioca festival her torture became more acute. Not being accustomed to read or converse, and having no domestic activities whatever, she spent the days lying or sitting down, brooding over the same idea: not to be married. It was a relief to cry. Whenever the postman came she still experienced a joyful hope. Perhaps? But the letter never came and she returned to her thought: not to be married.

As Dona Adelaide finished relating the disaster that had befallen the said Ismênia, she commented:

'That sort of thing ought to be punished, don't you think?'

'There's no reason to give up hope. Lots of people are lazy when it comes to writing,' said Coleoni, in a gentle, kind voice.

'Don't you believe it,' said Dona Adelaide. 'It's three months now, Senhor Vicente.'

'He won't come back,' said Ricardo authoritatively.

'Does she still expect him to, Dona Adelaide?' asked Olga.

'I don't know, my child. No one understands that girl. She hardly speaks, and when she does it's neither here nor there. She's so listless by nature. You can feel her misery, but she just won't say anything.'

'Is it out of pride?' persisted Olga.

'No, no . . . If it were pride she wouldn't refer to him from time to time. It's more like indolence, apathy . . . It seems she's afraid of saying anything for fear it might happen.'

'And what do her parents say about it?' asked Coleoni.

'I really don't know. But from what I can make out the general is not very upset, and Dona Maricota thinks she should find someone else.'

'That would be the best thing,' said Ricardo.

'I'm afraid she's a bit out of practice,' said Dona Adelaide, smiling. 'She has been engaged for so long . . .'

By the time Ismênia came to pay her daily call on Quaresma's sister the conversation had already drifted to other subjects. As she greeted them they all were aware of her distress. Suffering gave a certain vigour to her features. Her eyelids were dark, and her small, brown eyes wider and brighter. She asked after Quaresma, and there followed a brief silence. Finally Dona Adelaide asked:

'Have you had a letter yet, Ismênia?'

'Not yet,' she replied, half whispering.

Ricardo moved in his chair. His arm struck a shelf, knocking to the floor a small porcelain statuette which, almost soundlessly, shattered into a thousand fragments.

PART TWO

I
At The Haven

The place itself was neither ugly nor beautiful, but it had that peaceful, satisfied look of one who is well contented with his lot.

The house was situated on a narrow strip of land which formed a kind of terrace on the lower slopes of a small hill that rose up at the back. In front, seen through the bamboos of the hedge, a plain stretched away towards the distant mountains. This was cut, parallel to the line of the house, by the dirty, stagnant waters of a small stream. Further on, looking like a bright ribbon, the railway slashed its way across the plain; while to the left a cart-track, with houses either side, crossed the stream and wound its way on to the station. Quaresma's dwelling thus enjoyed an ample view; to the east there was the cool hillside, and the whitewashed walls made it gay and pleasant. Although the architecture was of the wretched sort common to our country houses, it boasted huge living-rooms, spacious bedrooms, all with windows, and a verandah with an irregular portico. Apart from this main building, 'The Haven', as Quaresma's country estate was called, possessed various outbuildings: the old flour-mill, with its wheel dismantled but the furnace still intact, and a stable with a thatched roof.

Less than three months had passed since he had come to occupy the house, in that secluded spot, two hours by rail from Rio, having spent six months in the asylum at Praia das

Saudades. Was he cured? Who can tell? He seemed to be: his gestures and actions were those of a normal man; but nevertheless there were signs that led one to believe that, though it could no longer be called madness, the dream he had nursed for so many years had not entirely forsaken him. Those six months had been valuable more for the rest and seclusion they afforded rather than for any psychiatric treatment.

The uncomplaining Quaresma had lived there, in the asylum, talking to his companions. There he saw rich men claiming they were poor, beggars behaving like rich men, the scholarly cursing knowledge, and fools protesting their wisdom. But of all of them the one that most astonished him was a peaceful old shop-keeper from the Rua dos Pescadores who thought he was Attila. 'I,' the inoffensive old fellow would say, 'am Attila, you know? I'm Attila.' He knew next to nothing about the warrior, merely the name. 'I'm Attila, I've killed lots of people . . .' And that was all.

The major left there more heavy-hearted than he had ever been before in all his life. Of all the sad things there are to see in this world, the saddest, the most acutely depressing, is madness.

The fact that our life goes on much the same, with this imperceptible, yet deep and almost always unfathomable derangement rendering it useless, causes us to think of something stronger than ourselves guiding us, driving us on, in whose hands we are nothing more than toys. At different times and in different places madness has been regarded as sacred, an idea that is justified by the feeling that overwhelms us when, on hearing the ravings of a madman, we immediately think that it is not he who is speaking, it is someone else, someone who sees for him, interprets things for him, is there behind him, invisible . . .

Quaresma left, deeply affected by the misery of the asylum. He went home; but the sight of familiar objects could not remove the strong impression that had stamped itself on his mind. His features, never particularly cheerful, now bore stronger signs of sorrow and depression than ever before, and it was in an attempt to raise his spirits that he had retired to that pleasant house in the country to live the life of a small farmer.

It was not he, however, who had thought of it; it was his god-daughter who had suggested that he spend the remainder of his days in that pleasant occupation. Seeing him so depressed, sad and moody, shut up in his house in São Cristóvão and unwilling to go out, she said to him one day in an affectionate, daughterly way:

'Godfather, why don't you buy a little farm? It would be so nice to grow things and have your own orchard and vegetable plots . . . what do you think?'

Irritable as he was, he could not help changing his expression as soon as he heard the girl's suggestion. It was an old ambition of his to obtain his food, his happiness and his livelihood from the soil, and it was with these former projects in mind that he answered:

'You are right, my child. What a wonderful idea of yours. There is so much fertile land that's not being made use of . . . Our country has the most fertile land in the world. Corn gives two harvests a year and a ratio of four hundred to one . . .'

Olga almost regretted having made the suggestion. It seemed that it might revive in her godfather's mind obsessions that had been eradicated.

'But don't you think, godfather, that every country has fertile land?'

'But comparable to ours,' he hastened to answer, 'there are very few. I'm going to do what you say: I shall grow corn, beans, potatoes . . . You'll see what I shall produce in my plantations and my orchard, and that will convince you just how fruitful our soil is.'

The idea, once planted in his brain, soon took root. The soil was already prepared and was only awaiting the seed. It did not bring happiness, which he had never known, but his moodiness and depression disappeared and there was a return of the mental activity of former days. He inquired the current prices of fruit, vegetables, potatoes and cassavas; he

73

calculated that fifty orange trees, thirty avocado pear, eight peach and other fruit trees, as well as pineapples (what a goldmine), pumpkins and other less important products would give an annual income of four thousand milreis clear of expenses. It would be idle to give here the details of his calculations, based as they were on everything that was laid down in the bulletins of the National Agricultural Association. He took into consideration the average yield of each fruit tree and each hectare under cultivation, together with wages and unavoidable losses; and as for the prices, he went to the market himself to check on them.

He planned his agricultural life with the care and precision that he put into all his projects. He looked at it from every angle, weighing the pros and cons, and was delighted when he discovered it to be financially attractive, not because of any desire to make a fortune, but because this was a further proof of the excellences of his native country.

It was with all this in mind that he bought the estate called 'The Haven', whose name was so well suited to the new life he had adopted after the storm that had shaken him for almost a year. It was not far from Rio, and although neglected and in bad repair, he had chosen it the better to demonstrate the power and capability of perseverance and love in agricultural work. He hoped for good harvests of corn, fruit and vegetables, so that, attracted by his example, a thousand other cultivators would appear, and before long the great capital would be surrounded by a veritable granary, so rich and abundant as to render imports from Europe and Argentina unnecessary.

How happy he had been to go there! He had practically no regrets for his old house in São Januário, now in the hands of strangers and possibly destined to be used for letting . . . It meant nothing to him that that spacious room, which had quietly sheltered his books for so many years, might become a frivolous ballroom, might witness the squabbles of quarrelling couples and family feuds. It was such a pleasant room, so snug and cosy with its high ceiling and unadorned walls, all of it impregnated with the desires closest to his heart and the fabric of his dreams . . .

He was contented. How easy it was to live off our land. Four thousand milreis a year to be earned from the soil with such ease, pleasure and joy! What a blessed land it was! How could people want to be civil servants, to rot behind a desk, servile and humiliated? How could anyone prefer to live in wretched little houses with no air or light, breathing a foul atmosphere and eating miserable food, when so easily one could have a life that was happy, abundant, free, gay and healthy?

It was only now that he had arrived at this conclusion, after having endured for so long the misery of the city and the enervating influence of government offices. It had come late, but not so late as to prevent him from experiencing, before he died, the idyllic rustic life and the fertility of the Brazilian soil. He decided then that his aim to bring about major reforms in institutions and customs was a vain one: what was vital to the greatness of his beloved country was a strong foundation based on agriculture and the cult of its fruitful soil, on which to build securely for the high destiny she was to fulfil. Moreover, the fertile land and varied climates, which permitted easy, profitable farming, made this the obvious path to follow.

Then he saw before his eyes the hillsides covered with rows of orange trees in blossom, snow-white and fragrant, looking like a procession of brides; the avocado pear trees with their rugged trunks laboriously supporting the heavy green fruit; the jabuticabas bursting from the firm branches; the pineapples, crowned like kings, receiving the warm blessing of the sun; the pumpkins spreading with their heavy, pollenladen flowers; the water-melons of such a vivid green they seem to be painted; the velvet peaches, the enormous breadfruit, the jambos, the huge mangoes; and amid all this the figure of a woman, her lap full of fruit, and one shoulder bare, smiling at him in gratitude, with the lingering, disembodied smile of a goddess: — Pomona, the goddess of orchards and gardens.

Quaresma spent his first few weeks at 'The Haven' making a systematic exploration of his new property. There was ample land, some old fruit trees, a dense virgin tract with red sage, bacurubus, prickle ashes, tibibuias, munjolos and other varieties of wild plant. Anastácio, who had accompanied him, was obliged to call upon memories of his days as a plantation slave, and it was he who taught their names to Quaresma, so widely read and knowledgeable in all things Brazilian.

Quaresma soon set up a museum of natural life at 'The Haven'. The specimens, taken from the woods and fields, were labelled with their common names, and wherever possible with the scientific ones too: the plants in a herbarium, and the woods in small blocks cut lengthwise and crosswise.

In his reading Quaresma had had occasion to study the natural sciences, and in his autodidactic fervour he had acquired a good groundwork of botany, zoology, mineralogy and geology.

It was not only the plants that were considered worthy of an inventory, but the animals too; however, as he did not have sufficient space, and because the preservation of the specimens required more care, Quaresma limited himself to making his museum on paper. From this he learned that his land was inhabited by armadillos, agoutis, opossums, a variety of snakes, shore-birds, rice-finches, seedeaters, tiés etc. It was poor in minerals: clay, sand, and here and there some crumbling blocks of granite.

When this inventory was finished he spent two weeks organizing his agricultural library and drawing up a list of the meteorological instruments needed to assist the work on the farm. He ordered Brazilian, French and Portuguese books, and bought thermometers, barometers, pluviometers, hygrometers, and anemometers. These arrived and were set up and suitably installed.

Anastácio watched all these preparations with amazement. What was all this stuff for—so many books, so much glass? Could his old employer be going in for pharmacy? The old negro's doubts did not last long. On one occasion when Quaresma was reading the pluviometer, Anastácio was nearby, gazing in astonishment as if it was some form of witchcraft. Noticing his servant's stupefaction, Quaresma said:

'Do you know what I'm doing, Anastácio?'

'No, boss.'

'I'm seeing if it has rained very much.'

'What you do that for boss? You can tell by looking how much it rains . . . Farm work means clearing the land, putting the seed in the soil, letting it grow and then harvesting . . .'

He spoke slowly and with assurance, in his soft African voice, scarcely sounding his 'r's.

Quaresma, without abandoning his instruments, gave heed to his servant's advice. The property was covered with weeds and brushwood. The orange trees, avocado pears and mangoes were uncared for, full of dead branches and covered with an unsightly growth of mistletoe; but as it was not the right season for pruning and cutting the branches Quaresma limited himself to weeding between the trees. Each morning at sunrise he and Anastácio would set out, hoe on shoulder, to begin the day's work. The sun was fierce and unrelenting; it was high summer, but Quaresma, brave and undaunted, insisted on going.

It was quite a sight to see him with his tiny figure, short-sighted, in a straw hat, wielding an enormous, rough-handled hoe, giving blow after blow in an attempt to uproot a stubborn screw-tree. His hoe looked more like a dredge or an excavator than a small agricultural instrument. Anastácio, beside him, looked on with a mixture of surprise and compassion. To go out and work under that sun just for pleasure, and without knowing how! You see all types in this world!

The two went on working: the old negro swiftly and deftly clearing away the undergrowth with his practised hand, his hoe gliding smoothly over the ground, cutting down the weeds; Quaresma furiously tearing up clods of earth here and there, held up for a long time at every bush, and sometimes, when he missed his aim and the blade bit into the ground, sending up a cloud of dust that made one think a troop of cavalry was passing by. On these occasions Anastácio would intervene, saying humbly but authoritatively:

'Not like that major, sir. You mustn't let the hoe go into the soil. Gently, like this.'

And he would teach his simple, inexperienced master the knack of using the ancient implement. Quaresma would seize it, place himself in position, and make a supreme effort to use it in the manner indicated. All in vain. The flange struck against the plant, the hoe rebounded, and overhead a little bird chirped mockingly, 'I see, I see.' The major lost his temper and tried again, exhausted and sweating, striking in rage with all his strength. Several times the hoe, missing both plant and earth, threw him off balance so that he fell to the ground, kissing the earth, mother of fruits and men. His pince-nez flew off and was smashed against a stone.

The exasperated major returned with redoubled energy to the task he had imposed on himself; and so firmly do our muscles retain the age-old memory of the sacred labour of wresting a living from the soil that Quaresma did not find it impossible to awaken in his the skill required to handle the venerable hoe. At the end of a month he could use it reasonably well; not continuously from dawn to dusk, but with long breaks for rest from time to time, as his age and lack of practice required.

Sometimes the faithful Anastácio would take a rest with him, and they would lie together, side by side, in the shade of one of the thicker fruit trees, with the heavy air of those summer days pressing through the foliage, and inducing in everything a sensation of morbid resignation. It was then, shortly after midday, when all around was as if drugged by the heat, and all life buried in silence, that the old major discovered the true nature of the tropics, composed, as it was, of contradictions such as he now saw: the bright, high, Olympian sun blazing down on the torpor of death, its own creation.

They had their lunch out there in the open, eating food from the day before quickly warmed up over an improvised stove made of stones, and then worked on until dinner time. There was in Quaresma a sincere enthusiasm, the enthusiasm of the idealist who wants to put his theories into practice. He was not dismayed by the initial ingratitude shown by the land, its morbid love of weeds and incomprehensible hatred of the fertilizing hoe. He laboured away, clearing the ground, until it was time for dinner.

He took more time over this meal, talking a little to his sister, telling her what he had done during the day which always consisted of an estimate of the area already cleared.

'You know, Adelaide, tomorrow the orange trees will be completely cleared, there won't be a single weed left.'

His sister, older than him, did not share his enthusiasm for rural life. It was too quiet, and if she had come to live with him it was only through the habit of always being with him. Of course she was fond of him, but she did not understand him: his actions and his inner conflicts were incomprehensible to her. Why hadn't he done as others did, taken a degree and become a deputy? That would have been so nice . . . But to bury his nose in books year after year and end up being a nobody was sheer stupidity. She had followed him to 'The Haven' and to pass the time had taken up raising chickens, much to the joy of her farmer brother.

'That's all very well,' she said, when her brother was telling her about the day's work. 'But don't you make yourself ill . . . Out in that sun all day long . . .'

'What do you mean, ill, Adelaide. Can't you see how healthy the people here are? If they get ill it's because they don't work.'

After dinner Quaresma went to the window which looked out onto the chicken-run and threw crumbs of bread out to the birds. The spectacle of the ducks, geese and hens, big and small, all engaged in a furious struggle pleased him: it seemed a picture of life in miniature, together with the rewards it offers. Later on he asked how the fowls were getting on.

'Have the ducklings hatched yet, Adelaide?'

'Not yet. There are eight days to go yet.'

And then his sister added:

'Your god-daughter is getting married on Saturday, aren't you going?'

'No, I can't go. All that formality would only upset me . . . I'll send a sucking pig and a turkey.'

'For heaven's sake, what a present to send!'

'What's wrong with that? It's traditional.'

That particular day the two of them were talking together in the dining room of the old country house when Anastácio came to inform them that there was a gentleman at the door. Ever since they had moved in no visitor, apart from a few poor people of the district asking, or in effect begging, for this or that, had knocked at Quaresma's door. He himself had made no acquaintances, so he received the old negro's communication with surprise. He hastened to receive his visitor in the main room, and found that the latter had already climbed the little front stairway and was on the verandah.

'Good evening, major.'

'Good evening. Please come in.'

The stranger entered and sat down. There was nothing unusual about him except that he was fat. His size was not excessive or grotesque, but was somehow disreputable, as if it had developed suddenly and he had stuffed himself with food for fear it might go down from one day to the next. Thus he was like a lizard that lays up fat in preparation for the hard winter. Through the plumpness of his cheeks one could see his natural, normal thinness. If he was destined to be fat, it was not at that age, little more than thirty, with no time for the rest of his body to put on weight; for though his cheeks were fat, his hands were still thin, with long, spindly, active fingers. The visitor spoke:

'I am Lieutenant Antonio Dutra, secretary of the inland revenue.'

'Is anything wrong?' asked Quaresma anxiously.

'No, nothing at all. We know who you are; everything is in order, there's nothing against you.'

The secretary coughed, took a cigarette, offered one to Quaresma and continued:

'Knowing that you were moving in here, major, I took the liberty to come and disturb you . . . It's nothing important . . . I hope, major . . .'

'Oh, not at all, lieutenant. Not at all.'

'I've come to ask for your co-operation in the form of a small contribution to the festival of Our Lady of the Immaculate

Conception, our patron; I am the secretary of the fraternity.'

'Of course. That's quite alright. Though I'm not a religious man, I'm . . .'

'One thing has nothing to do with the other. It is a local tradition that we ought to keep up.'

'Quite right.'

'You know,' went on the secretary, 'people hereabouts are very poor, and the fraternity too, so we are forced to call upon the good-will of those who are better off. And so, major . . .'

'No, wait a moment . . .'

'Oh major, please don't bother. It isn't urgent.'

He mopped his brow and put away his handkerchief. Then he looked outside and said:

'This heat. I've never seen a summer like this here before. How are you settling in, major?'

'Very well.'

'Do you intend to take up farming?'

'Yes, that's the reason I came into the country.'

'Nowadays it's no good, but years ago . . . This farm was a beauty, major. So much fruit. So much corn. Now the soil is worn out and . . .'

'What do you mean, worn out, Senhor Antonio! No soil is worn out. Europe has been cultivated for thousands of years, but . . .'

'But there people work.'

'Why don't they work here too?'

'How right you are! But with our land there are so many difficulties that . . .'

'But my dear lieutenant, there's nothing that can't be overcome.'

'You'll learn in good time, major. Here in our country the only thing that matters is politics, and nothing else. Just now there's a quarrel going on about the election of deputies . . .'

As he said this, the secretary threw a searching glance from under his fat eyelids at Quaresma's innocent features.

'What is it all about?' asked Quaresma.

The lieutenant, who seemed to be expecting the question, promptly asked with a smile:

'Don't you know?'

'No.'

'I'll tell you. The government's candidate is Doctor Castrioto, an honest man and a good speaker. But certain presidents of the Municipal Councils of the District have taken it into their heads to oppose the government just because Senator Guariba quarreled with the governor. And—bang—they've put up some fellow called Neves who's done nothing for the party and has no influence at all . . . What do you think of it?'

'Me? . . . Nothing.'

The officer of the inland revenue was astounded. Could there be a man in the world who, living in the municipality of Curuzu and knowing about the matter, remained unconcerned about the quarrel between Senator Guariba and the governor of the State? It was not possible. He reflected and gave a slight smile. Of course, he said to himself, this rascal wants to keep in well with both sides and do nicely for himself. Fishing very craftily . . . Sly upstart! It would be a good thing to clip the wings of this stranger who had appeared from God knows where.

'You are a philosopher, major,' he said, meaningfully.

'I'd like to think so,' said the ingenuous Quaresma.

Antonio pressed this important topic further, but despairing of discovering the major's secret intentions he cut short the conversation by saying blankly:

'Well major, you have no objection then to contributing towards our festival?'

'Of course not.'

They said goodbye. Leaning on the verandah, Quaresma watched him mount his little chestnut, shining with sweat, and bustling. As the secretary rode away and disappeared along the road the major was left thinking of the peculiar interest such people have in political rivalry and electoral intrigues, as if there were something important or vital about them. He could not imagine why a quarrel between two such notabilities should have to create dissension among so many people whose lives were so removed from their sphere. Wasn't the land there good for planting and growing? Didn't this require arduous labour each day? Why didn't they put the effort they employed in all the confusion of votes and minutes into the work of enriching the soil, taking from it life and sustenance, work equal to that of God and artists. It was foolish to be thinking of governors and Guaribas when our lives are dependent on the land, which demands of us tenderness and effort, toil and love . . .

Universal suffrage seemed to him to be a curse.

A train whistled and he lingered there to watch it arrive. Those who live in far off places feel a very special sensation at the arrival of the means of transport which puts them in touch with the rest of the world. There is a mixture of fear and joy. At the same time as you think of good news you think of bad news too. The double uncertainty . . . It is as if the train or steamer comes from the unknown, the mysterious, bringing with it not only the news, good and bad, but also something of our distant loved-ones, their voice or a smile.

Quaresma waited for the train. Brilliantly lit by the setting sun, it came puffing in and lay stretched out in the station like a snake. It did not stay long. Another whistle and it went on its way taking news, friends, wealth and disappointments to other stations down the line. The major got to thinking how ugly and inhuman it was, how the inventions of our days are so far removed from the conception of beauty handed down to us by our thinkers of two thousand years ago. He looked at the road which led to the station. Someone was coming . . . He was approaching the house . . . Who could it be? He cleaned his pince-nez and gazed at the man, who was walking quickly . . . Who was it? That hat, folded like a helmet . . . That long frock-coat . . . Short steps . . . A guitar. It was him!

'Adelaide, Ricardo's here.'

II
Thorns and Roses

The suburbs of Rio de Janeiro afford a most curious example
of city construction. This is no doubt partly the result of the
topography, with its fantastic pattern of mountains, but even
more of the haphazard nature of the construction itself. You
cannot imagine anything more irregular, more capricious or
more without a plan of any kind. The houses grew up as if
scattered by the wind, and the streets formed themselves
around the houses. Some of these begin as wide boulevards
only to end up as narrow lanes. They twist and turn, make
needless loops and seem to avoid the straight line with a
mysterious, implacable hatred. Sometimes they follow each
other in the same direction with an irritating persistence, at
others they diverge, leaving between them a tight space
packed with houses. Here, in a pathetically cramped area, the
houses are jammed one on top of the other; there, a vast bare
tract opens up a wide prospect to our eyes. And just as the
buildings grew up to no fixed plan, so too did the streets.

As for the houses themselves, they are of every different taste
and design. You go down a road and see a row of mean,
humble chalets with door and window set in the front wall;
then suddenly you come across a middle class villa, one of
those with a fancily decorated façade, lofty cellar and barred
basement windows. Once past this surprise you look beyond
and are confronted by a wattle hut with a roof of corrugated
iron or thatch, the centre of a swarming population. Further
on still there is an old rustic house with a verandah and pillars
of indeterminate style, which seems as if annoyed and wanting
to hide itself from that influx of ridiculous new buildings.

There is nothing about our suburbs to remind us of the
famous ones of the great European cities, with their peaceful,
comfortable villas and their fine paved roads. And as for those
trim, well-tended gardens, ours, if we have any, are usually
poor, unsightly and neglected.

The facilities provided by the municipal authorities are also varied and uncertain. Occasionally the roads have pavements in some parts but not in others; some roads are paved, but others of equal importance are still in a state of nature. At one point there is a small bridge, in good repair, over a dried-up river, while a few steps further on we have to cross a wide stream by means of a rickety foot-bridge.

On the roads you see elegant ladies in silks and brocade trying desperately to prevent the mud and dust from spoiling the magnificence of their dresses; you see workmen in clogs, dandies in the latest fashion and women in plain cotton. In the afternoon, when they are all returning from work or from an outing, you can see them intermingled together in the same street or even the same block, and almost always it is not the most elegant who walk into the best houses.

Apart from this, and without mentioning the epidemic flirting and endemic spiritualism, the suburbs have other interesting features, a unique example being the tenement houses (who would have thought to find them there). Houses which would scarcely do for one small family are divided and subdivided, and the microscopic quarters so obtained rented out to indigent inhabitants of the city. Here in these warrens are to be found the least regarded fauna of our society, who are as accustomed to misery as a Londoner is to fog.

It would be difficult to imagine humbler or more un-expected trades than those of the people who inhabit these places. In addition to cleaners and office boys in government departments, we find old women who make bone-lace, dealers in empty bottles, castrators of cats, dogs and cocks, sellers of charms, collectors of medicinal herbs, in short, a variety of wretched occupations quite unknown to our lower and upper middle classes. Frequently a whole family is crowded into one tiny cubicle, and there are occasions when the breadwinner has to go to town on foot for lack of a nickel to pay his train fare.

Ricardo Coração dos Outros lived in a poor tenement in one of the suburbs. Though not exactly sordid, it was still a tenement in the suburbs. He had lived there for years and liked the house, which, being perched on a hill, gave him a view from his bedroom window of a wide built-up area stretching from Piedade to Todos os Santos. Seen like this, from high up, the suburbs have a certain attraction. The tiny blue, white and ochre houses set amid the dark green of the mango trees, with here and there a tall, proud coconut or palm, make a pleasant sight; and the lack of any discernible pattern in the streets gives an impression of democratic confusion and perfect harmony among the inhabitants. And there too is a miniature train gliding swiftly through it all, turning to the left, veering to the right, its coaches, like vertebrae, as flexible as a snake moving through a pile of stones.

It was from that window that Ricardo scattered to the winds his contentment, his joy and his triumphs, as well as his sorrows and his suffering. He was there now, leaning over the window-sill with his chin cupped in his hand, contemplating a vast area of that beautiful, unique metropolis, the capital of a great country, of which in a certain way he, Ricardo, was, and felt himself to be, the soul. For was it not he who expressed its vague desires and dreams in verses which, though perhaps inadequate in themselves, gained from the plaintive tones of the guitar, if not full meaning, at least the semblance of the anguished cry of his infant native land, still in its formative state.

What was passing through his mind? He was not merely thinking, he was suffering too. It was that same negro who crazily persisted in trying to make the modinha say something, and who now had followers. He was mentioned by some as a rival to him, Ricardo; others declared that the lad was far ahead of Coração dos Outros; and there were even some ungrateful wretches who, forgetting the untiring work of the dedicated musician, did not so much as mention the name of Ricardo Coração dos Outros.

As he gazed with unseeing eyes Ricardo remembered his childhood, the village in the interior where he was born, his parents' little house with its corral and the lowing of the calves . . . And the cheese. That strong, appetizing cheese which was as ugly as the region that produced it, and as rich

86

too, for you only needed to eat one small slice to satisfy your hunger. And those parties! What memories! How had he come to learn the guitar? Wasn't it his teacher, Maneco Borges, who had foretold his future when he said, 'You'll go far, Ricardo. The guitar is in your heart'? Then why that hatred and those bitter attacks against him, the one who had brought the soul, the life-blood, the very essence of the country to this city of strangers?

The warm tears rolled down his cheeks, and he turned his gaze to the mountains, sniffing the salty air of the distant sea. How lovely it all was, so beautiful and majestic, but yet so harsh and ungrateful, with granite hills all round which turned black and evil when not softened by the green of the trees.

And he was there alone; alone with his glory and his agony, friendless, with no one to love or confide in; as alone as a god, or an apostle in a hostile land that refuses to hear his message. And he suffered the more that there was no friend or loved one to share those tears that were now falling to the indifferent ground. He remembered the famous lines:

'If I weep . . . the burning sands my tears do drink . . .'

At this he looked down to where, half-hidden from him, a black girl was busy at the wash-tank. She leaned on the clothes, pressing with her full weight; then she soaped them lightly, beat them against a stone, and began again. He felt sorry for the poor woman, doubly unfortunate in her class and her colour. Overwhelmed with tenderness, he began to think about the miseries of this world, grappling for a moment with the enigma of the wretchedness of our human destiny.

The girl, intent on her work, did not notice him and began to sing:

'The gentle breezes envious are
Of the sweetness of your eyes . . .'

It was one of his. Ricardo smiled in satisfaction; he felt like going down and kissing the poor woman and hugging her . . . Is that how things were? He received consolation from that simple girl: her sad, humble voice came to lighten his suffering. Then he recalled those lines of Padre Caldas, his fortunate predecessor, who had had an audience of noble ladies:

> 'Loreno gave joy to others,
> But joy himself he never knew . . .'

So it was a mission . . . The girl stopped singing and Ricardo could not help saying:

'Very good, Dona Alice, very good. If it wasn't, I shouldn't be asking for an encore.'

The girl looked up, recognized who was speaking, and said:

'I didn't know you were there or I shouldn't have dared to sing.'

'Shame on you. I can tell you it was very good, very good indeed. Go on singing.'

'Good heavens, no. Me sing for you to hear! . . .'

And despite his insistence she would sing no more. But the clouds seemed to have lifted from Ricardo's mind; he turned back into the room and sat down at the table to write. The furniture of his room was of the barest. There was a lace-fringed hammock, a pinewood table with writing material on it, a shelf of books, and hanging on the wall, the guitar in its leather case. There was also a coffee percolator.

He sat down and tried to begin a modinha about glory, that fugitive thing which one has without knowing, as impalpable and hard to seize as a breath of air; which disturbs, harrows, burns and consumes us like love. He arranged the paper and tried to begin, but it was no good. The emotion had been too strong; his whole nature had been shocked and upset at the idea of the outrage his merit was likely to suffer. He could not think clearly, the words would not come and the music refused to sound in his ears.

The morning wore on. In front the crickets chirped in the leafless tamarind tree. It grew hotter, and the sky turned a delicate pale blue. He wanted to go out, find a friend and enjoy his company. But who? If only Quaresma . . . Oh! Quaresma! He would be the one to bring comfort and consolation. It is true that this friend of his had lately shown but little interest in the modinha; but even so, he understood his aims, and the significance and purpose of the work to which Ricardo had dedicated himself. If only the major were close by; but he was so far away. He searched his pockets. His whole fortune did not amount to two milreis. How could it be done. He would arrange a pass and go. There was a knock at the door and they brought him a letter. Not recognizing the handwriting he tore open the envelope excitedly. What could it be? He read:

'My dear Ricardo, Greetings. My daughter Quinota is getting married tomorrow, Thursday, and she and her fiancé would be delighted if you could be present. If you have no prior engagement bring your guitar and come and have a cup of tea with us. Cordially yours, Albernaz.'

While he was reading the letter the singer's features began to change. Until then they had been gloomy and drawn; by the time he had finished reading he was beaming, his whole face wreathed in smiles. The general had not forsaken him: for the worthy soldier, Ricardo Coração dos Outros was still the king of the guitar. He would go there, and Quaresma's former neighbour would fix his journey for him. He gave a lingering look at his guitar, full of tenderness and gratitude, as if it were some benevolent idol.

When Ricardo arrived at General Albernaz' house the last toast had been drunk and everyone was making for the reception room in small groups. Dona Maricota was in pale green silk, and her short waist appeared even more bound and restricted in that expensive material, which seems to require bodies that are elegant and supple. Quinota was radiant in her wedding dress. Tall, with more regular features than her sister Ismênia, she was, despite her gracefulness, not so interesting, and her spirit and disposition were of a commoner sort. Lalá, the general's third daughter, was already quite the young lady, with plenty of make-up, and for ever patting her hair and smiling at Lieutenant Fontes. This marriage had general approval and was confidently awaited. Genelício, with his bride on his arm, was wearing a badly cut dress-coat which emphasized his round shoulders, and was limping badly in tight dress shoes.

Ricardo did not see them pass, as by the time he got there the general was going in, wearing his second best uniform of the good old days, and looking about as comfortable as a National Guardsman in his Sunday best. But the one who really looked important, prosperous and martial, and at the same time aristocratic, was Rear-Admiral Caldas. He was best man, and was impeccable in his dress uniform. His anchors glittered like the brass on a ship before captain's inspection, and his carefully combed sideboards, which broadened his face, seemed to be longing for the blustering winds of the vast, limitless ocean. Ismênia, in pink, was moving slowly and listlessly through the rooms, idly putting things in order. Lulu, the general's only son, was resplendent in his Military College uniform, full of gold lace and tassels, all the more so because he had passed his examinations, thanks to his father's influence.

The general hastened to speak to Ricardo, and the bride and groom, when he complimented them, showered him with thanks. Quinota even said, 'I am very happy . . .', hanging her head and smiling at the ground, a smile which filled the minstrel's heart with a transport of joy.

They started off the dancing and then the general, the admiral, Major Inocêncio Bustamente, who was also in his uniform, with its purple honorary stripe, Doctor Florêncio, Ricardo and two other guests went into the dining room for a chat.

The general was happy. For so many years he had dreamed of a ceremony like this in his house, and now for the first time he saw his dream come true. It was too bad about Ismênia . . . The ungrateful dog . . . But why think about that.

There were more congratulations.

'He's a fine young man, your new son-in-law,' said one of the guests.

The general took off his pince-nez, which was held by a thin gold chain, and while he cleaned it and peered short-sightedly, he said:

'I'm very pleased.'

Then he put on his pince-nez, straightened out the chain, and added:

'I think I have married my daughter quite well. He's an intelligent young man, a graduate and in a promising career.'

'And what a career,' retorted the admiral. 'It's not just because he is a relative of mine, but to be first accountant at the Treasury at the age of thirty-two is something unheard of.'

'Isn't Genelício in the Audit Office, wasn't he accepted?' asked Florêncio.

'Yes, he was accepted, but it's all the same thing,' replied one of the guests, who was a friend of the groom.

Genelício had, in fact, arranged a transfer, and it was not merely this that had decided him to get married. Having written a 'Synthesis of Scientific Public Accountancy', he found himself, without exactly knowing how, overwhelmed with praise by 'the press of this capital'. In recognition of the exceptional merit of the work, the minister had ordered him to be awarded a prize of two thousand milreis, and the edition was published at State expense by the National Press. It was a thick volume of four hundred pages of twelve point type, written in official language, and with a vast documentation of decrees and regulations occupying two thirds of the book.

The first sentence of the first part of the book, that portion that was truly scientific and synthetic, had in fact been much commented on and praised by the critics, not only for the originality of the thought, but also for the beauty of the expression. It read as follows: 'Public Accountancy is the art or science of correctly recording the expenses and revenue of the State.'

As well as the prize and the transfer, he was also given the promise of promotion to assistant director as soon as there was a vacancy.

Having heard all that was said by the general, the admiral and the other guests, the major could not help remarking:

'After the armed forces the best career is the Treasury, don't you think?

'Yes . . . Of course,' said Doctor Florêncio.

'Mind you, I've nothing against university men,' added the

major quickly.

'They . . .'

Ricardo felt himself obliged to say something, so he spoke the first words that came to his lips:

'When you get on well all professions are good.'

'I wouldn't say that,' said the admiral, stroking one of his sideboards. 'I don't want to belittle the others, but, well . . . our profession . . . hey Albernaz? Hey Inocêncio?'

Albernaz lifted up his head, as if to catch some memory floating about in the air, and then replied:

'Yes, but it has its drawbacks. When you're in a mess like at Curupaiti, with bullets flying all round, a fellow shot dead on one side, another screaming on the other . . .'

'Were you there, general?' asked Genelício's friend.

'No, I fell sick and returned to Brazil. But Camisão . . . You've no idea what it was like. You know though, don't you, Inocêncio?'

'Of course . . .'

'Polidoro was ordered to attack Sauce. Flôres on the left, together with our chaps, fell on the Paraguayans. But the devils had used their time well and were nicely entrenched . . .'

'That was Mitre,' said Inocêncio.

'You're right. We attacked furiously. There was a fearful row with the cannons thundering away, shots falling everywhere, men dying like flies . . . It was hell!'

'Who won?' asked one of the guests.

The others all looked at each other in astonishment, except the general, who had a very high opinion of the Paraguayans' capacities.

'The Paraguayans did; that is, they drove back our attack. That is what I mean when I say that ours is a fine profession, but it has its drawbacks . . .'

'That doesn't mean a thing. It was the same at Humaitá . . .' said the admiral.

'Were you aboard?'

'No, I went there later. There was some intrigue and I wasn't nominated because the appointment would have been equivalent to promotion . . . But at Humaitá . . .'

In the reception room the dancing went on gaily. Scarcely anyone left there to join them. The laughter, music and other things that could be guessed at did not distract the men from their warlike preoccupations, during which the general, the admiral and the major astounded the peace-loving civilians with accounts of battles that they had not seen and valiant combats in which they had not participated.

There is nothing like a peaceful, well-fed citizen, with a generous helping of wine inside him, for appreciating stories about war. He sees only the picturesque side, what we might call the immaterial aspect of the battles and encounters; the shots are those of a salute, and if they happen to kill anyone it is a matter of trifling consequence. In such accounts even death itself loses its tragic importance: three thousand killed, is that all! Moreover, as related by General Albernaz, the thing became inoffensive, war seen through rose-tinted spectacles, war in its popular image, where the customary butchery, brutality and ferocity do not appear.

Ricardo, Doctor Florêncio — the one who was employed as an engineer at the water-works — and Albernaz' two new acquaintances were held spellbound, open-mouthed and envious by the imaginary deeds of those three warriors, one of whom was an honorary soldier, probably the least docile of the three, and the only one who had ever taken part in any warlike operation, when Dona Maricota came in, active and bustling, livening up the party. She was younger than her husband; on her tiny head, which afforded such a contrast to her enormous body, her hair was still completely black. She was out of breath and spoke to her husband:

'What's all this, Chico. Here am I seeing to everything and looking after the girls and you hanging about here . . . Come on all of you, into the other room.'

'We'll be there in a minute, Dona Maricota,' said someone.

'Oh no you won't,' retorted the lady of the house. 'You're going now. Get along there, Senhor Caldas, and you, Senhor Ricardo, all of you.'

And she drove them in one by one, pushing them by the

shoulder.

'Hurry now, because Lemos's daughter is going to sing. And you're next, do you hear me, Senhor Ricardo?'

'Of course, madam. It's a command . . .'

As they were moving, the general paused, drew close to Coração dos Outros and asked:

'Tell me one thing: how is our friend Quaresma?'

'He's well.'

'Has he written to you?'

'Once or twice. General, I was wondering . . .'

The general drew himself up, adjusted his pince-nez, which was slipping, and asked:

'What?'

Ricardo, intimidated by the martial air with which Albernaz asked the question, hesitated a little before replying, but then for fear of losing his words he burst out:

'I was wondering if you could arrange me a ticket, a pass, to go and see him.'

'It'll be difficult, but come along to the office tomorrow.'

They walked on. As they did so Coração dos Outros added:

'I miss him, and I have several things on my mind. You know, a man in his position . . .'

'Come along tomorrow.'

Dona Maricota appeared ahead of them and spoke angrily:

'Aren't you two coming?'

'We're coming,' said the general.

And then addressing Ricardo, he said:

'Quaresma would have been alright, but he would meddle with books. Look at me now, it's forty years since I last picked up a book . . .'

They entered the room. It was vast. There were two huge oil paintings in heavy gilt frames, violent portraits of Albernaz and his wife, an oval mirror, a few small pictures, and the decoration was complete. It was impossible to judge the furniture as this had been removed to allow more space for the dancers. The bride and groom were seated on the sofa, presiding over the party. There were one or two low-necked frocks, a few dress coats, a number of frock coats, and a good many morning coats. Through the curtains of a window Ricardo was able to see the street. The pavement in front was crowded, for as the house was tall and had a garden it was only from there that curious passers by, and onlookers, were able to see anything of the party. Lalá, in one of the bay windows, was talking to Lieutenant Fontes. The general was watching them with an approving eye . . .

A girl, Lemos' famous daughter, was about to sing. She went over to the piano, placed the score in position, and began. It was an Italian *romanza*, which she sang with all the perfection and bad taste of a well educated young lady. At the end the applause was general, but somewhat cold.

Doctor Florêncio, who was standing behind the general, commented:

'A lovely voice that girl has. Who is she?'

'She's Lemos' daughter, Doctor Lemos of the Sanitary Department,' replied the general.

'She sings very well.'

'She's in the last year at the conservatory,' explained Albernaz.

It was now Ricardo's turn. He went to a corner of the room, took his guitar, tuned it and ran his fingers up the scale. Then, in the tragic manner of one who is about to play Oedipus Rex, he said in a deep voice:

'Ladies and gentlemen,' He stopped, modulated his voice, and went on: 'I am going to sing "Your arms", a modinha of my own composition, both the music and the lyrics. It is a tender, correct composition, and full of exalted poetry.' At this his eyes almost popped out of their sockets. He went on, 'I hope that no sound will be heard, otherwise the inspiration will be gone. And the guitar is an instrument that is very . . . ve . . . ry de-li-cate. Now.'

Everyone's attention was focused on him. He began: at first it was sweetly mournful, tender and plaintive like the sighing of a wave; then came a rapid, dancing measure with vigorous strumming of the guitar. These two measures were then alternated and the modinha came to an end.

Everyone was deeply affected by the music, for it appealed

both to the dreams of the girls and the desires of the men. Ricardo was warmly applauded. The general embraced him, Genelício rose to shake him by the hand, and so did Quinota in her immaculate wedding dress.

To escape from the compliments, Ricardo ran into the dining room. In the corridor he heard his name called, 'Senhor Ricardo, Senhor Ricardo.' He looked round and said, 'What can I do for you, madam?' It was a girl asking for a copy of the modinha.

'Don't forget,' she said in a cajoling voice. 'Don't forget; I love your modinhas so much . . . They're so tender and charming . . . Look, leave it with Ismênia to give to me.'

Cavalcânti's fiancée was coming up to them, and on hearing her name she asked,

'What is it, Dulce?'

The other explained. She undertook to deliver the modinha, and then in her turn, asked Ricardo in her sad voice:

'Senhor Ricardo, when is it you expect to see Dona Adelaide?'

'The day after tomorrow, I hope.'

'Are you really going there?'

'Yes.'

'Then ask her to write to me. I want so much to have a letter . . .'

And she furtively dabbed her eyes with her little lace handkerchief.

III
Goliath

On the Saturday of the week following that in which the general's daughter received as husband the solemn, round shouldered Genelício, glory and pride of our civil service, Olga was married. The ceremony took place with the pomp and splendour expected of people of her class. There were some imitation Parisian 'corbeilles' for the bride, and other 'chic' touches which did not annoy her, but gave her no greater satisfaction than they would have done to any ordinary bride. Perhaps even less.

Her going to church was far from being the expression of her own wishes and desires. She still could find within herself no reason for such a step, but she was apparently-uninfluenced by anyone else in her decision. Her husband was the happy one. Not so much on account of his bride, but because of the new direction his life was going to take. He was now rich, and being a doctor whose talents were sufficiently attested by his scholastic reports, he saw ahead of him an unbroken succession of triumphs in the medical industry, and in the positions he would occupy. He had no fortune whatever, but he considered his commonplace degree a title of nobility equal to those with which the genuine European aristocrats enhanced the birth of the daughters of Yankee sausage merchants. Although his father was an important farmer in some obscure spot somewhere in Brazil, his father-in-law had given him everything; and he had accepted it all with the indifference and disdain of a duke, a duke of class medals and 'passed with merit's, receiving the homage of a peasant who had never warmed the benches of an academy.

He believed that his bride had accepted him because of his wonderful parchment title, and this was, in fact, true. But it was not so much on account of the title but because he appeared to be intelligent, to love science, and to have the unbounded dreams of the educated man. This image Olga had of him was but a fleeting one. Later the tyranny and inertia of society, and the girl's natural timidity to break off, caused her to go through with the marriage. She even argued with herself that if it wasn't him it would be someone just the same: there was no point in putting it off.

And so it was that she was not marrying in obedience to her own clear-cut wishes, even though there were no extraneous circumstances obliging her to do so.

Despite the pomp she was far from being a striking bride. Though she was of pure European origin she was small, very small even, beside her tall, erect bridegroom whose face was beaming with joy. She tended to disappear inside the dress, the veils and the obsolete ornaments with which girls who are about to marry adorn themselves. Moreover, her beauty was not that striking beauty which, following the classical models, we demand to see in wealthy brides. There was nothing Grecian, authentic or counterfeit, about her features, nor had they anything of the majesty of grand opera. They were decidedly irregular, yet nevertheless they were profoundly individual. Not only did the brilliance of her eyes, so large they alone almost filled the sockets, light up her expressive face, but her small, well-shaped mouth revealed good nature and wit, and the general impression she gave was of prudence and curiosity.

Breaking with custom, they did not go out of town but settled down in the former constructor's house.

Quaresma did not go to the reception: he sent the traditional sucking-pig and turkey and wrote a long letter. All his attention was devoted to the farm, for the heat was coming to an end, the rains and the planting season were approaching, and he did not wish to be away from his property. It was only a short journey, but even so it would be like running away from the battle.

The orchard was now completely cleared and the vegetable plots were already prepared. Ricardo's visit tended to distract him rather, but did not keep him away from his agricultural pursuits.

This visit, which lasted a month, was a great success. The fame of Ricardo's name had preceded his arrival so that he was sought after and junketed by the whole municipality. The first thing he did was to have a look at the town. This was four kilometers beyond Quaresma's house, and had a railway station. Ignoring the road, Ricardo walked there along the railway track, if such a term may be used to describe a path, full of pot-holes, that went up hill and down dale, across level ground, and over rivers by means of primitive bridges. The town! . . . It had two main streets: the old one which had formerly been a road used by troops on the march, and the new one which had served to link this one to the railway. Together they formed a T, the vertical arm of which was the road to the station. Lesser roads ran from these, and the houses, which at first were huddled together in urban neighbourliness, gradually grew thinner and thinner to end in open country. The old road was called Marshal Deodoro (formerly Emperor) Street, and the new one Marshal Floriano (formerly Empress) Street. From one end of Marshal Deodoro Street a road led up to the parish church, a miserable, ugly building in the Jesuit style, that stood on top of a hill. To the left of the station a road, barely discernible between the widely scattered houses, led into an open space — Republic Square — where stood the Town Hall. This was a huge block of bricks, cornices and iron-barred windows, built in pure foreman of the works style. Such poverty of taste was enough to sadden the heart of whoever could recall the buildings of a similar nature erected in small French and Belgian communes during the Middle Ages.

Ricardo went into a barber's shop in Marshal Deodoro Street, the Salon Rio de Janeiro, and had a shave. He introduced himself, and the barber gave him information about the town. There were several bystanders, one of whom took him under his wing so that before long he had a wide circle of acquaintances. By the time he returned to the major's house he already had an invitation to the party being given by Dr Campos, Chairman of the Council, on the following Wednesday.

Saturday had come and gone and it was Sunday when Ricardo made his visit to town. There had been a mass, and

Ricardo watched the congregation coming out. This is never large in the country districts but Ricardo saw some of the typical girls of the interior, pale-skinned and sad, all decked out with bows, walking silently down the hill from the church, then spreading out along the road to enter the houses where they would spend another week of seclusion and boredom.

It was as they came out of church that he was introduced to Doctor Campos. The latter was the local doctor who lived out of town on his farm, and who had come in by dog-cart with his daughter, Nair, to attend the service. The doctor and the musician remained a few moments chatting, during which time the girl, very thin and pale, with long, lean arms, gazed down at the dusty surface of the road in affected annoyance. After they left Ricardo spent a minute or two reflecting on that daughter of Brazil's wide open spaces.

Doctor Campos' party was followed by others, which Ricardo honoured by his presence and enlivened with his voice. Quaresma did not accompany him, but was delighted at his success, for although he himself had given up the guitar he continued to admire this typically Brazilian instrument. The disastrous consequences of his petition had done nothing to shake his patriotic convictions. He still held to these deeply ingrained ideas, the only difference being that now he concealed them for fear of suffering from the incomprehension and malice of his fellow men. And so he was gratified by Ricardo's astonishing popularity, for it showed that amongst those people there still existed a core of national sentiment strong enough to resist the invasion of foreign taste and fashions.

Ricardo received all these honours and attentions without distinction of party, but it was Doctor Campos, the Chairman of the Council, who most plied him with favours. That morning he was even waiting for one of the councillor's horses to take him on a visit to Carico. While he was waiting he was talking to Quaresma, who had not yet left for the fields.

'You know, major, it was a good idea to come into the country. You can live well and get on . . .'

'I have no desire for that. You know that such things mean

100

nothing to me.'

'Yes . . . I know. But what I mean is, you needn't go asking for things, but if they are offered to you, you don't have to refuse, do you?'

'That depends, my dear Ricardo. I could not accept the responsibility of commanding a fleet.'

'No, I wouldn't go as far as that. But look, major: I love the guitar, even to the extent of dedicating my life to increasing its prestige; but if tomorrow the president were to say, "Senhor Ricardo, you're going to be a deputy," do you think for a minute I wouldn't accept, even knowing perfectly well that I would never be able to play again? I wouldn't think twice. You can't let an opportunity slip by, major.'

'Everyone has his own ideas.'

'Of course. And by the way, major: do you know Doctor Campos?'

'By name.'

'Do you know that he is Chairman of the Council?'

Quaresma gave a quick, suspicious glance at Ricardo, who noticing nothing, added:

'He lives a league away from here. I've already been to his house, and today I'm going for a ride with him.'

'I'm glad to hear it.'

'He wants to meet you. May I bring him along?'

'By all means.'

At that moment Doctor Campos' emissary came through the gate bringing with him the promised horse. Ricardo rode away, and Quaresma set off for the fields to meet his two employees. There were now two, for in addition to Anastácio, who was more a member of the household than an employee, he had taken on Felizardo.

It was a summer morning, but the uninterrupted rain of the previous days had brought down the temperature. The light was intense and the air soft. Quaresma walked along listening to the varied sounds of life: the murmur of the woods and the cries of the birds. Red tiés and seedeaters fluttered here and there, and the ani birds stood out as little black specks against the green of the trees. Even the flowers, our miserable wild

101

flowers, seemed to have come out into the light of day, not merely for propagation but to show off their beauty.

Quaresma and his employees were now working further off, clearing a new field, and it was to assist with this service that he had contracted Felizardo. The newcomer was tall and thin, with long arms and legs like a monkey. He had a coppery complexion and a light beard, and though he gave the appearance of weakness there was no tougher worker than he. Added to this he was a tireless gossip. By the time he arrived at six o'clock in the morning he already knew all the local scandal.

This clearing was intended to win back some ground on the north side of the property that had been taken over by brushwood. Once cleared, the major planned to plant several acres or so of corn, interspersed with potatoes — a new crop in which he had high hopes. The felling had been completed and the fireguards prepared, but Quaresma would not set fire to it. By this he avoided burning the ground and destroying those elements affected by fire. Now his work was to separate the thicker trunks which could be used for timber; the lesser branches and leaves he carried off to be burnt in small heaps. This required time, and caused the major many falls, unaccustomed as he was to lianas and tree stumps, but it promised to bring beneficial results.

During the work Felizardo would go on telling the news to pass the time. Some people sing; he talked, and it mattered little to him whether anyone listened or not.

'People is all het up down there,' he said as soon as the major arrived.

Most of the time Quaresma would listen to him, and occasionally ask him a question. Anastácio remained grave and silent. He never spoke, but worked on, stopping from time to time, deep in thought, in the hieratic posture of a Theban mural.

'Why, what's happening, Felizardo?' asked the major.

His companion rested the thick trunk on the pile, wiped away the sweat with his fingers, and replied in his soft, lisping voice:

102

'Politics . . . Lieutenant Antonino and Doctor Campos almost came to blows yesterday.'

'Where?'

'At the station.'

'What about?'

'Some party matter. From what I hears Lieutenant Antonio supports the governor and Doctor Campos supports the senator . . . It's a real to-do, boss.'

'And which one do you support?'

Felizardo did not answer right away. He seized his sickle and slashed at a branch that was tangled round the trunk he was removing. Anastácio was standing watching his garrulous companion. At length he replied:

'I don't know . . . Crows don't mix with peacocks. That's more a matter for you, boss.'

'But I'm the same as you, Felizardo.'

'Ah boss, if it was only true. Why only three days ago, boss, they tells me you's a good friend of the marshal.'

He went off with his log. When he returned Quaresma asked anxiously:

'Who told you?'

'Can't say, boss. Just happened like I overhears it in the Spaniard's store, and they say too that Doctor Campos is swelled up like a frog 'cause of it.'

'But it's not true, Felizardo. I've never been a friend of his . . . I knew him . . . But I never told anyone here about that! . . . What do they mean, a friend!'

'Ah!' exclaimed Felizardo with a broad, knowing smile. 'What you doing, boss, is playing innocent.'

No efforts by Quaresma could remove from that childlike head the idea that he was a friend of Marshal Floriano. 'I met him at work'—said the major, to which Felizardo with a grin replied, 'Ah boss, you's as crafty as any snake!'

Such obstinacy had its effect on Quaresma. What could it mean? And what about Ricardo's words, those hints he had thrown out that morning . . . He believed the singer to be an honest man and a faithful friend, incapable of laying traps for him; but he could be deceived by his enthusiasm and his wish to be a good friend, and so become the instrument of any trouble-maker. Quaresma remained thinking for a while, neglecting to remove the branches that had been cut. Before long, however, he forgot about it and his worries evaporated.

In the evening, when he went in for dinner, he no longer remembered the conversation, and the meal went off as usual, neither very gay nor very sad, but without the slightest shadow of any preoccupation on his part. Dona Adelaide, as always wearing her cream house-coat and black skirt, was sitting at the head of the table with Quaresma on her right and Ricardo on her left. It was the old lady who always encouraged Ricardo to talk.

'Did you enjoy your outing, Senhor Ricardo?'

She could not bring herself to say 'Seu' instead of 'Senhor'. The ladylike upbringing she had received years ago would not allow her to use the popular, familiar form of address. She had heard her parents, Portuguese through and through, saying 'senhor', and she continued to use it naturally and without affectation.

'Very much. What a place. There's a waterfall . . . It's magnificent. For inspiration, give me the country!'

He said this in an attitude of ecstasy, his features assuming the expression of a Greek tragedian's mask and his deep voice rumbling like distant thunder.

'Have you composed very much, Ricardo?' asked Quaresma.

'I finished a modinha today.'

'What's it called?' asked Dona Adelaide.

' "Carola's lips." '

'How nice! Have you written the music yet?'

It was Quaresma's sister who asked. Ricardo, who was lifting his fork to his mouth, left it suspended between his lips and the plate and replied firmly:

'The music, madam, is the first thing I compose.'

'You must sing it to us in a little while.'

'With pleasure, major.'

After dinner Quaresma and Coração dos Outros went out for a stroll round the farm. This had been the only concession that Policarpo had made to his friend as regards his agricultural affairs. He always took with him a piece of bread, and scattered the crumbs in the hen-house in order to see the furious struggle amongst the fowls. When it was over he would remain a moment or two in thought, considering their lives that were maintained and protected in order to sustain his own. He smiled at the chickens, picking up the featherless chicks that were so lively and ravenous; and he paused to wonder at the stupidity of the turkey that stalked so proudly about, giving off its presumptuous cries. Then he would go to the pig-sty and help Anastácio pour out the ration into the troughs. The enormous hog would get to its feet with difficulty and come and plunge its head into the container, while in the next compartment the piglets came grunting with their mother to wallow in the food. Utterly repulsive as was the greed of these animals, their eyes held a certain gentle, human appeal that made them attractive.

These inferior forms of life were little to Ricardo's liking, but Quaresma would spend whole minutes watching them, forgetful, rapt in silent communion. They sat down on a tree trunk, and while Quaresma gazed up at the sky Ricardo told him some story or other. The evening was closing in: the earth was relaxing after the long, burning kiss of the sun. The bamboos sighed; the crickets chirped; the doves cooed amorously. Hearing steps, the major turned round.

'Godfather.'

'Olga.'

No sooner did they see each other than they were clasped in each other's arms, and when they separated they remained holding hands, gazing at one another. Then, as in all happy meetings, there came the silly but affecting phrases: 'When did you get here? I didn't expect . . . It's so far . . .' Ricardo looked on, enraptured by this show of affection, while Anastácio removed his hat, gazing at the 'young mistress' with the kindly, vacant expression of the African.

Once the emotion had passed Olga leaned against the pig-sty and looked around her.

'Where's your husband?' asked Quaresma.

'The doctor? . . . He's inside.'

Her husband had been most unwilling to accompany her there. He was not at all pleased with this intimacy with some fellow with no academic titles and possessing neither wealth nor social position. He could not understand how his father-in-law, who after all was a rich man and quite out of his sphere, could have maintained and cultivated a relationship with a petty employee of an unimportant government office, even to the extent of making him godfather to his daughter. If it were the other way round it might be credible, but as things were it toppled the whole hierarchy of Brazilian society. But when, as it happened, Dona Adelaide received him with exaggerated respect and especial consideration, he was mollified, and all his little vanities received their due satisfaction.

Dona Adelaide was an elderly lady of the time when the Empire was giving birth to this academic nobility, and doctors she held in particular reverence and awe. So it was not difficult for her to give evidence of this when she found herself in the presence of Doctor Armando Borges, of whose scholastic reports and awards she had exact information. Even Quaresma received him with the sincerest expressions of admiration, and the doctor, basking in this superhuman prestige, spoke slowly, sententiously and dogmatically. And as he talked, possibly so as not to destroy the effect, with his right hand he kept twisting the huge symbolic ring, the talisman, which covered the knuckle of his left index finger like an awning.

They talked for a long time. The young couple described the political troubles in Rio and the rebellion of the Santa Cruz Fortress, while Dona Adelaide told the epic story of their removal, of the breakages and smashed furniture. They retired to bed, perfectly happy, at midnight, while from the stream in front of the house the bullfrogs offered up their solemn hymn to the transcendental beauty of the immense, black, starlit sky.

They awoke early. Quaresma did not go to work immediately but remained chatting over coffee with the doctor. The postman came with a newspaper for him. He tore it open and read the name. It was *The Citizen*, a local weekly put out by the government party. As the doctor had gone away he took advantage of the opportunity to glance at it. He put on his pince-nez, sat back in his rocking chair and unfolded the paper. He was on the verandah; outside the bamboos were swaying gently in the breeze. He began to read. The editorial was entitled 'Intruders', and consisted of a vituperative attack on those who lived in the place without having been born there—'strangers who come poking their nose into the private and political life of the Curuzu family, disturbing its peace and tranquillity'.

What the deuce did that mean? He was about to lay the thing aside when he thought he noticed his name among some verses. He found the place and came across the following lines:

CURUZU POLITICS
Quaresma, my dear Quaresma,
Quaresma of my dreams,
Forget about potatoes
And give up planting beans.
A farmer, dear Quaresma,
You were never meant to be;
So get your pen, and once again
Start writing in Tupí.
Eagle Eye.

The major was stupefied. What could it mean? What was the reason? Who had done it? Try as he might he could find no reason, no justification for the attack. His sister had come in, accompanied by Olga, and Quaresma held out the paper to her with trembling hand: 'Read this, Adelaide.'

Seeing immediately how upset her brother was, the old lady took it hastily and read it with care. She had that generous, motherly nature common to most spinsters, for it seems that having no children of their own serves to increase their interest in and sympathy for the sufferings of others. While she was reading Quaresma said, 'But what have I done? What interest have I got in politics?' And he scratched his head, where the hair was already turning grey.

'Don't worry, Policarpo. Is this all? . . . For goodness' sake!'

Olga read the lines too, and asked her godfather:

'Haven't you ever interfered in local politics?'

'Never . . . In fact, I'm going to declare that . . .'

'Don't be crazy!' cried the two women at the same time.

'That would be giving way . . . That's what they want . . . Don't do that,' added his sister.

The doctor and Ricardo came in from outside and found the three of them engaged in this discussion. They noticed the change in Quaresma, pale, moist-eyed and for ever scratching his head.

'What's the matter, major?' asked the singer.

The ladies explained and showed them the verses, whereupon Ricardo told them what he had heard in the town. Everyone believed that the major had come there for political reasons, for didn't he give alms, allow the people to gather wood on his property, distribute medicines among them . . . Antonio had said that such a Tartuffe ought to be exposed.

'But didn't you deny it?' asked Quarcsma.

Ricardo said that he had done so but the secretary would not believe him and had repeated his intention of attacking Quaresma.

The major was deeply upset by all this, but his force of character asserted itself so that while his friends were there he was able to conceal his feelings and give no indication of being worried.

Olga and her husband stayed about a fortnight at 'The Haven,' though after a week he was getting tired of it. There were not many places to see. In general our small villages are far from being picturesque, but there are one or two famous spots and, as in Europe, each one has its own historical curiosity to offer.

In Curuzu the most popular excursion was to Carico, a waterfall two leagues from Quaresma's house in the direction of the mountains away on the horizon in front. Doctor Campos had already made acquaintance with the major, and it was he who provided the horses, and also a side-saddle so that Olga could go there too.

They set off in the morning, the Chairman of the Council and his daughter, and the doctor and his wife. It was quite a pretty spot. In a triple fall of about fifty feet the water hurled itself, a boiling turmoil, down the side of a mountain into a large stone basin, where it shattered itself into spray with a deafening roar. The vegetation was thick, so that like most waterfalls it was roofed in by trees, and only with difficulty did the rays of the sun filter through to sparkle in round and oblong shapes on the water and the pebbles. Perched on the branches, the parakeets with their more brilliant green looked like engravings on the walls of that fantastic chamber.

Olga was able to explore everything at will, walking from one side to the other, for the chairman's daughter kept as silent as the tomb, and the father was gleaning the latest medical information from her husband: How do they cure erysipelas nowadays? Is tartar still used as an emetic?

What most impressed her during the excursion was the general misery about her: the lack of cultivation, the wretchedness of the houses and the gloomy dejection of the poor people. Brought up in the city, she had always believed that country dwellers were healthy, carefree and gay. With so much water and clay about, why were the houses not made of bricks and roofed with tiles? There was nothing but that deadly thatch, and the mud brick which showed the pattern of the sticks like the skeleton of a sick man. Why didn't they plant anything round the houses, a garden or an orchard? Wouldn't it be easy, just a few hours' work? And there was no livestock of any kind, scarcely a goat or a sheep. Why should it be? Even on the farms the situation was not much more encouraging: all were squalid and gloomy, with little in the way of a pleasant orchard or fertile garden. Apart from coffee and maize here and there, there were no other crops that she could see, no other signs of agricultural activity. It could not be just laziness or indolence. For his own use and consumption man has always had energy to work: even those peoples most accused of idleness do a certain amount of work. In Africa, India, Indo-China, everywhere married couples, families and tribes do some planting for themselves. Could it be the soil?

What was the reason? All these questions aroused her curiosity, her desire to know, and at the same time her pity and compassion for those wretched scarecrows, pariahs with scarcely a roof to their heads, probably half-starved . . .

She imagined herself a man. If she were one she would spend months and years there, and in other places, making enquiries and observations until she discovered the reason and the remedy. What she had seen was the peasant of the Middle Ages and the beginning of our era: it was La Bruyère's famous animal with a human face and an articulate voice.

Next day she took a walk over to her godfather's newly cleared field, so she seized this opportunity to question the talkative Felizardo about the matter. The work was nearly completed, there being a large tract of almost entirely cleared land which climbed a little way up the hill at the back of the property. Olga found him down at the bottom, chopping up some of the larger pieces of wood with an axe, while above him, at the edge of the forest, Anastácio was raking together the fallen leaves. She spoke to him.

'Good morning, miss.'

'You're working very hard, aren't you?'

'What we can, miss.'

'Yesterday I went to Carico, it's a pretty place . . . Where do you live, Felizardo?'

'The other side, on the road to town.'

'Is it very big, your place?'

'Got a fair bit of ground, yes miss.'

'Why don't you grow things for yourself?'

'Get away with you, miss. And what would we eat?'

'Whatever you produce or whatever you buy with the money the crops bring in.'

'There now miss, you be a thinking something, but it just ain't like that. And while crops be a growing, what then? Eh miss, that's about it, isn't it?'

He gave a blow with his axe but the log slipped off. He placed it more firmly on the block, but before striking again he said:

'Land ain't kid's play . . . And there's them ants . . . We

ain't got tools . . . Not so bad for them Italians or Germans, government give them everything . . . government don't like us . . .'

He brought down the axe firmly and surely, and the rough log split into two almost equal parts of a light yellowish colour where the dark heartwood began to appear.

She walked back vainly trying to drive out of her mind the complaints voiced by Felizardo. He was right. For the first time she became aware that the government's 'self-help' was only directed towards their own nationals; for the others every assistance and facility was provided, even without taking into consideration their previous education and the support of their compatriots. Wasn't the land his? And who owned all the abandoned land that was to be found in those parts? She had even seen farms closed down with their houses in ruins . . . Why this flight from the land; why these huge, useless, unproductive estates? Her attention wandered and she was no longer able to consider the problem. She hurried back: it was dinner time and she was hungry.

She arrived to find her husband and godfather talking. The latter had lost a little of his gloom and there were times when he was more like his normal self. When she arrived he was exclaiming:

'Fertilizers! How can any Brazilian get such an idea in his head. Our soil is the most fertile in the world.'

'But it's getting worn out, major,' explained the doctor.

Dona Adelaide was silent, her attention being given to the crochet she was doing. Ricardo was listening, wide-eyed. Olga broke into the conversation:

'What's this all about, godfather?'

'Your husband is trying to convince me that our soil needs fertilizers . . . That's almost an insult . . .'

'You can be sure, major,' went on the doctor, 'that if I were you I'd try some phosphates . . .'

'That's right, major,' put in Ricardo. 'When I began to play the guitar I didn't want to study music. Why study, it's inspiration that counts! . . . Now I know that it's necessary . . . It's just like that,' he concluded.

111

They all glanced at each other; all except Quaresma, who then said with the most sincere conviction:

'Doctor, Brazil is the most fertile country in the world, the most truly blessed, and her soil needs no such additions to be able to serve man. You may be sure of that.'

'There is land more fertile than ours.'

'Where?'

'In Europe.'

'In Europe?'

'Yes, in Europe. The black lands of Russia, for example.'

The major gazed at him for a moment and then said triumphantly:

'You're no patriot. Those lands . . .'

Dinner went off more calmly. Ricardo even talked some more about the guitar, and at night sang his latest composition, 'Carola's lips'. Rumour had it that Carola was one of Doctor Campos' maids, but no one made any reference to this. He was listened to with interest and warmly applauded at the end. Olga played on Dona Adelaide's old piano, and before eleven o'clock they were all in bed.

Quaresma went to his room, undressed, put on his nightgown, lay down, and began to read an old eulogy of the wealth and resources of Brazil.

The whole house was silent; outside, not the slightest sound was to be heard. The bullfrogs had temporarily suspended their nocturnal choir. Quaresma went on reading, and he remembered how Darwin had enjoyed listening to that concert from the marshes. How strange everything is in this world, he thought. From the store-room, which was next to his bedroom, there came a peculiar noise. He pricked up his ears and listened. The bullfrogs began again their hymn. There were basses, and other voices higher and shrill; they followed each other, and at one moment they were all joined together in a sustained unison. Then suddenly the music ceased. The major listened intently: the noise went on. What could it be? There was a light snapping sound like twigs being broken and falling to the ground . . . The bullfrogs began again: the conductor tapped with his baton and in came the basses and tenors. It lasted a long time; Quaresma was able to read five pages or so. The choristers fell silent once more, but the noise continued. Quaresma got up, seized his candlestick, and just as he was, in his nightgown, went to the room where the noise was coming from.

He opened the door but could see nothing. He was just about to examine the corners when he felt a sting in his foot. It almost made him cry out. He lowered the candle to see better and discovered an enormous sauva ant clinging furiously to his thin skin. He had found out the cause of the noise. Ants had invaded the store-room through a hole in the floor and were carrying off his reserves of corn and beans, the bins having been inadvertently left open. The floor was black; dense masses of them were bearing off the grains and plunging into the earth in search of their subterranean dwelling.

He tried to drive them off. He killed one, two, ten, twenty, a hundred; but they were thousands, and at every moment the army increased. One came and bit him, then another, and they went on biting his legs and feet and climbing up his body. He could stand it no longer, and kicking and screaming he let the candle fall.

He was in darkness. He struggled to the door, found it, and fled from that insignificant enemy, which even in the broad light of day he would probably be unable to discern clearly . . .

IV
'Stand Firm, I'm On My Way'

Dona Adelaide, Quaresma's sister, was four years his elder. She was a find old lady of medium build, with a thick, white head of hair, a complexion that was beginning to give signs of advancing age, and a calm, gentle expression. Unemotional, unimaginative, and with a clear-sighted intelligence, she was in everything a complete contrast to her brother; and if there existed no insuperable barrier between them, neither was there a perfect understanding. Her brother's nature remained a mystery to her, and she made no attempt to penetrate it. As for him, he was quite uninfluenced by that methodical, orderly, organized woman whose commonplace ideas were so simple and straightforward.

Though she was already past fifty, and he getting on that way, they were rarely ill, and their healthy appearance gave promise of many more years to come. The calm, orderly existence they had led until then had contributed much to the good health they both enjoyed. Quaresma had kept his eccentricities in incubation until he was past forty, and she had never had any.

Life, for Dona Adelaide, was something very simple; it consisted of living; that is of having a house, meals and clothes, all very modest and unassuming. She had no ambitions, passions or desires. As a girl she had not dreamed of beautiful things, triumphs, Prince Charmings or even of a husband. She did not marry because she felt no need for it; sex meant nothing to her, and with regard to body and soul she had always felt herself complete. Within the family setting her tranquil appearance and the calm of her gentle, emerald green eyes served to focus and accentuate her excitable brother's uneasiness and disquiet. That is not to say that Quaresma went about raving like a madman. Fortunately that was not the case. In appearance one might even think that there was nothing disturbing his spirit; but a more careful examination of his habits, mannerisms and attitudes soon

114

revealed that peace and serenity found no place in his mind.

There were times when, lost in reverie, he would stay minutes on end gazing at the horizon; at others, when working in the field, he would remain motionless with his eyes fixed on the ground and one hand scratching the other, and then with an exclamation carry on with his work. Sometimes he made no attempt at all to repress his comments and exclamations. On such occasions Anastácio would cast a furtive glance at his employer, but say nothing. The former slave was unable to look at him directly. Felizardo, on the other hand, would carry on with his account of Custodio's daughter's elopement with Manduca from the store; and so the work went on.

Quite naturally Dona Adelaide remained unaware of all this for the simple reason that, except early in the morning and at dinner, they lived separate lives: he at work in the fields, and she looking after the house. Their other acquaintances, since they lived far off, also remained in ignorance of the major's all-absorbing preoccupations.

It was more than six months since Ricardo had visited him. The latest letter he had from his god-daughter and her father was a week old; he had not seen her since her visit with Ricardo, while as for her father, he had not seen him for almost a year, that is since he had moved to 'The Haven'.

During all this time Quaresma had dedicated himself to the improvement of his property. His habits had not changed and his activities remained always the same, though the truth is that he had abandoned his meteorological instruments. The hygrometer, the barometer and the like were no longer consulted and their readings noted down in a book. His experience with them had not been a happy one. Whether it was due to his inexperience and his ignorance of basic theory, or whatever it was, the fact is that all his forecasts based on the information they afforded turned out wrong. If he forecast fine weather it rained, and if he predicted rain there was a drought.

In this way he lost a lot of seed, and Felizardo even showed his contempt for the instruments with his broad troglodyte's grin:

'You see, boss. Rain come when God say.'

The aneroid barometer still hung in a corner with its needle swinging unheeded; the maximum and minimum temperature thermometer remained on the verandah, never receiving a single friendly glance; the pluviometer bucket was in the hen-house being used as a drinking bowl for the fowls; only the anemometer continued stubbornly spinning away, cableless, at the top of the mast, as if protesting against Quaresma's display of contempt for science.

Quaresma lived on in this way feeling that the campaign that had been begun against him, though no longer public, was developing slowly behind the scenes. Both by character and temperament he longed for it to be brought to a head. But how, if they didn't accuse him or bring anything against him directly? It was a contest with shadows and ghosts which it would be ridiculous to accept.

Moreover, the general conditions around him, the misery of the country people, which he had never hitherto suspected, the abandonment of the land to unproductivity, brought painful reflections to his meditative, patriotic soul. It grieved him to see that those humble people lacked any sense of solidarity or of mutual assistance. Nothing at all would bring them together; they lived separate, isolated, in families that were usually irregular, feeling no need of communal effort to work the land. And yet near at hand there was the example of the Portuguese who, in groups of six or more working together, were able to run reasonable farms and make a living and a profit. Even the old customs relating to collective work had disappeared.

How could this be changed?

Quaresma was in despair . . .

The excuse, often given, of lack of hands seemed to him either mischievous or stupid; and stupid or mischievous must be the government that went on bringing in people by the thousand without concerning itself with those who were already there. It was as if in a pasture that could scarcely support half a dozen cattle, three more were added to increase the supply of manure! . . .

From his own experience he fully appreciated the difficulties and obstacles in the way of making the land productive and rewarding. An incident gave him eloquent proof of one aspect of the matter. Once the mistletoe and the effects of so many years of ill-usage and neglect had been overcome, the avocado pear trees produced a crop which, if not particularly abundant, more than supplied the needs of his own household. He was overjoyed. For the first time he would put in his pocket money he had earned from the land, his ever fruitful, ever virgin land. He tried to sell. But how, and to whom? Nearby there was the odd customer who would buy for a ridiculously small price. In his determination he went to Rio in search of a buyer. He went from door to door but no one wanted them: there was a glut. They told him to try a certain Senhor Azevedo, a fruit merchant in the market. He went there.

'Avocado pears. Oh, I've got plenty . . . They're dirt cheap.'

'But,' said Quaresma, 'only today I asked in a greengrocer's and they wanted five milreis a dozen.'

'Ah, but in quantity . . . You know how it is . . . Well, if you want to send them . . .'

Then he jingled his heavy gold chain, stuck a hand in the armhole of his waistcoat, and almost with his back to the major, said:

'I'd have to see them . . . Depends on the size . . .'

Quaresma sent them, and when he received the money he experienced the proud satisfaction of the hero who has just won a glorious battle. One by one he caressed the grubby notes, studied their number and design, laid them alongside each other on a table, and for a long time could not bring himself to change them.

In order to estimate his profit he discounted the freight by rail and cart, the cost of the crates and the salary of his assistants. This calculation, which was not too difficult, revealed a profit of one thousand five hundred reis, neither more nor less. Senhor Azevedo had given him for a hundred the price one paid for a dozen.

Even so his pride was not diminished, and he saw in those pitiful earnings a source of contentment greater than if he were paid a fine, fat salary.

And so he returned to his work with redoubled energy. Next year the profits would be greater. Now the job was to clean the fruit trees. To help him deal with these old trees he hired another employee, Anastácio and Felizardo being kept busy out in the fields. It was this new man, Mané Candeeiro, that he set to work to prune the trees, sawing off the dead branches and those in which the parasite had embedded its roots. The work was arduous and difficult. Sometimes they had to climb right up to the top to cut off the affected branch, with thorns tearing their clothes and flesh, and not infrequently with the danger of Quaresma, saw and companion all toppling to the ground.

Mané Candeeiro rarely spoke, unless it was something to do with hunting; but he sang like a bird. Whilst sawing he would sing simple country ballads in which, as the major was surprised to observe, there was no mention of local plant or animal life, or of customs related to the country. They were extravagantly sensual and sentimental, cloyingly so in fact. By chance in one of them a local bird was named, which caused the major to pay attention:

> 'I'll say my farewell
> As does the bacurau,
> With one foot on the highway
> And the other on the bough.'

This reference to the bacurau was particularly gratifying to Quaresma: the interest of the local people was being attracted to their surroundings; there was an emotional response which indicated that our race was already putting down its roots into the immense land it inhabited. He copied the verse and sent it to the old poet in São Cristóvão. Felizardo said that Mané Candeeiro was a liar because all those stories of hunting peccaries, jacus and panthers were made up. Nevertheless he respected his poetical talent, especially at the musical contest. Ah, he was a stout lad at that.

He was light-skinned and had regular, commanding

features whose harsh strength was somewhat softened by African blood. Quaresma looked to see if he could find some of that evil nature that Darwin discovered in half-breeds, but completely without success.

With Mané Candeeiro's help Quaresma managed to clean the fruit trees of that old farm that had stood idle and deserted for almost ten years. Once the job was done he was saddened to see the old trees all cut back and amputated, with leaves in one part and bare in another . . . They seemed to be suffering, and he thought of the hands that had planted them some thirty or forty years ago, slaves possibly, miserable, despairing creatures . . .

But it was not long before the buds sprouted once more turning everything green again, and it was as if the rebirth of the trees brought joy to the flocks of wild birds. In the morning the red tiés fluttered about uttering their feeble cries; this bird is so useless but of such gorgeous plumage that it seems to have been born to adorn ladies' hats. Flocks of brown and copper-coloured pigeons hunted for food on the newly cleared ground. As the day wore on the clouds of seedeaters appeared and the tanagers sang from the topmost boughs. And in the evening they all joined together cheeping, chirping and twittering in the tall mango trees, in the cashews and the avocado pears, as if hymning the praises of the stubborn, productive toil of old Major Quaresma.

This joy was short-lived. An unexpected enemy appeared with the daring rapidity of a consummate general, who until then had shown himself timid, only sending out scouting parties.

After that attack on Quaresma's provisions the ants had been driven off and had not reappeared. But that morning, when Quaresma looked at his field of maize, his heart froze, and he remained motionless with the tears rushing to his eyes. The maize had sprung up, at first with tiny green shoots, shy like a child, and had then grown half a palm above the surface of the soil. He had even brought copper sulphate solution to wash the potatoes that were to be sown between the rows. Every morning he would go there to see his fully grown maize

119

with its white blossom and its tufted, wine-coloured ears swaying in the breeze. That morning there was nothing. Even the tender stalks had been cut and carried off. 'Might be a man's work,' said Felizardo. It was, however, the sauva ants, those terrible hymenoptera, diminutive pirates who fell on the crop with the rapacity of a Turkish brigand . . .

They had to be dealt with. Quaresma immediately set to work; he located the main entrances to the ant-hill and burnt lethal formicide in each one. The days passed and the enemy seemd to be routed. But one night while walking to his orchard to enjoy the starlit sky he heard a strange noise, as of dead leaves being crushed. There was a crack . . . It was nearby . . . He struck a match and, my God, what did he see! Almost all the orange trees were black with enormous sauva ants. There were hundreds of them swarming all over the trunks and branches, moving about like the population of a huge city in busy, well-directed streets: some were climbing, others descending, but all without the slightest disorder or confusion. The work proceeded as if directed by bugle calls. Those on top cut off the leaves by the stalk; below, others sawed them into pieces, while yet a third party carried them off along a smooth trail in the low grass, holding them over their immense heads as they marched in long files.

For a moment the major was struck with despair. This was an obstacle he had not reckoned with, nor had he imagined it so great. It was obvious that he was up against an intelligent, organised society that was both bold and stubborn. There came into his mind that sentence of Saint-Hilaire: 'If we had not driven out the ants they would have driven us out.' He was not sure whether these were the exact words, but the sense was the same, and he wondered that it had not occurred to him before.

By next day his confidence had returned. He bought the necessary materials, and then he and Mané Candeeiro opened up paths and racked their brains trying to discover the main centres, the underground nests of these terrible insects. These were then subjected to a veritable bombardment, deadly and lethal, of burning, exploding sulphide.

From then on the battle raged without a pause. Immediately an opening appeared formicide was put down, for otherwise no cultivation was possible. And even though the ants were eliminated from his land, it would not be long before the ant-hills on his neighbours' and the common land were linked to his by communicating channels.

It was a punishment, a torture, a Dutch dyke kind of vigil, and Quaresma realised that only some central authority or government, or an agreement among the farmers could bring about the elimination of that scourge that was worse than hail or frost or drought, for it was there all the time, summer and winter, autumn and spring.

Despite this day to day struggle the major was not disheartened, and was even able to harvest some of the crops he himself had sown. If his joy had been great when he sold his fruit, it was even more acutely felt as he watched the successive cartloads of pumpkins, cassavas and sweet potatoes in baskets covered with stitched sacking, set off for the station. The fruit was partly the work of others: the trees had not been planted by him. But these, no; they were the result of his own work, sweat and initiative.

He even went to the station to see the baskets off, with the tenderness of a father watching his son depart in quest of triumph and glory. Some days later he received the money and set to work to calculate his profit. He did not go to the fields that day as the work of book-keeper took the place of that of farmer. Concentrating on figures did not come so easily to him nowadays, and it was not until about midday that he was able to say to his sister:

'Do you know how much profit we made, Adelaide?'

'No. Less than with the avocado-pears?'

'A little more.'

'Well . . . How much?'

'Two thousand five hundred and seventy reis,' answered Quaresma separating his syllables for emphasis.

'What?'

'That's right. On freight alone I paid a hundred and forty two thousand five hundred.'

Dona Adelaide remained for a while with her eyes lowered, following her sewing, then she looked up and said:

'For heaven's sake, Policarpo, you'd better give it up . . . You've been spending so much money! . . . Just on the ants! . . .'

'Oh come now, Adelaide. Do you think I want to make a fortune? I'm doing this to set an example, for the sake of agriculture, to make the best use of our fertile soil . . .'

'Yes, I know . . . You want always to be the queen bee! . . . Have you ever seen any of our leading men making such sacrifices? . . . Just go and see if they make any! Nonsense! . . . They go in for coffee, which is given every form of assistance . . .'

'But I make them.'

Adelaide returned to her sewing; Policarpo rose and went to the window that looked out onto the chicken-run. The weather was dull and unpleasant. He adjusted his pince-nez, stared out for a moment and then said:

'Adelaide, isn't that a dead chicken?'

The old lady gathered up her sewing and went to the window to see for herself:

'You're right. That's the second one that has died today.'

After this brief conversation Quaresma went back to his study. He was contemplating important agricultural reforms, having already sent for catalogues, which he was going to examine. He already had in mind a double plough, a mechanical cutter, a sower, a grubber and some harrows, all of steel, and all American, which would do the work of twenty men. Until then he had not looked kindly on these innovations: the richest soil in the world did not need these processes, which seemed to him artificial, in order to produce. But now he was prepared to use them on an experimental basis, though in the matter of fertilizers he refused to budge. As Felizardo used to say, turning the earth is fertilizing it; and so it seemed to Quaresma a profanation to apply nitrates, phosphates, or even common manure to Brazilian soil . . . It was an insult. It seemed to him that the day he should become convinced they were necessary, his whole system of ideas would collapse, and the motivating force of his life disappear.

He was thus engaged in choosing from various types of ploughs, 'Planets', 'Bajacs' and 'Brabants,' when his little servant announced the visit of Doctor Campos.

In came the huge figure of the jovial, smooth-tongued councillor. He was tall and fat, with something of a paunch; he had brown eyes, set evenly in his face, a straight forehead of average width, and a badly shaped nose. Being rather swarthy, and with thin greying hair, he was what people thereabouts called a caboclo, despite his curly moustache. He was from Bahia or Sergipe, not Curuzu, though he had lived there for twenty years, married there, and prospered, thanks to his wife's dowry and his medical practice. The latter demanded little in the way of mental effort: he had some half dozen prescriptions, and for a long time now had managed to embrace all the local ailments within this restricted formula. As Chairman of the Council he was one of the most distinguished citizens of Curuzu, and Quaresma held him in particular esteem because of his familiar, affable manner and his simplicity.

'The top of the world to you, major. And how's life around here. Plenty of ants? Back home we've none left.'

Quaresma's reply was a little less enthusiastic and jovial, but he was pleased by the doctor's unembarrassed cheerfulness. Quite at ease, the latter went on:

'You know what brings me here, major? You don't, do you? Well, I've come to ask a small favour of you.'

The major was not surprised; he quite liked the man, and expressed his anxiety to help.

'As you know, major . . .'

His voice was now soft, subtle, insinuating; the honeyed words gushed persuasively from his lips:

'As you know, major, we're going to have elections in a few days' time. "Our party" is certain of victory: every division is on our side, except one . . . Now this is the point, major; if only you . . .'

'But how can I help if I haven't got a vote? I don't interfere, and don't wish to interfere in politics,' said Quaresma

123

innocently.

'Just for that reason,' replied the doctor in a loud voice. Then gently: 'The polling station is in your district, over there in the school. Now if . . .'

'If what?'

'I've got here a letter addressed to you from Neves. If you wrote back (right away would be best) to say that there was no election . . . What do you say?'

Quaresma fixed his gaze on the doctor, stroked his beard for a moment, and then replied clearly and firmly:

'Certainly not.'

The doctor did not get angry. Putting even more unction and persuasiveness into his voice, he produced arguments: it was for the sake of the party, the only one that was fighting for the interests of the farmer. Quaresma was inflexible; he refused, declaring that such disputes were absolutely repugnant to him, that he had no party, and that even if he had, he would not avouch anything when he did not know whether it was true or false.

Campos showed no signs of annoyance, but talked a little about unimportant matters, and then amiably, and with the utmost joviality, took his leave.

This took place on the Tuesday, that dull, unpleasant day. In the afternoon there was a thunderstorm and heavy rain. The weather only cleared on the Thursday, on which day the major was surprised by a visitor wearing an old, disreputable uniform, and bearing an official letter to the 'proprietor of "The Haven",' as the uniformed messenger himself put it.

In conformity with local bye-laws and dispositions, read the document, Senhor Policarpo Quaresma, proprietor of the estate, 'The Haven', was required, under pains laid down by these same bye-laws and dispositions, to cut and clear all stretches of the said estate that abutted on the public highway.

The major thought for a while. Such an intimation was surely impossible. Was it, though? A joke . . . He read it again, and saw Doctor Campos' signature. It was quite correct . . . But how ridiculous it was to compel him to cut and clear a stretch that amounted to one thousand two hundred metres in length, for the front of his estate bordered on one road, and one of the sides followed another for eight hundred metres—how was it possible?

The old corvée . . . It was outrageous. Let them confiscate the estate first. When he consulted his sister she advised him to speak to Doctor Campos, whereupon he told her about the conversation he had had with him some days earlier.

'Don't be so stupid, Policarpo. He's the one . . .'

Light dawned in his mind . . . That system of rules, regulations, laws and dispositions, in the hands of such ruling chiefs became a rack, an instrument of torture with which to torment their enemies and oppress the people, robbing them of initiative and independence, crushing and demoralizing them.

He saw before his eyes the haggard, yellow faces that were to be seen idling outside the shop doors; he saw too the dirty ragged children with hangdog looks, surreptitiously begging in the streets; he saw the holdings, deserted and useless, given over to weeds and destructive insects; he saw the despair of a good active, hardworking man like Felizardo with no initiative to plant a grain of maize on his own land, and spending on drink all the money that passed through his hands—this picture flashed through his mind with the speed and sinister brilliance of lightning. Its effect only disappeared when he came to read the letter his god-daughter had sent.

It was a gay, lively letter. She told of small, everyday incidents, her father's forthcoming trip to Europe, her husband's mortification when he happened to go out one day without his ring; she asked after her godfather and Dona Adelaide, and respectfully requested the latter to take great care of 'Duchess's' white ermine mantle.

'Duchess' was a huge, white duck with soft-looking white feathers, whose slow, majestic gait, long neck and firm step had prompted Olga to give it that noble name. The animal had died some days ago. And what a death! A disease that had struck down two dozen ducks, carried off 'Duchess' too. It was a kind of paralysis that first affected the legs and then spread to the rest of the body. She took three days to die. She lay on her breast, her beak glued to the ground, with the ants attacking her; the only sign of life she gave was a slight pulsation of the throat near her beak, as she tried to drive off the flies that tormented her in her last moments. And it was strange how the pain and suffering of that creature, so different from us, affected the human beings, as if they too shared in its agony.

The hen-house was left like a devastated village, with disease attacking hens, ducks and turkeys, now in one way, now in another, killing them off until the population was reduced to less than a half. No one could cure it. In a country whose government maintained so many schools turning out so many learned men, there was not one who, with drugs and prescriptions, was able to reduce these serious losses.

All these difficulties and setbacks disheartened the enthusiastic farmer of the first few months, but even so it never entered Quaresma's head that he should abandon his projects. He bought veterinary manuals, and was even about to purchase the agricultural equipment described in the catalogues.

One afternoon, however, while he was waiting for a team of oxen that he had ordered for the ploughing, a police constable appeared at the door with an official letter. He remembered the intimation from the municipal authorities. He was intending to contest it, and was not greatly concerned. He took the paper and read it. It was not from them but from the taxation office, whose secretary, Antonio Dutra, as stated in the document, summoned Senhor Policarpo Quaresma to pay a fine of five hundred milreis for having despatched farm produce without payment of the necessary taxes.

He saw just how much of this was mere petty revenge, but, in his sincere patriotism, his thoughts soon turned to wider aspects of the matter. Forty kilometres from Rio, did one have to pay taxes to send a few potatoes to the market? After Turgot and the Revolution were there still internal customs houses? How could agriculture flourish in the face of so many obstacles and impositions? If one added to the monopoly of the Rio profiteers the exactions of the State, how was it possible to earn a decent living from the land?

126

And he saw again the vision that had passed before his eyes when he received Doctor Campos' intimation, this time even more frightful and horrifying; he foresaw the time when the people would be forced to eat toads, snakes and dead animals, as were the French peasants in the days of the great kings.

Quaresma remembered his Tupí, his folklore, his modinhas and his attempts at agriculture—all seemed now so insignificant, puerile and childish. His work must be on a much vaster scale: it was necessary to change the whole administration. He imagined a government that was strong, respected and intelligent. One that would sweep away these shackles and impediments: Sully and Henri IV laying down wise agricultural laws, assisting the farmer . . . Ah yes! Then the granaries would be well stocked and his native land be happy!

Felizardo handed him the paper that he sent·for every day from the station, and said:

'I's not coming to work tomorrow, boss.'

'Of course not, it's a holiday . . . Independence day.'

'It's not for that.'

'What is it then?'

'Government's in trouble, and folks says they're recruiting. I'm off into the bush . . . That's not for me.'

'What kind of trouble?'

'It's in the papers, boss.'

He opened the newspaper and immediately saw the news that ships of the Fleet had rebelled and ordered the president to resign. He recalled his thoughts of a few moments ago: a· strong government, even to the extent of tyranny. . . . Agricultural reform . . . Sully and Henri IV . . .

His eyes shone with hope. He dismissed his servant. He went into the house, and, saying nothing to his sister, took his hat and hurried to the station. He went to the telegraph office and wrote:

'Marshal Floriano, Rio. Stand firm. I am on my way.— Quaresma.'·

V

The Bard

'Don't you see, Albernaz, you just can't go on like that . . .
Some fellow in a ship trains his guns on the shore and says,
"Out you go, Mr President," and the man gets up and goes?
. . . Oh no. You have to make an example . . .'

'I'm of the same opinion, Caldas. The republic must be
strong, united . . . This country needs a government that will
compel respect . . . It's incredible. A country as rich as ours,
perhaps the richest in the world, is despite all this, poor, and
in debt to everybody . . . Why? Because of the governments
we've had, with no prestige, no power . . . That's the reason.'

They were walking in the shade of the huge, majestic trees
of the abandoned park; both were wearing uniform and
sword. After a pause, Albernaz went on:

'Look at the Emperor Pedro II . . . There wasn't a single
rag of a newspaper that didn't call him a booby, and other
things . . . Used to go out during Carnival . . . I've never seen
such disrespect. What happened? He bolted like an intruder.'

'And he was a good man,' observed the admiral. 'He loved
his country . . . Deodoro never realised what he had done.'

They walked on. The admiral stroked one of his sideboards,
and Albernaz glanced about him, lit a cigarette, and then
took up the conversation again:

'He died penitent . . . Wouldn't even be buried in his
uniform . . . As there's no one listening, between ourselves he
was an ungrateful wretch: look how much the emperor had
done for all his family; don't you agree?'

'There's no doubt about it. Albernaz, you want to know
something: say what they like, we were better off then . . .'

'Who's denying it? There was more morality . . . Where is
there a Caxias? a Rio-Branco?'

'And more justice too,' said the admiral firmly. 'What I
suffered wasn't on account of the "old man", it was that
scum . . . Things were cheaper . . .'

'I can't understand,' said Albernaz, with particular em-

128

phasis, 'why people still want to get married . . . We seem to be doomed.'

They glanced up at the old trees of the Imperial Residence where they were now walking. They had never looked at them before; and now it seemed to them that they had never seen trees so proud and beautiful, so peaceful and secure as those, spreading the cool, grateful shade beneath their gigantic branches. It was as if they flourished because they felt that that ground belonged to them: spared by the axe, they would never be dragged off to be used in the construction of miserable hovels; and this feeling had given them strength to sink their roots and an immense urge to grow. The soil they grew in belonged to them, and they showed their gratitude by shooting out their branches, crowding together and interweaving their foliage so as to provide coolness for the good mother earth, and protection from the fury of the sun.

Most pleasing of all were the mango trees, whose long, leafy branches almost kissed the earth. The breadfruit trees stretched up, while on either side of the path the bamboos leaned over, covering the earth like a green vault.

The old imperial building stood on a small hill. They could see the foundations, the oldest part, which dated back to the time of D. João, with the clock tower a little way off, separated from the main building. There was nothing at all beautiful about the palace; it was, in fact, vulgar and monotonous. Its ancient appearance, narrow windows and low rooms were unimpressive. Nevertheless, there was something self-assured about it: it had an air of confidence and dignity that is not often found in our houses, a quality proper to the person who feels he is living not for the instant, but for years, for centuries . . . The palm trees that surrounded it stood up stiff and erect, their lofty, green plumes standing out against the sky, looking like the guard of the old imperial residence, a guard proud of its service and its duties.

Albernaz interrupted the silence:

'How's this all going to end, Caldas?'

'Who knows.'

'The "chief" must be in a mess . . . First there was Rio

Grande, and now Custodio . . . Hum!'

'Authority is authority, Albernaz.'

They were walking towards São Cristóvão station, and crossed the old imperial park from the Cancela gate to the railway lines. It was morning and the weather was clear and fresh. They took short, firm steps, but were in no hurry. Just as they were about to leave the grounds they came across a soldier asleep under a bush, and Albernaz decided to wake him: 'Come on, my man. Come on.' The soldier got up in utter bewilderment, but on seeing the two senior officers rapidly pulled himself together, saluted, and then stayed with his hand at his cap, rigid at first, but soon slackening.

'Lower your hand,' said the general. 'What are you doing here?'

Albernaz spoke in a sharp commanding tone. The private, in fear and trembling, explained that he had been on shore patrol all night. His company had returned to barracks and he had been given permission to go home, but he was so worn out that he had rested there for a time.

'Well, how are things going?' asked the general.

'Don't know, sir. Can't say, sir.'

The general examined the soldier for a while. He was white, with fair hair, though of a shabby, dirty fairness; his features were ugly, with prominent cheekbones and a bony head, and all about him was angular and disjointed.

'Where are you from?' continued Albernaz.

'Piauí, sir.'

'The capital?'

'Please sir, from the interior. From Paranaguá, sir.'

So far the admiral had not spoken to the soldier, who was still frightened and answering haltingly; so in order to calm him, Caldas resolved to speak kindly to him.

'Can't you tell us, lad, what ships they have?'

'The *Aquidabã* . . . The *Luci*.'

'The *Luci* isn't a ship.'

'Please sir, that's right. The *Aquidabã* . . . a whole crowd of 'em sir.'

The general broke in, speaking with an almost paternal

130

gentleness, using the more intimate, familiar expressions one uses when addressing inferiors:

'Well, take a rest, son. But you'd better go home . . . They might steal your sword, and you're on duty.'

The two officers walked on and before long were on the station platform. The little station was quite busy. A large number of officers, active, retired and honorary, lived in the vicinity, and the placards ordered them all to report to the competent authorities. Albernaz and Caldas were saluted as they walked along the platform. The general was well known by virtue of his post, but not the admiral. As they walked by he heard people ask, 'Who is the admiral?' This pleased Caldas, who felt a surge of pride at his position and his incognito.

There was a solitary woman on the platform, a young girl. Albernaz glanced at her, and for an instant thought of his daughter, Ismênia. Poor girl . . . Would she ever get better? Those crazes of hers. Where would it all end? Tears came to his eyes, but he fought them back. He had taken her to half a dozen doctors, but not one had been able to prevent her losing her reason; it was as if this were escaping little by little from her brain.

These thoughts of his daughter were driven away by the noise of an express train which thundered by with a clanking of metal, whistling furiously, and sending up clouds of heavy smoke into the air. The monster was crammed with soldiers in uniform. The rails continued to vibrate long after it had passed.

Bustamente appeared. He lived in the outskirts, and had come to take the train to report for duty. He was wearing his old Paraguayan uniform, cut in the style of the Crimean War. With his cone-shaped hat stuck forward, his red belt and short jacket it was just as if he had stepped straight out of a painting by Vítor Meireles.

'Hallo . . . What are you doing here?' asked the honorary officer.

'We came by the park,' said the admiral.

'Nothing to be surprised about! Those trams run very close to the sea front . . . I'm not bothered about being killed, but I want to die fighting. To get yourself knocked off to no purpose, and not knowing how, doesn't go down well with me . . .'

The general had spoken loud, and the young officers who were nearby looked at him with ill-concealed disapproval. Albernaz noticed, and immediately added:

'I know something about shelling . . . I've been under fire enough times . . . You know, Bustamente, at Curuzu . . .'

'It was ghastly,' agreed Bustamente.

The train drew into the station. It approached slowly and quietly, the jet black locomotive puffing and sweating, with its huge lantern in front, like a cyclops' eye, giving the impression of a supernatural apparition. It came on, and then finally shuddered to a halt.

It was full, with a large number of officers in evidence. Judging by the looks of it, Rio must have had a garrison of a hundred thousand men. The soldiers chatted gaily, but the civilians were silent, downcast and even nervous. If they spoke at all it was in whispers, casting furtive looks at the seats behind them. The city was swarming with secret agents, 'members' of the Holy Republican Office, and denunciations were the currency with which one obtained positions and rewards.

The slightest suspicion was sufficient to make you lose your job, your liberty and — who knows — your life. We were then still at the beginning of the revolt, but the régime had already made its intentions known, and all were warned. The chief of police had drawn up a list of suspects. No distinction was made with respect to position or intellectual capacity. A poor office boy and an influential senator, a professor and a humble office worker, all were submitted to equal persecution by the government. This was a time to take mean revenge, to settle old scores . . . Everyone was in command; authority was delegated to countless hands. In Marshal Floriano's name, any officer, or even civilian, holding no public office whatever, used the power of arrest. And woe betide whoever ended up in jail, for there he would remain, suffering all the tortures of the Inquisition, completely forgotten about. Officials vied with each other in fawning and servility. It was a reign of terror, but it was half-hearted, ignoble, bloody, furtive, futile, purposeless and irresponsible . . . There were executions; but there never appeared a Fouquier-Tinville.

The soldiers were in their element, especially the junior officers, the ensigns, lieutenants and captains. For most of them their satisfaction was due to the belief that their authority over their platoon or company, and over that whole flock of civilians, was to be reinforced. But for others this feeling was purer, more disinterested and sincere. These were the disciples of that pernicious, hypocritical positivism; that narrow, tyrannical pedantry that justified all violence, all murders, all outrages in the name of the preservation of order. This was the condition, so it was said, of progress and the coming of the new order — the religion of humanity — when the adoration of the Grand Fetish would be celebrated with the blaring music of cornets and pitiful verses, and paradise itself appear, with inscriptions in phonetic script and the chosen wearing rubber-soled shoes . . .

The positivists discussed and cited theorems of mechanics to justify their ideas on government, which were identical to those of an oriental potentate. The mathematics of positivism was never anything more than a mere clamour, which in those days succeeded in intimidating everyone. There were even some who were convinced that mathematics had been specially created for positivists, as if the Bible had been written solely for the Roman Catholic Church and not also for the Anglican. Their prestige, however, was enormous.

The train moved on, and after stopping at one more station took them to the Praça da República. The admiral, glued to the walls, made his way to the naval arsenal; Albernaz and Bustamente went to the General Headquarters. They entered the huge building that echoed with bugle calls and the clinking of swords; the immense courtyard was full of soldiers, flags, cannon, stacks of rifles, and bayonets glittering in the slanting rays of the sun . . .

On the upper floor, near the minister's office, there was a coming and going of gilded and multi-coloured regimentals, uniforms of the different services and regiments, amidst which the dark suits of the civilians looked as obtrusive as flies. There were officers of the National Guard, the Police, the Navy, the Army, the Fire-Service and of volunteer battalions that were being formed.

They reported together to the Adjutant-General and the War Minister, and then remained talking in the corridors. They were happy to do so as they had just met Lieutenant Fontes, and they were both anxious to speak to him: the general because he was now engaged to his daughter, Lalá, and Bustamente because he would learn from him some of the names of the modern weapons.

Fontes was full of horror and indignation, cursing the rebels and proposing the severest punishments.

'They'll see what happens . . . Pirates! Bandits! If I were the marshal and got my hands on them . . . They'd know it!'

Far from being harsh and cruel, the lieutenant was actually kind and goodhearted; but he was a positivist holding religious, transcendental ideas about his Republic, which for him was the depository of all human happiness; and he would not admit that some might wish it other than what seemed good to him. Outside this there was no honesty or sincerity; they were all self-seeking heretics, and like an inquisitor in his Phrygian cap restraining his fury at not being able to burn them in autos-da-fé, he saw pass before his eyes a long procession of criminals — the penitent, backsliding, stubborn, treacherous, crafty — all unmasked, and walking about freely.

Albernaz did not share this rage against their opponents. Deep in his heart he even wished them well; he had friends there, and for a man of his age and experience such differences counted for nothing. Nevertheless, he was hoping for great things from the marshal. He was in financial difficulties, as his pension and the gratification he received as organizer of the Largo do Moura archives were not enough; he was hoping to obtain another commission, which would ease the strain when he bought Lalá's trousseau.

The admiral, too, had great confidence in the warlike and statesmanlike qualities of Floriano. His lawsuit was not going very well. He had lost it at the first hearing, and was spending a lot of money. The government was needing naval officers as nearly all of them had joined the revolt. Perhaps they would give him a squadron to command . . . It is true that . . . But what the devil! If it was a ship it would be a different story: but a squadron wouldn't offer any difficulty; all you needed was the guts to fight.

Bustamente had great faith in Marshal Floriano Peixoto's capacities; so much so that he was thinking of raising a battalion of patriotic volunteers, to which he ·had already given the name, 'Southern Cross'. He, naturally would be the commander, and enjoy all the privileges that go with the rank of colonel.

Genelício, whose activities were anything but warlike, also expected much from the energy and firmness of Floriano's government. He aimed at becoming assistant director; there was no other course open to a serious, honest, energetic government if they wished to put the department in order.

These secret ambitions were more general than is supposed. Our lives depend on the government, and the revolt brought into confusion the jobs, honours and positions distributed by the State. People under suspicion opened up vacancies, and their titles and posts were assumed by the faithful. Moreover, the government, needing as it did support and men, was obliged to create, invent and scatter with a liberal hand offices, salaries, promotions and gratifications.

Even Olga's husband, Doctor Armando Borges, the serene and dedicated scholar of his student days, saw in the revolt the realization of his most ambitious dreams. Though a doctor, and a wealthy one thanks to his wife's fortune, he was not satisfied. Greed for money and desire for fame acted like a spur. He already had a position as doctor in the Syrian Hospital, where he went three times a week, and in half an hour attended to thirty or more patients. When he arrived the nurse would give him the information, and he would go from bed to bed asking, 'How do you feel?' 'Better, doctor,' the Syrian would answer in his guttural voice. At the next, he would enquire, 'Are you feeling better?' And that was his visit.

135

On arriving at his office he would write out his prescriptions: 'Patient number one, repeat the prescription; patient number five . . . which one's that?'—'It's the one with the beard.'—'Ahh!' And he gave the prescription.

But being doctor in a private hospital does not bring fame to anyone; the important thing is to have a government appointment, otherwise he would be no more than a mere general practitioner. He wanted an official post as doctor, director or even professor in the Faculty. This, in fact, would not be difficult provided he could arrange good recommendations, for he was already fairly well known as a result of his activities and his private resources. From time to time he would write a paper: 'Shingles: Aetiology, Prophylaxis and Treatment' or 'A Contribution towards the Study of Scabies in Brazil,' and send it, some forty or sixty pages, two or three times a year, to the newspapers that were interested in him: 'the energetic Doctor Armando Borges, illustrious physician, skilled doctor of our hospitals' etc. etc. Not content with this, he would write articles, long-winded compilations in which there was nothing original, but which were rich in quotations in French, English and German.

The post he most coveted was that of professor, but it was the examination that filled him with fear. He had made his contacts, and moved in the right circles, where he was highly thought of; but the idea of that disputation terrified him.

Not a day passed without him buying books in French English and Italian. He even engaged a German teacher so as to enter the world of German science; but he lacked the energy for any protracted study, and the little he had had as a student had disappeared as a result of his easy circumstances. The front room of the high basement had been transformed into a library, the walls being lined with shelves that groaned under the weight of thick treatises. At night he opened the venetian shutters, lit the gas lamps, and dressed all in white, sat down at the table with an open book in front of him.

Sleep never failed to overtake him after the fifth page . . . This was the very devil! He had the idea of getting his wife's books. These were French novels: Goncourt, Anatole France,

Daudet, Maupassant, but they put him to sleep just the same as the treatises. He was incapable of appreciating the greatness of their analysis and description, or their interest and value to society at large through the revelation of a whole new world—the life, feelings and sufferings of their characters. His pedantry, his pseudo-science and the poverty of his general education made him see these as toys, pastimes, gossip, the more so since the reading of such books put him to sleep. But it was necessary for him to delude himself; and his wife! Furthermore, they could see him from the road, and if he were to be seen slumbering over his books! . . . He ordered some novels by Paulo de Kock, changed the names on the covers, and drove away his sleep.

Meanwhile, his practice prospered. By arrangement with her tutor, he managed to make six thousand milreis treating a rich orphan for a violent fever. His wife had for long been aware that his show of intelligence was mere pretence, but that disreputable action roused her indignation. What necessity was there for him to do it? Wasn't he rich already? Wasn't he a young man? Didn't he have the privilege of a university degree? Such an act seemed to the girl lower, more despicable than a jew's usury or a ghost-writer's fee . . .

It was not disgust or contempt that she felt for her husband; it was rather a calmer, more passive feeling: she simply lost interest, and detached herself from him. She felt that all the moral links that bound them together, the ties of sympathy and affection, had been broken. Even before she was married she had seen through such things as his love of study, his interest in science, the true nature of his ambitions; but she had forgiven him. Many times we deceive ourselves about our strength and capabilities: we dream of being Shakespeare, but turn out to be a hack. This could be forgiven. But a charlatan? That was too much.

An unworthy idea passed through her mind. But what would be the use of such a near-indignity? . . . All men must be the same, so there was no point in changing this one for another . . . She was conscious of an enormous relief when she arrived at this conclusion, and her whole physiognomy lit up again, as if the cloud that had obscured her bright eyes had suddenly lifted.

In his desperate scramble for easy fame, the doctor failed to perceive the change in his wife. She disguised her feelings, more for the sake of dignity and decorum than for any other reason, and he lacked the intelligence and sharpness to penetrate the disguise. They continued to live together as if nothing had happened; but what an immense distance there was between them!

Such was their situation at the time of the revolt, and for the three days since it had broken out the doctor had been meditating on the social and financial possibilities it afforded.

His father-in-law had put off his trip to Europe, and that morning, as was his custom after lunch, he was relaxing in a deck-chair reading the newspapers. The doctor was getting dressed, and Olga was busy with her correspondence, sitting at the end of the dining-room table, writing. She had her own study, a luxurious one with books, book-cases and writing-desk, but in the morning she preferred to do her writing there, beside her father. It seemed to her that the room was brighter, the view of the mountain, though ugly and overwhelming, helped to sober her thoughts, and the vastness of the room gave her more liberty to write.

She was writing and he reading, when suddenly he spoke:

'Do you know who's coming here, Olga?'

'Who?'

'Your godfather. He sent a cable to Floriano saying he was coming . . . It's here in the *Nation*.'

It was not difficult for her to guess Quaresma's motives, or realize the effect these events would have on his ideas and feelings. She wanted to feel disapproval and reproach, but she saw that this was so in accordance with his character, so at one with the nature of the life he had built for himself, that she could only give an indulgent smile:

'Godfather . . .'

'He's crazy,' said Coleoni. '*Per la madonna*. For a man who's nicely, calmly settled, to come and get mixed up in this infernal mess . . .'

The doctor, now dressed to go out, had joined them; he was wearing his black frock coat and carrying a shining top-hat in his hand. He was radiant, his round face glowing, except where his large moustaches cast a shadow on it. Overhearing his father-in-law's last words, he asked:

'What's the matter?'

Coleoni explained, and repeated the comments he had just made.

'But that's nothing to the point,' said the doctor. 'It is the duty of every patriot to fight for the Republic . . . What's age got to do with it? Forty or so isn't all that old . . . He can still fight for the Republic . . .'

'But he'll gain no advantage from it,' objected the old man.

'And is it only those who stand to gain advantage who should fight for the Republic?' asked the doctor.

Olga, who had just finished reading the letter she had written, without even looking up, said:

'Of course.'

'And now you come along with your theories, my child. A man's patriotism isn't in his belly . . .'

And he gave a false smile, made even more unnatural by the dull gleam of his false teeth.

'But are you the only ones to talk about patriotism? What about the others? Have you got the monopoly of patriotism?' asked Olga.

'Yes we have. If they were patriots they wouldn't be shelling the city, paralysing and demoralizing the activities of the legally constituted authorities.'

'Ought they, then, to stand by and watch the arrests, the deportations, the executions and all the other outrages that are being committed here and in the south?'

'Deep down, you're a rebel yourself,' said the doctor, closing the discussion.

Which is what she was. The sympathy of those with no interests to pursue, that is, of the population as a whole, was with the insurgents. Not only does this always happen everywhere, but in Brazil in particular, for a variety of reasons, this is the normal thing. Governments, with their inevitable recourse to violence and hypocrisy, become estranged from the sympathy of those who believe in them; and then, forgetful of their essential impotence and incapability, they are led to promise what they are unable to perform, so creating malcontents who are always crying for changes and yet more changes.

It is not surprising, therefore, that Olga supported the rebels, while her father, a foreigner, and with a life's experience of our authorities, concealed his sympathies under a prudent cloak of silence.

'You won't do anything that would compromise me, will you Olga?'

She had risen to accompany her husband to the door. She paused, fastened her bright gaze upon him, and with a slight contraction of the lips, said:

'You know perfectly well I wouldn't.'

The doctor went down the steps from the verandah, crossed the garden, and at the gate turned to wave goodbye to his wife, who was leaning on the verandah watching him leave in the manner of all couples, happily or unhappily married.

At this same time, Coração dos Outros was happily dreaming, remote from earthly preoccupations. He was still living in his tenement house in the suburbs, whose view stretched from Todos os Santos to Piedade, taking in an immense built up area, a panorama of houses and trees. His rival was now no longer spoken of, and his wound was healed. Nowadays his triumph was uncontested: the whole city held him in due esteem, so that he almost considered his career was at an end. Only Botafogo still withheld recognition, but he was quite sure of obtaining this. He had already published more than one volume of songs, and was now thinking of publishing yet another.

For some days he had stayed in the house, scarcely going out, preparing his book. He used to remain shut up in his room, lunching on bread and coffee, which he made himself; in the evening he would go to a tavern near the station for dinner. He had noticed that whenever he arrived the carters and workmen having dinner at the dirty tables would lower their voices and look at him suspiciously; but he paid no attention . . . Though he was popular in the neighbourhood he had not seen a single familiar face during the last three days. He himself was shy of speaking, and in the house he limited himself to exchanging a 'good morning' or 'good afternoon' with his neighbours.

He liked to spend days like that, bound up in himself, listening to the voices within him. He did not read the newspapers so as not to distract his attention from his work, but spent his time thinking of his modinhas, and the book which was destined to be one more victory for his beloved guitar.

That afternoon he was sitting at the table revising one of his works, one of the latest; in fact it was the one he had written on Quaresma's farm — 'Carola's Lips'. First of all he read it through, humming as he did so; then he read it once more, seized his guitar the better to capture the effect, and began to sing:

> 'She's prettier far than Margaret and Helen,
> When round her fan an artful smile she slips.
> The illusion that alone makes life supportable,
> Is no place else but in Carola's lips.'

Just then he heard a shot, then another, and another . . . What the devil, he thought. They must be saluting some foreign ship. He plucked the strings of his guitar once more, and continued his song in praise of Carola's lips, where he found the illusion that alone makes life supportable . . .

PART THREE

I
The Patriots

For over an hour he had been waiting there, in one of the large rooms of the palace, able to see the marshal, but without succeeding in speaking to him. There was scarcely any difficulty in getting admitted to his presence, but to be able to speak to him was by no means so simple.

The easy-going atmosphere of the palace, bordering as it did on slovenliness, was characteristic and significant. In the other rooms it was not uncommon to see aides, messengers and attendants chatting together, sprawling unbuttoned on the divans. There was slackness and laxity everywhere. Cobwebs hung in the corners of the ceiling, while a heavy tread on the carpets brought forth dust as from a badly swept street.

Quaresma had been unable to come immediately as he had announced in his telegram. It had been necessary to put his affairs in order, and find someone to keep his sister company. Dona Adelaide had put a thousand difficulties in the way of his departure: she pointed out that the risks he would run in the war and the fighting were out of all proportion to his age, and too much for his strength. But he put his foot down and refused to be dissuaded, for he was convinced that all his intelligence and will-power, all he possessed of life and energy should be put at the disposal of the government, so that then . . . oh!

He spent the days drawing up a petition to give to Floriano. In it he outlined the measures necessary for the improvement of agriculture, and described the difficulties caused by the existence of large estates, government taxes, heavy freight charges, lack of markets and political interference.

Holding the manuscript in his hand, the major thought of his house in a far off corner of that ugly plain, from which, on a bright clear day, you could see the long line of mountains on the western horizon. He thought of his sister, and of the strange, impassive look in her calm, green eyes as she watched him leaving. But what he remembered most at that moment was his old negro servant, Anastácio, looking long at him, not this time with the passive affection of a domestic animal, but rolling the whites of his eyes in astonishment, fear and pity, when he saw him step into the railway carriage. It was as if he could scent misfortune . . . He did not often act in this way; he must have discovered ominous signs of disasters to come . . .

Quaresma had stationed himself in a corner watching the various people come in, and waiting for the president to summon him. It was early yet, just a few minutes short of midday, and Floriano even had a tooth-pick in his mouth, a relic of lunch. He spoke first of all to a commission of ladies who had come to offer their life-blood in defence of their native land and its institutions. The speaker was a small, fat woman with a short waist and large, prominent bosom, who was waving a closed fan in her right hand as she spoke. It was impossible to say exactly of what colour or race she was; she presented a mixture of so many of them, one blotting out the other, that she defied accurate classification.

While she spoke, the little woman gazed at the marshal with her large eyes flashing fire. Their blaze seemed to make Floriano uncomfortable, as if he was afraid of melting before the warmth of a look that seemed more expressive of seduction than of patriotism. He avoided looking at her, hanging his head like a boy and tapping with his fingers on the table . . . When it was his turn to speak, he raised his head a little, but without looking at the woman, and with a harsh, heavy, farmer's smile declined the offer on the grounds that the Republic was still possessed of sufficient strength to achieve victory.

The last sentence was spoken slowly, almost ironically. The ladies took their leave. The marshal looked round the room, and his eyes fell on Quaresma:

'Well now, Quaresma?' he said familiarly.

The major was about to go up to him, but suddenly he stopped short and remained where he was. A throng of junior officers and cadets surrounded the dictator and captured his attention. It was impossible to make out what they were saying, for they were speaking in his ear, whispering and clapping him on the shoulder. The marshal hardly said a word, just nodded his head or uttered a monosyllable, as Quaresma was able to perceive by the movement of his lips.

They began to leave, shaking the dictator by the hand, and as they did so one of them, heartier and more familiar than the others, squeezed his limp hand, patted him affectionately on the shoulder, and in a loud voice, with much emphasis, said:

'Strong action, marshal.'

All this seemed so natural, so normal, having become part of the new ceremonial of the Republic, that no one, not even Floriano himself, felt the slightest surprise. On the contrary, some went so far as to smile happily at the sight of their caliph, their khan, their emir transmitting something of his sanctity to the impudent subaltern. Not all of them left immediately; one of them remained behind to have a confidential word with the country's supreme authority. He was a cadet of the Military Academy, with his turquoise uniform, shoulder-belt and private's sword.

The cadets of the Military Academy formed a sacrosanct body, enjoying privileges and rights of every description. They took precedence over ministers in interviews with the dictator, and abused his support to annoy and oppress the entire city. Their minds had been affected by odd scraps of positivism, producing a very special kind of religious feeling. This transformed Floriano's authority, and in a vague way the Republic itself, into an article of faith, a talisman, a Mexican idol, on whose altar all outrages and crimes were a worthy oblation, a valuable offering to secure its satisfaction and perpetuity.

The cadet remained there . . .

This gave Quaresma a better opportunity to observe the physiognomy of the man who, for almost a year, was to wield such supreme power, the power of a Roman Emperor, directing and controlling everything with not a thing to oppose the full play of his wishes, whims and foibles; not laws, nor customs nor common human mercy.

It was gross and disheartening. With his drooping moustache, his loosely hanging lower lip with its tiny beard, his coarse, flaccid features, not even his expression or the set of his chin revealed any personality or trace of superior talent. His look was dull and lifeless, expressing little other than sadness; not a sadness personal to him, but ingrained, of the race itself. He gave the impression of softness, nervelessness.

The major was unwilling to see in these signs any indication of his character, intelligence or temperament. Such things don't count, he told himself. His enthusiasm for this political idol was strong, sincere and disinterested. He believed him to be energetic, shrewd, far-seeing, stubborn and well-informed of his country's needs; wayward at times, perhaps, a kind of combination of Louis XI and Bismarck.

But he was not like that at all. With a total lack of intellectual qualities, there was one dominant feature of Marshal Floriano's character: lukewarmness; and by temperament he was extremely lazy. His laziness was not of the ordinary sort which every one of us knows, but was of a morbid nature, a lack of nervous vitality caused by insufficient fluid in his organism. Wherever he went he became notorious for his indolence and his reluctance to perform the duties of his position. As director of the Pernambuco arsenal he had not the energy to sign the necessary despatches, and during the time when he was Minister of War he spent months without going near the Ministry, leaving everything unsigned, and bequeathing a mountain of work to his successor.

Those who are familiar with the bureaucratic activities of a Colbert, a Napoleon, a Philip II, a William I of Germany, or, generally speaking, of all great statesmen, are unable to understand Floriano's indifference to communicating to his

146

officers his orders and his explanations of his wishes and opinions. Certainly such communication was necessary so that his superior judgement should make itself felt, and have its influence on governmental and administrative affairs.

This mental and physical inactivity was the cause of his silence, his mysterious monosyllables which were invested with the authority of Sybilline pronouncements, his famous 'successions of perhapses' which produced such an effect on the intelligence and imagination of the people, avid for heroes and great men. Another result of this unhealthy laziness was that he walked about in slippers, a habit that gave him the appearance of unassailable calm, the calm of a great statesman or general.

The first months of his government are still fresh in everyone's mind. Faced with the insurrection of the prisoners, soldiers and non-commissioned officers of the Santa Cruz fortress, he ordered an investigation, but then backed down for fear that those listed as instigators should rebel a second time. Not content with this, he gave the most liberal rewards to these very same men.

Moreover, it is inadmissible in a great man, a Caesar or a Napoleon, to allow his subordinates such degrading intimacies, to condescend to them as he did, even permitting his name to be used as a shield for a long series of crimes of every nature. One instance is enough. Everyone knows in what an atmosphere of hostility Napoleon assumed the command of the army in Italy. Augereau, who used to call him 'the gutter general', said to someone after having spoken to him: 'That man put the fear of God into me.' And the Corsican was master of the army with no backslapping, and no tacit or explicit delegation of his authority to irresponsible subordinates.

Furthermore, the slowness with which the revolt of 6th September was put down clearly reveals the weakness and hesitancy of a man who had all those unlimited resources at his command.

There is another side to Marshal Floriano which does much to explain his actions and his behaviour. This was his love of his family: a deep-rooted, old-fashioned patriarchal love, of the type that is passing away with the onward march of civilization.

As a result of the failure of his efforts to farm two of his properties he was in a precarious position financially, and he did not want to die before he was sure of leaving his property to his family unencumbered by debts. Honest and upright as he was, his only hope lay in what he could save from his salaries. Hence his caution, his playing for safety, so necessary if he was to keep the rich prizes; hence, too, the stubbornness with which he clung to the Presidency of the Republic. The mortgage of his two properties — 'Brejão' and 'Duarte' — was his Cleopatra's nose.

His idleness, his half-heartedness and his fervent love of his home produced this 'perhaps-man' whose image, distorted by the mental and social needs of his contemporaries, was transformed into that of a statesman, a Richelieu. He became a leader who succeeded in putting down a serious rebellion more by obstinacy than vigour; who was given men and money, and even inspired enthusiasm and fanaticism. But this enthusiasm and fanaticism which so assisted, encouraged and supported him, only became possible after he had been adjutant-general of the Empire, senator and minister — that is after he had created his legend before the eyes of the world, and stamped it firmly in the minds of all.

His conception of government was not despotism; neither was it democracy or aristocracy: it was a domestic tyranny. If the child has behaved badly you punish it. On a grand scale, behaving badly meant opposing him, holding opinions contrary to his, and the punishment was no longer a slapping, but imprisonment and death. If there is no money in the Treasury you put back into circulation the notes that have been withdrawn, just like what you do at home when visitors arrive and there is not enough soup: you add more water.

Moreover, his military education and rudimentary culture gave greater force to this childlike conception, tainting it with violence, not so much directly, through his own natural perversity and contempt for human life, but indirectly, by the

148

weakness with which he cloaked and failed to restrain the ferocity of his lieutenants and followers.

All this was far from Quaresma's mind. He was one of the many honest, sincere men of that time who had been gripped by the contagious enthusiasm that Floriano had succeeded in arousing. He was thinking of the great work that Destiny had reserved for that calm, melancholy figure; of the drastic reforms he would bring to the tottering framework of his native land, that country that the major had been accustomed to believe the richest in the world, even though he had lately had some doubts of this in certain respects. Surely he would not destroy such hopes, and his powerful action would make itself felt throughout Brazil's eight million square kilometers bringing roads, security, protection to the weak, guaranteeing work and promoting wealth.

He did not pursue this train of thought for long. After the marshal had addressed him so familiarly another man, who was also awaiting his turn, began to take an interest in that small, taciturn figure wearing pince-nez. He worked his way nearer to Quaresma, and when he was quite close he said, as if communicating a fearful secret:

'They'll see the "caboclo" . . . Have you known him long, major?'

Quaresma answered him, and the other questioned him further; but the president was now alone and the major went up to him.

'Well now, Quaresma?' said Floriano.

'I have come to offer my humble services to Your Excellency.'

The president gazed for a moment at that tiny figure and with much difficulty gave a faint smile of satisfaction. He recognized in the gesture a sign of the strength of his popularity and the justice of his cause.

'I'm very grateful to you . . . Where have you been? I know that you left the arsenal.'

Floriano had that ability to remember the faces, names, jobs and positions of the subordinates he dealt with. There was something of the Asiatic about him: he was cruel and paternal at the same time.

Quaresma told him of his life, taking advantage of the opportunity to speak about agrarian laws, and reforms that would help to put the country's agriculture on a new footing. The marshal listened absentmindedly, a little crease of annoyance forming at the corners of his lips.

'I have gone so far as to bring this memorandum for Your Excellency.'

The president gave a gesture of irritation, as if to say, 'Don't bother me,' and said idly:

'Leave it there . . .'

The dictator laid the manuscript on a table, and then turned to Quaresma's interlocutor of a few moments before:

'What is it, Bustamente? How's the battalion coming along?'

The man, a little scared, drew nearer:

'Quite well, marshal. We need barracks. If Your Excellency would give orders . . .'

'Of course. Speak to Rufino in my name and he'll fix you up . . . Better still, take him this note.'

He tore a piece from one of the first pages of Quaresma's manuscript and there and then, on that little scrap of paper, wrote a few words in blue pencil to his War Minister. Only when he had finished did he realize the discourtesy:

'Oh, I'm sorry Quaresma, I've torn your memorandum. It doesn't matter, though . . . It was the top part and had nothing written on it.'

Quaresma confirmed this, and the president then addressed Bustamente:

'Find a place for Quaresma in your battalion. What rank would you like?'

'Me?' repeated Quaresma stupidly.

'Fine. You two arrange things between you.'

They took their leave of the president and slowly went down the stairs of the Itamariti palace. Not a word passed between them until they reached the street. Quaresma was a little cold. It was a bright warm day, and the traffic in the city did not seem to have changed appreciably. There was the same confusion of trams, carriages and carts, but the faces of the people gave signs of anxiety and terror: it was as if some fearful dread were hanging over everything.

Bustamente introduced himself. He was Major Bustamente, now Lieutenant Colonel, an old friend of the Marshal from the days of the Paraguayan War.

'But we've already met,' he exclaimed.

Quaresma looked at the old, dark mulatto, with his long, Mosaic beard and his shrewd eyes, but he did not remember having met him.

'I don't remember . . . Where?'

'In General Albernaz' house . . . Don't you remember?'

Policarpo had a vague recollection, and then the other went on to explain the formation of his patriotic battalion, 'The Southern Cross.'

'Would you like to join?'

'Very much,' said Quaresma.

'We're having a bit of trouble . . . Uniforms, boots for the soldiers . . . With these initial expenses we ought to help the government . . . It wouldn't do to bleed the Treasury, would it?'

'Of course not,' said Quaresma enthusiastically.

'I'm delighted you agree with me . . . I can see you are a patriot . . . So I've decided we'll have a subscription amongst the officers in proportion to their rank: a second lieutenant contributes a hundred milreis, a lieutenant two hundred . . . What rank would you like? Ah, but of course, you're a major, aren't you?'

Quaresma then explained why it was that they called him major. An influential friend in the Ministry of the Interior had included his name, with that rank, in a list of the National Guard; and although he had never paid the necessary fee he found himself always addressed as major, and the title had stuck. At first he had protested, but as they insisted he let things be.

'That's fine,' said Bustamente. 'You can carry on as major.'

'What is my contribution?'

'Four hundred milreis. A bit steep, but . . . It's an important position, you know. What do you say?'

'Agreed.'

Bustamente took out his pocketbook, made a note with a stub of pencil, and took a cheerful leave of the major:

'Right then, major: six o'clock in the provisional barracks.'

The conversation took place at the corner of the Rua Larga and Campo de Sant'Ana. Quaresma was going to take a tram to the centre of the city with the intention of visiting his friend in Botafogo, and so pass the time until his initiation into military life.

There was little traffic in the square: the trams passed by with a rhythmical clip-clop of the mules' hoofs. From time to time there was a bugle call and a rattle of drums, and out through the central gate of the general headquarters would come a column with rifles on their shoulders, the fixed bayonets of the recruits dancing and glittering with a harsh, sinister brilliance. As he boarded the tram some artillery shots were heard, and the dry crack of rifles. It did not last long; before the tram had reached the Rua da Constituiçao all the sounds of war had ceased, so that anyone who did not know might have thought that things were normal.

Quaresma sat down in the middle of the seat and was about to read the newspaper he had bought. He was unfolding it slowly when he was interrupted by a tap on the shoulder. He turned round.

'Oh. General.'

They greeted each other warmly. General Albernaz loved these occasions; it gave him such pleasure, such an exquisite emotion to renew acquaintanceships that had grown weak through absence. He was wearing his old, battered uniform, but without his sword, and his pince-nez were as usual fastened by a gold chain that passed behind his left ear.

'So you've come to watch the fun?'

'Yes. I've already seen the marshal.'

'Those lads are going to find out who they're up against. They think they're dealing with Deodoro, but they're making a big mistake. Thank God the Republic now has a real leader . . . The "caboclo" is as tough as they come . . . In Paraguay . . .'

152

'You knew him there, didn't you general?'

'Well . . . We didn't actually meet; but Camisão . . . He's as hard as nails. I'm in charge of munitions . . . He's a crafty one, the "caboclo": he didn't want me on the shore. He knows me pretty well, and knows that any munitions that come from my hands will be the real stuff . . . I don't let a single crate out of the stores without examining it myself . . . You have to . . . In Paraguay there was a lot of confusion and pilfering: they sent a good deal of lime instead of powder — did you know that?'

'No.'

'That's how it was. I wanted to go to the beaches, into the firing line, but the old man wants me in munitions . . . The captain orders and the sailor obeys . . . He knows . . .'

He turned his back, adjusted the chain that had fallen from his ear, and was silent for a moment.

'How's the family?' asked Quaresma.

'They're well. Did you know that Quinota is married?'

'Yes, Ricardo told me. And how is Dona Ismênia?'

The general's features clouded over, and he answered with seeming reluctance:

'She's much the same.'

A father's embarrassment prevented him from telling the whole truth. His daughter had gone mad. It was a meek, childish form of madness: she would spend whole days sitting quietly in a corner, gazing stupidly about her, as expressionless as a statue, lifeless and imbecile. Then suddenly she would comb her hair and adorn herself, and run to her mother, saying, 'Get me ready, mother. My husband is coming . . . Today is my wedding day.' At other times she would cut up pieces of paper in the form of wedding announcements, and write: 'Ismênia de Albernaz and So-and-so (the name varied) are pleased to announce their engagement.'

The general had already consulted a dozen doctors, spiritualists, and had now brought in a miracle-working witch-doctor, but none could cure his daughter. The craze never left her, and her mind became more and more bound up with the obsession of marriage, the appointed goal in her life which she

153

had never attained. And so, in their full bloom, she lost both her mind and her youth.

Her condition cast a gloom over that house, formerly so gay and lively. There were fewer parties, and when they were obliged to give one for the important occasions, by dint of every care and every kind of promise she was taken to the house of her married sister. There she would remain while the others danced, forgetting for a moment the sufferings of their sister.

Albernaz did not wish to disclose this tragedy of his old age. He suppressed his emotion, and he went on in a natural tone of voice, the same familiar, intimate tone he used with everybody:

'It's a disgrace, Senhor Quaresma. What a setback for the country. And the cost. A port like this closed to trade, how many years is that going to set us back.'

The major agreed with him, and showed the necessity of upholding the government so as to make any further uprisings and rebellions impossible.

'You're right,' said the general. 'Otherwise we shan't get ahead, there'll be no progress. And what a bad impression abroad!'

The tram arrived at the Largo de São Francisco and the two went their separate ways: Quaresma to the Largo do Carioca, and Albernaz to the Rua do Rosário.

Olga saw her godfather come in without her usual warm sense of pleasure. It was not that she felt indifferent; what she felt was rather surprise, astonishment, almost fear, even though she knew perfectly well that he was about to arrive. Yet nothing had changed about Quaresma; his features, his body, his whole appearance were the same. He was the same small, pale man with the pointed goatee, and the penetrating look behind his pince-nez. He was not even more sunburned, and his way of compressing his lips was just the same as she had known for years. But he seemed different; it was as if he had come in goaded by some strange, compelling force. Yet when she considered it, he had entered quite naturally with his short, firm step. What was it that had oppressed her and taken

154

away the joy she felt at seeing such a well-loved face? She could not guess. She was reading in the dining-room, and Quaresma, as was his old habit, had come straight in without being announced. She was still under the gloomy impression his entrance had caused when she answered his question:

'Father is out, and Armando is downstairs, writing.'

He was, in fact, writing, or rather translating into 'classical language' a lengthy article on 'Firearms' wounds'. This classical style was his latest intellectual artifice. By this he sought to be different, to distinguish himself from those young fellows who write stories and novels in the newspapers. He, a scholar, and above all a doctor, could not write as they did. His superior learning and his academic title would never allow him to use the same language and expressions, the same syntax as those poetasters and hacks. Then there came to him the idea of the classical style. The method was simple: he wrote in the normal manner, using everyday words and phrases; then he inverted the order of the clauses, divided up the sentence with commas, substituted 'incommode' for 'trouble', 'around' for 'round', 'enquire' for 'inquire', 'eschew' for 'avoid', 'voluminous' for 'large', finally turned it all back to front, and so obtained his classical style, which was already winning the admiration of his colleagues and the public in general.

The expression 'provoke dissension' was much over-worked: he used it on every possible occasion, and when he wrote it on the whiteness of the paper he imagined it gave the force and brilliance of Pascal to his style, and a transcendental quality to his ideas. At night he used to read Padre Vieira, but sleep overtook him after the first few lines, and he would dream he was a respected physician of the seventeenth century prescribing negus and warm water, just like Doctor Sangrado.

His translation was nearly finished. He was now quite expert, for with time he had acquired an adequate vocabulary, and the final version was almost half done mentally while he wrote out the first draft. He received his wife's message, informing him of the visit, with slight annoyance; but as he had been unable to find a classical equivalent of

155

'orifice', he felt that the interruption might be useful. He wanted to put 'hole', but that was plebeian; although 'orifice' was much used, it was nevertheless more dignified. Perhaps on his return he would find it, he thought, and went up to the dining room. He was in a good humour as he walked in, with his large, unkempt moustache and round face, to find his wife and her godfather engaged in a discussion about authority.

She was saying:

'I can't understand that tone of sanctity you adopt when you discuss authority. No one now governs in the name of God, so why all this respect, this veneration with which you try to surround our rulers?'

The doctor, who had heard the whole sentence, could not refrain from saying:

'But it is necessary, indispensable . . . We know they are men like us, but you are going to bring everything down in ruins.'

Quaresma added:

'It exists because of the internal and external requirements of our society . . . Take ants, take bees . . .'

'I agree. But bees and ants have their revolutions too. And do they maintain their authority by means of assassinations, exactions and violence?'

'Who knows . . . Who knows? Maybe . . .' said Quaresma evasively.

The doctor had no doubts, and spoke straight out:

'What have we got to do with bees? Are we human beings, nature's supreme creation, to go to insects for our standards?'

'It's not that, my dear doctor; what we seek to find from their example is certainty regarding the generality of the phenomenon, its immanence so to speak,' said Quaresma gently.

He had not finished his explanation when Olga added:

'If only such authority brought happiness. But it doesn't; so what is it worth?'

'But it will bring it, ' declared Quaresma categorically. 'It is a question of consolidating it.'

They stayed talking for a long time. Quaresma described his

visit to Floriano and his enlistment in the 'Southern Cross' battalion, the doctor feeling a twinge of envy when he referred to the familiar way he was treated by the president.

After a light snack Quaresma left. He felt the need to see once more these narrow streets with their dark, cavernous shops where the attendants moved about as if in a subterranean passage. How he had missed the tortuous Rua dos Ourives, the pot-holed Rua da Assembléia and the elegant Rua do Ouvidor!

Life was just the same. There were people standing about in groups, girls out for a stroll and crowds packing the Café do Rio. Here were the avant-garde, the 'jacobins', the dedicated custodians of the Republic, so intransigent that in their eyes moderation, tolerance, and respect for the life and liberty of others constituted crimes of *lèse-patrie*, symptoms of criminal monarchism and dishonest capitulation in the face of the foreigner. The foreigner meant principally the Portuguese, which did not prevent there being extravagantly jacobin newspapers published by Lusitanians of the first water.

Apart from this passionate, gesticulating group, the Rua do Ouvidor was unchanged. Lovers met and girls passed by. If a shell went humming through the bright, blue sky overhead, the girls, squealing like cats, would rush inside the shops, wait a little while, and then come out again smiling, the blood little by little returning to their white, scared faces.

Quaresma dined at a restaurant before making his way to the barracks, which was provisionally installed out at Cidade Nova in an old tenement house that had been condemned by the Sanitary Authorities. The house had two storeys, both of which had been divided into cubicles the size of a ship's cabin. At the level of the first floor there was a verandah made of planks, which was reached by means of a rickety wooden stairway that swayed and creaked at the lightest step. The administration was in the first room of the first floor, and the yard, now without its washing lines, but with the flagstones still stained by detergent and soapy water, served as a parade-ground for the recruits. The instructor was a somewhat lame, retired sergeant who had been admitted to the battalion with the rank of second lieutenant, and would bawl with majestic deliberation: 'Shoul . . . der . . . arms!'

The major handed his subscription to the colonel who proceeded to show him the model of their uniform. This proved to be a most unusual lace-maker's phantasy: the jacket was bottle-green with bluish piping, and had gold braid and four silver stars in the shape of a cross on the collar.

The sound of confused shouting reached the verandah. Down below, surrounded by soldiers, a man was struggling, weeping and imploring. Now and again they struck him with the butt of a rifle.

'It's Ricardo,' exclaimed Quaresma. 'Don't you know him, colonel?' he asked, filled with interest and pity.

Bustamente, on the verandah, remained impassive. He replied only after a pause:

'Yes, I know him . . . He's an insubordinate volunteer, a rebel.'

The soldiers brought the 'volunteer' upstairs. As soon as he set eyes on the major, Ricardo burst out:

'Save me, major.'

Quaresma called the colonel to one side, begging and imploring him, but all to no purpose . . . They needed men . . . However, he'd make him a corporal.

Ricardo, who was following the conversation from a distance, guessed that he was being refused and cried out desperately:

'Alright, I'll join; but let me have my guitar.'

Bustamente drew himself up and shouted to the soldiers:

'Give Corporal Ricardo back his guitar.'

II
You, Quaresma, are a Visionary

Eight o'clock in the morning. The mist still hangs over everything. On land the lower parts of nearby buildings are scarcely discernible, while at sea no eye can penetrate those rolling white clouds, that opaque wall of vapour that dissolves here and there into phantastic shapes and appearances. The sea is silent but for a faint murmur at long intervals. A small stretch, covered with seaweed, is visible from the beach; the mist seeming to make its heavy smell more pungent. To left and right there is the unknown, the mysterious. Yet that dense, diffusely lit mass is peopled with sounds. The whine of nearby saws, the whistles of factories and trains, and the creaking winches of ships' cranes pierce the thick morning gloom. Another sound, too, is heard; the rhythmic splash of oars dipping in the water. It must be Caronte bringing his boat across to that Stygian shore.

Action stations! Every eye scans the dense curtain of mist. Faces are tense, as if expecting a horde of devils to rush upon them from the fog . . .

The sound disappears: the boat has passed on. Sighs of relief all round . . .

It is neither night nor day; neither dawn nor dusk; it is the hour of dread and of treacherous half-light. At sea there is neither star nor sun to guide by; on land the birds batter themselves to death against the white walls of the houses. Our wretchedness is the more complete, and the absence of all that silent evidence of human activity underlines our isolation amid the vastness of nature.

The sounds continue, but as there is nothing to be seen it is as if they come from the depths of the earth, or are nothing more than aural hallucinations. Reality exists only in the narrow strip of sea that is visible, murmuring gently at long intervals, fearful of its encounter with the sea-weed strewn sand of the beach.

After the sound of the oars, the soldiers, in groups, stretch

159

themselves out on the grass above the beach. Some dozen others gaze upwards, trying to penetrate the mist that moistens their faces. Corporal Ricardo Coração dos Outros, with rifle at his waist and cap on his head, sits apart from the others, alone on a rock, contemplating the terror of the morning. He had never before seen fog so close to the sea, where its sinister power is felt to the full. He was accustomed to seeing the clear, rosy sunrise, soft and fragrant; that ugly, misty dawn was a new experience for him.

Under his corporal's uniform the minstrel is not unhappy. The free life of the barracks suits him well enough; his guitar is there inside, and in his leisure moments he can play it, humming to himself in a low voice. He must not let his fingers get rusty . . . His only small grievance is not to be able to open up his lungs from time to time. But the commander of the troop is Quaresma, who might give his permission . . .

The major is inside the house, which serves as a barracks, reading. Nowadays his favourite study is artillery. He bought compendiums on the subject; but, as his knowledge is insufficient, from artillery he goes to ballistics, from ballistics to mechanics, from mechanics to calculus and geometrical analysis, and so on down the scale to trigonometry, geometry, algebra and arithmetic. He runs through this chain of interconnected sciences with the faith of an inventor, gaining the most rudimentary notions after a whole cycle of consultations in one compendium after another. And so he passes those days of wartime idleness delving into mathematics, that science that is so inimical and distasteful to brains that are no longer young.

The unit possesses a Krupps cannon, but he has nothing to do with this death-dealing weapon. Despite this he studies artillery. The officer in charge of it is Lieutenant Fontes, who refuses to take orders from the patriotic major. This does not bother Quaresma, who carries on slowly learning how to use the gun and putting up with his subaltern's arrogance.

Bustamente, the long-bearded commander of the 'Southern Cross' is in the barracks engaged in the administration of the battalion. There are very few officers and relatively fewer men, but the State has four hundred on the pay-roll. There is a shortage of captains, but there are enough second lieutenants and almost enough lieutenants; they have one major, Quaresma, and the commander, Bustamente, who out of modesty made himself merely a lieutenant-colonel.

The unit commanded by Quaresma consisted of forty men, with three second lieutenants and two lieutenants; but the officers rarely put in an appearance, being either sick or on leave. The only ones on duty were himself, the former agriculturalist from 'The Haven', and Second Lieutenant Polidoro, who came only at night.

A soldier came into the room:

'Sir, may I go to lunch?'

'Yes. Call Corporal Ricardo for me.'

The private hobbled out in his heavy boots. These were a penance to him, so as soon as he found himself in the woods on the way home he took them off, and felt the breath of liberty blowing on his cheek.

Quaresma went to the window. The mist was already dissolving, and the sun could be seen, like a dull golden disc in the sky.

Ricardo Coração dos Outros appeared looking comic in his corporal's uniform. The jacket was far too short, revealing the whole length of the wrist, while the absurdly long trousers trailed on the ground.

'How are you, Ricardo?'

'Fine. And you, sir?'

'Alright.'

Quaresma surveyed his friend and subordinate with his leisurely, penetrating look:

'You've been rather unhappy lately, haven't you?'

Ricardo was pleased by the major's interest:

'No . . . What's the use of admitting it, major? . . . If it goes on like this to the end it won't be too bad . . . It's hell when they start shooting though . . . There is one thing, major: when there's nothing to do, wouldn't it be possible to go into the woods and sing? . . .'

The major scratched his head, stroked his goatee and said:

161

'I don't know . . . It's . . .'

'You know, singing in a low voice is like rowing on dry land . . . They say that in Paraguay . . .'

'Alright. You can sing there; but not too loudly, mind.'

They were silent for a moment. Ricardo was about to leave when the major added:

'Tell them to send me my lunch.'

Quaresma lunched and dined there, his meals being provided by a nearby eating-house, and not infrequently slept there too. He slept in one of the bedrooms of the imperial building where his unit was billeted, for it had once belonged to the emperor, being situated in the former royal park of Ponta do Caju. Also within the royal precincts were the Rio Douro Railway Station and a large noisy sawmill. Quaresma went to the door and looked out at the dirty beach. He wondered that the emperor should have liked going there to bathe.

The mist was now lifting, and in the heart of the rolling clouds the various objects were beginning to assume a definite shape, as if satisfied that the nightmare had gone. First of all the lower parts slowly appeared, followed, almost in an instant, by the upper parts. To the right there were the houses of Saude and Gamboa, and cargo ships emerging from the mist: three masted galleys, tramp steamers and tall sailing ships, giving the momentary impression of a Dutch landscape; to the left Rapôsa bay, Retiro Saudoso, the dreadful Sapucaia, Governador island and the blue Orgãos mountains reaching to the sky; in front was Ferreiros island with its coal dumps; and looking further out across the calm waters of the sea, Niteroi, whose mountains, in the tardy morning light, had just become visible against the blue of the sky.

The mist disappeared and somewhere a cock crowed. It was as if joy had returned to the earth; it was an alleluia! Those whines, whistles and creaks now assumed a gay note of satisfaction.

Lunch arrived, and the sergeant came in to inform Quaresma that there were two desertions.

'Two more?' said the major in surprise.

162

'Yes sir. A hundred and twenty-five and three hundred and twenty didn't answer at roll-call today.'

'Register it, sergeant.'

While Quaresma was having lunch Lieutenant Fontes, the officer in charge of the gun, arrived. He rarely slept there, spending the nights at home and coming during the day to see how things were getting along.

There was one morning when he didn't turn up. It was still dark, and the sentry made out a dark shape far out at sea, gliding over the surface of the water. It carried no light, and only the movement and the slight phosphorescence of the water betrayed that it was a ship. The sentry gave the alarm; the men ran to action stations, and Quaresma appeared.

'Advance the cannon. Stand by,' ordered the commander.

Then a few moments later he nervously added:

'Wait a minute.'

He ran to the house to consult his compendiums and tables. Meanwhile the launch drew nearer, and with the soldiers all on tenterhooks, one of them took the initiative, loaded the gun and fired.

Quaresma ran back in alarm panting for breath:

'Did you . . . estimate . . . the distance . . . the aim . . . the angle? You must always bear in mind the accuracy of your fire.'

Next day when Fontes came and learned of the incident he burst out laughing:

'Really major, do you think you're out in the training ground doing practical exercises? . . . Open fire!'

And that is actually how it was. Almost every afternoon there was a bombardment, the fortresses firing on the ships, and the ships on the fortresses, with both ships and forts emerging unscathed from their terrible ordeal.

There was one occasion, however, when they did score a hit, and the newspapers announced, 'Yesterday the Acadêmico fort gave a marvellous display of gunnery. With such and such a cannon they put a shell into the "Guanabara".' The following day the same paper published a rectification at the request of the Pharoux Dock battery, which was the one that had fired the lucky shot. Some days later, when the incident was almost forgotten, there came a letter from Niteroi claiming the honours for the Santa Cruz Fortress.

Lieutenant Fontes arrived and began to examine the cannon with his expert touch. There was a trench with bales of alfalfa, and the muzzle of the gun poked out from behind the straw looking like the gullet of some wild animal hidden in the bushes. After examining it carefully he focused his eyes on the horizon, and was looking at Cobras Island when he heard the sound of a guitar, and a voice singing:

'I promise by the Holy Sacraments . . .'

He made his way to where the sounds were coming from and was confronted by a most charming spectacle: in the shade of a large tree the soldiers were sitting or lying in a circle round Ricardo Coração dos Outros, listening to his plaintive songs.

The men had just had their lunch and drunk their rum, and they were so absorbed in Ricardo's singing that they did not notice the presence of the young officer.

'What's all this?' he said sternly.

The soldiers leapt to their feet and saluted; and Ricardo, standing to attention, with his right hand at his cap and his left holding his guitar, which rested on the ground, explained:

'Please sir, the major said we could. You know we wouldn't be playing about unless we had permission, sir.'

'Very well. I don't want any more of it, though,' said the officer.

'But Major Quaresma . . .' objected Ricardo.

'There's no Major Quaresma here. I've already said I want no more of it.'

The men dispersed, and Lieutenant Fontes proceeded to the old imperial house to have a word with the 'Southern Cross' battalion's major. Quaresma was still engaged in his studies, a sisyphean labour, but voluntarily undertaken for the glorification of his country. Fontes entered and said:

'What's this, Senhor Quaresma. Do you allow the men to have sing-songs?'

Quaresma, who had completely forgotten about the matter,

164

was astonished by the lad's stern, harsh manner. The latter repeated:

'So you allow the men to sing modinhas and play the guitar while on duty?'

'What harm does it do? They say that on campaign . . .'

'What about discipline? What about respect?'

'Alright. I'll forbid it,' said Quaresma.

'That won't be necessary. I've already done so.'

Quaresma was not offended. He saw no reason to be annoyed, and replied simply:

'Quite right.'

He went on to ask the young officer how to find the square root of a decimal fraction. The lad showed him, and they remained talking about everyday matters. Fontes was engaged to Lalá, General Albernaz' third daughter, and he was waiting for the revolt to end before getting married. For an hour the conversation between the two of them turned upon this simple family matter, linked as it was to those explosions, the shooting, that grave contest between two ambitious rivals.

Suddenly the air was pierced by the metallic call of the bugle. Fontes pricked up his ears, and the major asked:

'What call is it?'

'Action stations.'

The two ran out; Fontes faultlessly dressed, the major vainly fumbling with his shoulder belt and tripping over his venerable sword, which insisted on getting between his short legs. The men were already in the trenches, armed. The necessary ammunition was in place beside the cannon. A launch was moving slowly towards them, its high prow aimed directly at their position. Suddenly a puff of white smoke rose up from its deck. 'They've fired,' yelled a voice. Everyone ducked, and the shell whined harmlessly high overhead. The launch came on fearlessly.

As well as the soldiers there were some curious onlookers and small boys watching the firing. It was one of these who had shouted the warning. It was always like that. Sometimes they went right up to the troops, close to the trenches, getting in everyone's way. At other times some fellow or other would go up to the officer and very politely ask, 'Would you give me permission to fire a shot?' The officer agreed, the men loaded the gun, and the man aimed it and fired.

As time passed the revolt assumed the aspect of a party, an entertainment for the city . . . Whenever a bombardment was announced the terrace of the promenade was filled in a trice. It was just like the old days in the Dom Luis de Vasconcelos gardens when it was fashionable, on moonlit nights, to go and look at the solitary planet lighting up the sky and silvering the surface of the water. You could hire binoculars, and both young and old, men and women, followed the bombardment as if it were a stage show: 'The *Santa Cruz* has fired. Now the *Aquidabā*. There she goes.' In this way the revolt became part of everyday life, entering into the habits and customs of the city.

The little boys in the Pharoux Docks—newspaper-boys, shoe-shine boys and fruit sellers—used to shelter behind doorways, urinals and trees, watching, waiting for the projectiles to fall. Then when one landed nearby they would rush out together to pick it up as if it were a coin or a sweet.

Bullets became fashionable: there were tie-pins, trinkets for watches and pencil-cases made of small rifle bullets; medium sized ones were also collected, and their cases, scoured and polished, used to decorate the side-tables of middle-class houses; the large ones, which were popularly called 'melons' or 'pumpkins', ornamented the gardens, being used as pots or statues.

The launch went on firing. Fontes, too, fired a shot. The cannon disgorged its shell, recoiled, and was immediately put in position again. The launch replied, and the boy shouted out, 'They've fired.'

It was always these urchins who announced the enemy's shots. No sooner did they see the brief explosion and the heavy smoke slowly spurting from the ship than they yelled, 'They've fired.' There was one lad in Niteroi who had his hour of fame. They called him 'Thirty Réis'. At the time the newspapers gave a good deal of attention to him, even running a subscription for him. He was a hero. But with the end of the

166

revolt he was forgotten, just like the *Luci*, a fine launch that captured the interest and imagination of the city, winning for herself both enemies and admirers.

The launch gave up annoying the Caju post, and Fontes, after giving instructions to the second in charge, went away.

Quaresma shut himself up in his room, devoting himself once more to his warlike studies. The remaining days that he spent there at the extremity of the city were no different from that one. The same things happened, and the war became a banal repetition of similar events. Occasionally, when boredom overtook him, he went out. He would go into the city, leaving the post in the charge of Polidoro, or Fontes if he was there. He rarely left during the day because Polidoro, the keenest of them, and a carpenter by profession, was working in a furniture factory and only came at night.

By night the centre of the city was carefree and gay. There was plenty of money about as the government was paying double salaries as well as the occasional gratuity. Moreover, death was always present, and all this together was an incentive to merry-making. The theatres were crowded and the restaurants too.

Quaresma, however, did not care to get engaged in the bustle of the semi-besieged town. He sometimes went in mufti to the theatre, and as soon as the show was over he would go back to his room in the city or to the post.

Other evenings, as soon as Polidoro arrived, he would go for a walk along the nearby roads and beaches as far as Campo de São Cristóvão. Looking at those suburbs, one vast cemetery with white tombstones scattered over the hillsides like freshly clipped sheep grazing, and the meditative cypresses watching over them, it was as if that part of the city was the feudal domain of death. The houses had a funereal appearance, isolated and half-hidden; the sea murmured lugubriously against the muddy banks; the palm trees sighed in sorrow, and even the tinkling of the trams' bells was mournful.

He walked on as far as the square, and once there he felt the urge to see his old house again. He ended up by going into General Albernaz' house, for he owed him a visit and decided to take advantage of this opportunity. They had dinner, and dining with the general, as well as Lieutenant Fontes and Admiral Caldas, was Quaresma's commander, Lieutenant-Colonel Inocêncio Bustamente.

Within the barracks Bustamente was a most active commander. As regards concern for the books, for the good handwriting in which the ledgers, registers, company lists and other documents were kept, he had no equal. With their help the organization of his battalion was irreproachable, and in order to keep a watchful eye on the accounts he visited the different posts from time to time.

Quaresma had not seen him for ten days. Immediately after they had exchanged greetings the colonel asked:

'How many desertions?'

'Nine to date,' said Quaresma.

Bustamente scratched his head in desperation and said:

'I don't know what's got into these people . . . There's no accounting for it . . . They've no patriotism.'

'And they're perfectly right, believe me,' said the admiral.

Caldas was pessimistic and indignant. His petition was not going well, and so far the government had not come up with anything for him. His patriotic fervour diminished as his hopes of one day becoming a vice-admiral slowly evaporated. It was true that the government had not yet organized its fleet, but according to the rumours going round he would not be commanding even a squadron. It was a disgrace. He was a little old, it was true; but never having had a command before he would have conserved all his youthful energy.

'Admiral, you shouldn't talk like that . . . Our feeling for our native country is only one step below our feeling for humanity in general.'

'My dear lieutenant, you're still young . . . I know about these matters . . .'

'But we shouldn't despair . . . We're not working for ourselves but for others, those who come after us,' went on Fontes persuasively.

'What have I got to do with them?' said Caldas angrily.

Bustamente, the general and Quaresma listened quietly to

this debate, the first two smiling a little at Caldas' rage as he moved his leg about restlessly and stroked his long, white sideboards. The lieutenant replied:

'A great deal, admiral. We must all work so that better days will come, bringing order, happiness and higher moral standards.'

'Better days! There never have been and never will be,' snapped Caldas.

'I agree,' said Albernaz.

'Things will always be the same,' added Bustamente, sceptically.

The major said nothing; he seemed uninterested in the conversation. In the face of this opposition Fontes, unlike others of his faction, did not lose his temper. He was thin and dark-skinned, with hollow cheeks breaking the oval of his face. After listening to all of them, he shook his right hand in the favourite gesture of the preacher, and in his drawling, nasal voice said benevolently:

'There has already been an attempt at it: the Middle Ages.'

No one there could contradict him. Quaresma knew only Brazilian history, and the others none whatever.

Fontes' affirmation reduced them all to silence though it did not quiet their doubts. The Middle Ages is a curious period: with its high moral standards, you never know quite where to place it, in what year. If you say, 'In Clothair's time, he himself, with his own hands set fire to the hut where his son, his son's wife and children were sheltering,'—the positivist will object: 'The church had not yet completely established its ascendancy.' Then you say, 'St Louis wished to execute a feudal lord because he had ordered three children to be hanged for killing a rabbit in his grounds.' The faithful believer replies: 'Don't you know that the Middle Ages continue until the appearance of the *Divine Comedy*? St Louis' times were those of decadence . . .' If you cite the epidemics of nervous complaints, the misery of the peasantry, the armed robbery of the barons, the hallucinations of the millennium, the barbaric slaughter of the Saxons by Charlemagne, they reply either that the moral ascendancy of the church had not yet

169

been established or that it had already disappeared.

Nothing of this was objected to by the young positivist and the conversation turned to the revolt. The admiral criticized the government severely: they had no plan whatsoever and were just fighting aimlessly. In his opinion they should have done everything possible to occupy Cobras Island, even though it cost rivers of blood. Bustamente had no firm opinion about this, but Quaresma and Fontes were against it: it would be a risky undertaking and serve no purpose at all. Albernaz had not yet given his opinion, and when he did it was in the following terms:

'But we reconnoitred Humaitá without too much difficulty.'

'But you didn't take it,' said Fontes. 'It was a different situation altogether, and even so the reconnaissance was quite useless . . . You ought to know, you were there.'

'Well, er . . . I fell sick a little before and returned to Brazil, but Camisão told me it was a close thing.'

Quaresma lapsed into silence. He wanted to see Ismênia. Fontes had told him of her condition, and for some reason the major felt deeply concerned by her illness. He had seen all the others: Dona Maricota, active and bustling as always; Lalá, signing with her eyes, trying to drag her fiancé away from that interminable conversation; and the others who, from time to time, came from the reception room to the dining room where he was. Finally, unable to restrain himself any longer, he asked after her. He was told that she was in the house of her married sister and getting worse; she had succumbed more and more to her obsession, and was declining in health.

The general recounted all this frankly to Quaresma, and when he had finished describing this personal tragedy of his, he said with a long sigh:

'I don't know, Quaresma . . . I just don't know.'

It was ten o'clock when the major left. He took the tram back to Ponta do Caju and went straight to his room. It was a lovely night, and, as it does with all of us, the soft, milky light of the moon had produced its strange effect on him. The body experiences a sensation of relief, of voluptuousness, as if we are stripped of our material being and are left pure soul, floating

170

amid dreams and chimeras. Quaresma was not aware of the transcendental feeling, but experienced, without perceiving it, the effect of the pale, cool light of the moon. He lay down for a while fully dressed, not because he was sleepy, but by reason of the sense of rapture induced by the silent planet.

Before long Ricardo came to rouse him: the marshal had arrived. It was his habit to go out at night, sometimes at dawn, visiting the different posts. When the public got to know of this, it captured their imagination to an extraordinary extent, consolidating even more his fame as a consummate statesman.

Quaresma went to meet him. Floriano was wearing a wide-brimmed, soft felt hat, and a short, shabby overcoat. He gave the impression of a criminal or of an exemplary head of the family engaged in an extramarital adventure.

The major greeted him, and informed him of the attack made on his post some days earlier. The marshal, gazing about him, answered lazily in monosyllables. Just as he was about to leave he spoke a little more, saying slowly and hesitatingly:

'I'll have to get a searchlight installed here.'.

Quaresma accompanied him as far as the tram. They walked through the former pleasure grounds of the emperors. A short distance from the station a partially lit locomotive was puffing away. It seemed to be snoring in its sleep; and its small carriages, bathed in the light of the moon, seemed to be peacefully sleeping too. The aged mango trees, with here and there a bough missing, were as if scattered with silver. It was a magnificent moonlit night. The two men walked on. Suddenly the marshal asked:

'How many men have you?'

'Forty.'

The marshal muttered, 'Not very many,' and fell silent. For a second Quaresma saw his face lit up by the moonlight. He though the dictator's expression looked more friendly. What if he should speak . . .

He prepared the question but had not the courage to speak out. They went on walking. The major thought furiously: why not? There was no disrespect. They were drawing near to the gate. Suddenly he thought he heard a noise behind them; he glanced back but Floriano scarcely turned his head. The roofs of the sawmill looked as if they were covered with snow, so bright was the moonlight. The major still chewed over his question. It must be now: the gate was only two steps away. He gathered all his courage and said:

'Have you read my memorandum yet, Your Excellency?'

Floriano replied slowly, with scarcely a movement of his drooping lip:

'Yes.'

Quaresma became enthusiastic:

'You see, Your Excellency, how easy it is to put this country on its feet. Once you brush aside all those difficulties I indicated in the memorandum you were kind enough to read; once you have put right the errors of a defective legislation that is ill-suited to the needs of the country, Your Excellency will see how everything will change, how instead of being dependent on others we shall be truly free . . .'

As he spoke, Quaresma's enthusiasm warmed. He was unable to see the dictator's face, covered as it was by the brim of his felt hat; but if he could have done so it would have frozen him on the instant, such was the chilling mask of annoyance that it wore. The president was angry. Quaresma's words and his appeal for legislation and government measures were going to sink into his mind despite his wishes to the contrary. Suddenly he said:

'Do you really think, Quaresma, that I'm going to put a hoe into the hand of every one of those idle rogues . . . It would need an army . . .'

Utterly taken aback, it was a moment or two before Quaresma could answer:

'But that's not what I mean, Marshal. With your power and prestige, Your Excellency, and with energy and the right legislation you can encourage people to work, stimulate enterprise, make it profitable . . . For example, all you need . . .'

They passed through the gate of Pedro I's old park. The

moon was still shining with its opalescent splendour, so bright that it seemed to add doors and windows to a large unfinished building in the road, transforming it into a palace of dreams.

Floriano listened to Quaresma with the keenest displeasure. The tram arrived, and as he parted from the major he said, in his customary expressionless voice:

'You, Quaresma, are a visionary . . .'

The tram departed. Overhead, the moon poured down its borrowed light upon the world, illuminating all things, and stirring dreams within the souls of men . . .

III

. . . And They Fell Silent . . .

'I've tried everything, Quaresma, but I don't know . . . they can't do anything.'

'Have you taken her to a specialist?'

'Yes. I've been round all the doctors, spiritual healers, even witch-doctors.'

The old man's eyes grew moist behind his pince-nez. The two had met at the War Ministry pay-office and were strolling through Sant'Ana square, talking. The general was taller than Quaresma, but whereas the latter had a long neck, the former's head was sunk between two prominent shoulders that looked like stubs of wings. Albernaz went on:

'And as for medicines! Every doctor prescribes something different. The spiritualists are the best; they use homoeopathy. The witch-doctors use infusions, prayers and incense I just don't know, Quaresma.'

He lifted his eyes up to the greyish sky, but his pince-nez did not allow him to keep that posture for long. It began to slip. Quaresma lowered his head, and walked for a while examining the stones of the path. After a few moments he looked up and said:

'Why don't you put her in a nursing home, general?'

'The doctor has already advised me to . . . But my wife won't hear of it, and with the state the girl's in now it's hardly worth while . . .'

He was referring to his daughter, Ismênia, whose condition, both mental and physical, had grown visibly worse during those last few months. She was always feverish, languishing in bed, and declining rapidly towards the cold embrace of death.

Albernaz spoke no more than the truth: in order to cure her madness and other ailments they had tried everything, accepting advice from anyone, no matter who it might be. It gave food for thought to see that man, a general, a distinguished servant of the government, having recourse to mediums and witch-doctors in an attempt to save his daughter.

Sometimes he even took them home. The mediums would go up to the girl, give a shuddering convulsion, and with wild, staring eyes scream, 'Come out, brother.' And they passed their fluttering hands rapidly and nervously to and fro between their breast and the girl so as to sprinkle her with the miraculous fluids.

The witch-doctors had other methods, and their ceremonies for communicating with the occult forces around us were long and drawn-out. Usually they were African negroes. When they arrived they lit a small stove in the bedroom, took a stuffed toad or other odd thing from a basket, beat about with bundles of herbs, performed dances and uttered unintelligible words. The ritual was complicated and could not be hurried.

When it was over, Dona Maricota, now less active and bustling than before, would look gratefully at the sorcerer's huge black face, made venerable and imposing by its white beard, and ask:

'Well?'

The negro would pause and consider for a moment as if receiving a final communication from the other world, and then say with the majestic air of the African:

'I go see, lady . . . I listen spirits . . .'

She and the general had watched the ceremony; their love for their child, together with that element of superstition that is to be found in all of us, winning for it their respect, almost their faith.

'So it was witchcraft that did this to my daughter?' asked Dona Maricota.

'That right, lady.'

'Who is responsible?'

'Saint won't say.'

And that obscure, aged negro and former slave, dragged half a century ago from the depths of the African continent, would take his departure, leaving in both their hearts a fleeting ray of hope.

It was a most interesting situation, that of this African negro. With the sufferings of his long captivity still fresh in his mind, here he was, resorting to the relics of his primitive tribal beliefs—relics that had with difficulty survived their forced removal to lands of other gods—and using them for the benefit of his former masters. It was as if the gods of his childhood and of his race, those bloodthirsty idols of mysterious Africa, were avenging him in the legendary manner of the Christ of the Gospels . . .

The sick girl watched all this without understanding or finding any interest in the antics of these all-powerful men, who were able to summon and command spirits and immaterial beings from the other world.

The general called all this to mind as he walked beside Quaresma. It filled him with bitterness against science, spirits, and sorcery, and against the God, who, remorselessly and pitilessly, was slowly taking his daughter from him.

In the face of such overwhelming grief, the major did not know what to say. It seemed to him that any words of consolation would be ridiculously inadequate. Finally he said:

'General, would you mind if I had another doctor see her?'

'Who is he?'

'My god-daughter's husband . . . You've met him . . . He's young, and you never know. What do you think? There might be a chance, mightn't there?'

The general agreed, and the hope of seeing his daughter cured smoothed some of the lines from his cheeks. He drew encouragement from every doctor he consulted, every spirit-healer and every witch-doctor, for from every one he expected a miracle. That same day Quaresma went to speak to Doctor Armando.

The revolt was already four months old, and any advantages the government had gained were problematical. In the south the insurrection had reached the gates of São Paulo, only Lapa holding out stubbornly in one of the few noble passages of the whole desperate affair. The defences of the little town were entrusted to the energetic, purposeful Colonel Gomes Carneiro, who proved himself a serene, confident and fair commander. He did not allow himself to be driven to reckless bloodshed, but he obeyed to the letter the trite, grandiloquent command, 'Fight to the death.'

Governador Island had been occupied, and Magé taken. The rebels, however, commanded the harbour entrance and the bay, which they entered and left unperturbed by any opposition from the fortresses.

The outrages and crimes committed by the government forces during these two operations reached Quaresma's ears, causing him considerable unease. On Governador Island there was a virtual removal of all furniture, clothing and other belongings. What could not be carried off was destroyed by fire and axe. The occupation left the most bitter memories, and even today people recall fearfully the cruelty and rapacity of a Captain Ortiz, who belonged either to the Volunteers or the National Guard. On one occasion a fisherman passed by with a basket of fish. Ortiz called the wretched man:

'Here, you.'

The man came up, trembling with fear, and Ortiz asked:

'How much do you want for that?'

'Three milreis, captain.'

176

The captain gave a twisted smile and haggled with him in a friendly way:

'Won't you let it go for less? . . . That's too expensive. Look, it's nothing out of the ordinary, only carapebas.'

'Alright, captain. Two fifty.'

'Take it inside.'

He was standing at the door of the house. The fisherman came back and hung about, obviously waiting for his money. Ortiz shook his head and said sarcastically:

'Oh, it's money you want. Charge it up to Floriano.'

On the other hand Moreira Cesar is well remembered, and even today people gratefully recall some kind service or other rendered them by the famous colonel.

The rebel forces appeared to be no weaker; nevertheless, they had lost two ships, one of these being the *Javari*, whose reputation during the revolt was of the very highest. The land forces in particular dreaded her. She was a monitor of French construction, low built, lying squat in the water like a steel crocodile or turtle. Her guns were held in terror; but what most infuriated her adversaries was her low freeboard: sitting so low in the water she offered no target to their uncertain marksmanship. Her engines did not work, so the huge turtle had to be towed into battle by a tug.

Then one day, near Villegagnon, she sank. No one knew what happened, and to this day the matter has never been satisfactorily explained, the government claiming that it was a shell from Gragoatá, while the rebels maintained that it was due to the opening of a valve, or some accident of that nature. Like that of its sister ship, the *Solimões*, off Cape Polônio, the loss of the *Javari* is still shrouded in mystery.

Quaresma, still with the Caju garrison, had gone to receive his pay. He had left there Polidoro, all the other officers being either sick or on leave, and also Fontes who, being a kind of inspector-general, had broken with custom and slept the night in the little imperial house, and was going to stay until evening.

Ricardo Coração dos Outros had been miserable ever since the day he had been forbidden to play the guitar. They had taken from him his life-blood, the whole moving force of his existence, and he now spent his days gloomily leaning against the trunk of a tree, silently cursing the incomprehension of his fellow men and the fickleness of fortune. Fontes noticed his low spirits, and in an attempt to lessen his suffering obliged Bustamente to make him a sergeant. This was no mean achievement, for the old Paraguay veteran held this rank in very high esteem, only conferring it in exceptional circumstances or when requested by very important people.

Thus the minstrel's life was that of a blackbird in a cage. From time to time he would venture further off and open up his lungs to see if he still had any voice left, or whether it had disappeared in the smoke of the bombardment.

Knowing that the post was in good hands, Quaresma resolved to delay his return, and after leaving Albernaz he walked to Coleoni's house to keep the promise he had made to the general.

His friend had not yet decided on his trip to Europe. He was in two minds, waiting for the end of the rebellion which did not seem to be any nearer. It was nothing to do with him, and until then he had kept his opinions hidden from everyone. If pressed, he would plead his status as a foreigner, and maintain a prudent silence. But the requirement of a passport, which had to be obtained from police headquarters, was what really worried him. In those days everyone was scared of dealing with the authorities. There was such ill-will towards foreigners, and the officials themselves were so arrogant, that he was afraid to go for the document for fear that some careless word, look or gesture might be misinterpreted by an over-zealous officer and cause him some anxious moments.

It is true that he was Italian, and that Italy had just given the dictator cause to remember that she was a great power. But the case he was thinking of concerned a sailor, whose death at the hands of the government forces had cost Floriano the sum of a hundred thousand milreis. But he, Coleoni, was not a sailor, and he had serious doubts whether, in the event of his arrest, his country's diplomatic representatives would take the same interest in securing his release.

Moreover, not having declared his intention of retaining his nationality following the government's famous naturalization decree, it was quite possible that one or other would invoke this, either to wash their hands of him or confine him in the notorious Gallery No 7 of the Reformatory, transformed, by a stroke of the pen, into a state prison.

It was a time of fear and uncertainty, and Coleoni could speak openly only to his daughter. His son-in-law was becoming an even more fervent jacobin and supporter of Floriano, and had had some bitter things to say about foreigners.

Nor was the doctor very far wrong: he had already obtained one favour from the government. He had been appointed to the Hospital de Santa Bárbara in the place of a colleague who, in the public interest, had been dismissed for his suspicious behaviour in visiting a friend in prison. But as the hospital was situated on the island of the same name, which was inside Guanabara Bay opposite Saude, and this was still in the hands of the rebels, he had nothing to do, especially as the government had so far declined his offers to assist in treating the wounded.

The major found father and daughter at home. The doctor had gone out for a walk round the city, displaying his dedication to the government cause by conversing with the most fanatical jacobins in the Café do Rio, and not forgetting to let himself be seen in the corridors of the Itamarati by the adjutants, secretaries and other persons who had the ear of the president.

When Quaresma walked in Olga again experienced that peculiar sensation that the presence of her godfather had been causing her lately. This was heightened by his accounts of his company's engagements with the enemy, being under fire, exchanging shots with the launch, all of which he described simply and naturally as if it were part of a game, a competition or some other pastime in which death was not present. She noted, too, that he was worried; certain phrases he used showed he was discouraged and despondent.

The major was, in fact, deeply troubled. His sincerity, his

179

enthusiasm and his opinion of the dictator had been severely shaken by Floriano's reception of his suggested reforms. Confident of finding a Henri IV and a Sully, he found himself face to face with a president who called him a visionary, who was incapable of appreciating the significance of his projects, never even giving himself the trouble to examine them, and who displayed a lack of interest in the higher aspects of government as if he were not president at all! . . . And was it to maintain such a man in power that he had left the peace of his own home to risk his life in the trenches? Was it for this man that so many were dying? By what right did he have power of life and death over his fellow citizens if he was not interested in their welfare and happiness, in the improvement of the country, the development of its agriculture and the good of its rural population?

There were times when such thoughts reduced him to utter despair, and his anger would be turned against himself. But then he would reflect: the man's up against it, he can't do anything now; later on he's bound to do something . . .

It was this constant, agonizing doubt that was the cause of the gloom and despondency that Olga had recognized in his downcast features.

Before long, however, Quaresma turned from the subject of his military life and explained the reason of his visit.

'Which one is it?' asked his god-daughter.

'The second one, Ismênia.'

'The one who was engaged to the dentist?'

'That's right.'

'Ohhh!'

This drawn-out 'Ohhh' was uttered with such emphasis as if it expressed her whole opinion about the matter. She understood the girl's despair, and saw only too clearly that the cause of it lay in the idea that is dinned into girls' minds of the necessity of getting married at all costs, making marriage the sole aim and goal of life, so that to remain single is a dishonour and an insult. Marriage has nothing to do with love or motherhood; it is simply marriage, something meaningless, unrelated either to our deepest instincts or to our necessities.

180

As a result of Ismênia's weak nature and feeble-mindedness, Cavalcânti's flight had been transformed into the certainty that she would never get married, and it was this shattering idea that had destroyed her.

Coleoni was interested and very much affected. In the days when he was struggling to make a fortune he had turned hard and callous; but he was essentially good-hearted, so that when he became rich he lost this veneer of harshness, for he realised that to be good you must also, in some way or another, be strong.

As for the major, tormented as he was with his own problems his interest in Albernaz' unfortunate daughter had fallen off a little lately and she had not occupied a constant place in his thoughts, yet nevertheless in his tender warm-heartedness he felt for her.

He did not stay long at his friend's house. Before returning to the Caju post he wanted to call at battalion headquarters. He was hoping to arrange a short leave of absence in order to visit his sister whom he had left behind at 'The Haven'. Although he had letters from her three times a week and her news was always satisfactory, he felt the need to see her again, and Anastácio too. Theirs were faces he had been accustomed to see every day for year after year, and he missed them. Perhaps they might help restore his tranquillity and peace of mind.

In Dona Adelaide's last letter there was a sentence that made him smile now when he remembered it: 'Don't take any risks, Policarpo. Be very careful.' Poor Adelaide! Did she think that a bombardment was no different from a shower of rain?

The headquarters was still in the old condemned tenement house out at Cidade Nova. As soon as Quaresma appeared round the corner the sentry let out a lusty bellow and made an impressive noise with his rifle. The major walked in, taking off his hat as he did so, for he was in civilian dress and had discarded his top-hat for fear that this might offend the republican susceptibilities of the jacobins.

In the yard the instructor was breaking in the new volunteers, and his majestic, long drawn-out commands —

'Shoulder . . . arms! About . . . turn!' rose up to the heavens and re-echoed round the walls of the former royal lodge.

Bustamente was in his room, or rather his office, immaculate in his bottle-green uniform with its gold lace and blue piping. With the help of a sergeant he was examining the writing in one of the official books.

'Red ink, sergeant. It's laid down in the 1864 instructions.'

He was referring to an amendment or something similar.

As soon as he saw Quaresma come in the commander exclaimed delightedly:

'Major, you must have guessed!'

Quaresma calmly put down his hat, had a drink of water, and Colonel Inocêncio explained his satisfaction:

'You know we've got marching orders?'

'Where are we going?'

'I don't know . . . I've just had orders from Itamarati.'

He would never say from general headquarters, or even from the Minister of War; it was always from Itamarati; from the president; from the supreme authority. Put like that it seemed to give more importance to himself and his battalion, making it into a kind of élite guard, favoured and beloved by the dictator.

Quaresma was neither surprised nor dismayed. He realized that his leave was now out of the question, and that moreover he would have to change his studies, abandoning the artillery and passing on to the infantry.

'You'll be in charge, major. Did you know?'

'No, colonel. Aren't you going?'

'No,' said Bustamente, stroking his long beard and speaking out of the left side of his mouth. 'I've got the organization to put straight and I can't . . . But don't worry, I'll be joining you later . . .'

It was almost evening by the time Quaresma left headquarters. The lame instructor was still bawling with majestic deliberation, 'Shoulder . . . arms!' The sentry was unable to repeat his performance with the rifle as he only noticed Quaresma when he was already far off.

182

The major went into town and called in at the post office. There was some intermittent firing. In the Café do Rio the high-priests were still discussing the consolidation of the Republic. Before he reached the post-office Quaresma suddenly remembered his forthcoming departure, so he rushed to a bookshop and bought some books on infantry. He would also need the regulations, but those he could get at general headquarters.

Where was he going? To the South, to Magé, to Niteroi? He did not know . . . He did not know . . . Oh, if only this were to bring about the realization of his dreams and desires! But who knows? . . . It could be . . . perhaps . . . Later on . . .

He passed the rest of the day tormented by doubts about the use to which he was devoting his life and his energies.

Olga's husband made no fuss about going to see the general's daughter. He was firmly convinced that with his new scientific methods he would be able to do something: Such, however, was not to be.

Although the girl's obsession was not now so pronounced, her health continued to decline. She was so thin and weak that she could scarcely sit up in bed. Her mother spent most of her time with her, for her sisters, being young, lost a little of their interest and had their attention directed towards other things. Dona Maricota had lost all her former enthusiasm for parties and dances; she was constantly at her daughter's bedside, comforting and cheering her, and there were times when, looking long at her, she felt herself to be in part responsible for her plight.

Illness had given greater strength to Ismênia's features, tautening the slackness and removing the lifelessness from her eyes. The paleness of her face enhanced the beauty of that glorious head of chestnut brown hair, flecked with gold.

She rarely spoke very much, so on that day Dona Maricota was astonished at her garrulity.

'Mother, when is Lalá getting married?'
'When the rebellion's over.'
'Isn't the rebellion over yet, then?'
Her mother answered her, and she remained quiet for a

while, gazing at the ceiling. After a short reflection she said:

'Mother . . . I'm going to die . . .'

'You mustn't say that,' said Dona Maricota. 'What do you mean, going to die! You're going to get well. Your father's going to take you to Minas where you'll get fat and get your strength back . . .'

Her mother spoke slowly, stroking the girl's cheek as if she were a child. Ismênia listened patiently, and then answered calmly:

'Come now, mother; I know! I'm going to die, and I want to ask you one favour . . .'

Dona Maricota was surprised by her firmness and seriousness. She looked round, and seeing the door half open got up to close it. She wanted to drive that idea from her daughter's mind, but Ismênia returned to it patiently and serenely:

'I know, mother!'

'Well then. Supposing it is true, what is it that you want?'

'I want to be buried in my wedding-dress, mother.'

Dona Maricota still tried to make a joke of it, but her daughter rolled over on her side and fell asleep, her breathing coming slowly and gently. She left the room with tears in her eyes; she was deeply moved, and knew in her heart that her daughter was speaking the truth.

The confirmation of this soon came. Doctor Armando had visited her that morning for the fourth time. She seemed better: for some days she had been able to sit up in bed, and she conversed sensibly and with obvious pleasure. Dona Maricota had to go and pay a visit, so that the invalid was left in the care of her sisters. They went to the bedroom from time to time to be sure she was sleeping, and passed the time amusing themselves.

Ismênia woke up, and through the half-open door of the wardrobe she saw her wedding dress. Wanting to have a closer look at it, she got up bare-foot and laid it on the bed to admire it. Then she felt the urge to try it on. As she put on the skirt there came back memories of her wedding that never was. She remembered her fiancé, Cavalcânti, with his bony nose and

184

staring eyes. But she remembered him, not with hatred, but just as if she was calling to mind some place she had visited a long time ago that had impressed her.

The one whose memory filled her with rage was the fortune-teller. Accompanied by a maid she had succeeded in eluding her mother and going to consult Mme Sinhá. How casually she had told her, 'He won't return!' How that had hurt! What an evil woman! Ever since that day . . . Ah! . . . Unable to find the corset she buttoned the skirt over her bodice and went to the mirror. When she saw her bare shoulders and her deathly white bosom she was astonished. Was that all part of her? She felt herself, and then placed the veil over her head. It caressed her shoulders like the fluttering of a butterfly's wings. Suddenly she came over weak, gave a little moan and fell backwards onto the bed,. her legs 'hanging out. When they came to see her she was dead. The veil was still over her head, and one breast, white and round, had escaped from the bodice.

She was buried the next day, and for two days Albernaz' house was as crowded as it had been during his most successful parties.

Quaresma went to the funeral. It was not a ceremony he enjoyed, but he went. He saw the poor girl in her coffin, dressed as a bride and covered with flowers, looking as immaculate as a statue. She had changed but little. It was really she who was there: it was the wretched, nervous Ismênia, with her delicate features and her glorious hair who was there in that wooden box. Death had fixed her childlike prettiness, and she went to the grave with the insignificance, the innocence and the colourlessness that had been hers in life.

Looking at those sad remains, Quaresma saw in his mind's eye the hearse stopping at the gate of the cemetery, going up the path between the tombs, thousands of them, huddled together, struggling for room in the confined space on the level and on the sides of the hills. Some tombs seemed to look lovingly at each other and want to draw closer, while others betrayed their repugnance at being so near. There, in that silent laboratory of decomposition, were to be found

185

incomprehensible yearnings, repulsion, attraction and animosity; the tombs themselves were arrogant, vain, proud, humble, gay and sad, while many of them gave evidence of an extraordinary effort to escape from the levelling influence of death with its annihilation of rank and fortune.

Quaresma was still gazing at the dead girl when this vision of the cemetery with its dense lines of sculptures passed before his eyes. Some of the tombs had urns, crosses and inscriptions; others had pyramids of rough stone, portraits, grotesque shelters, and extravagant, baroque ornaments in an attempt to escape from the anonymity of the grave, the end of everything.

There are inscriptions in abundance: long and short, with names, dates, surnames, pedigree — a complete birth certificate of the corpse down below, who being but putrefied clay is no longer able to make himself known.

And one is disappointed at not coming across a single familiar name, not one celebrity or notability whose name has resounded for decades, and who sometimes, even when dead, seems to want to go on living. All are unknown; all those who seek to rise from the tomb and engrave themselves on the memories of the living are no more than fortunate mediocrities, nonenties who made no mark in their passage through the world. It was to this place that Ismênia would come, to the oblivion of that dark hole, leaving behind her no trace of her person, her feelings, or her soul.

Quaresma went into the house in an effort to drive away this melancholy vision. He had been in the reception room where Dona Maricota was surrounded by ladies, friends of the family, who did not speak to him. Lulu, in his college uniform with a mourning band on the arm, was dozing in a chair. The sisters were continually coming and going. The general was waiting quietly in the dining-room, with Fontes and some other friends beside him. Caldas and Bustamente were standing apart, talking together in a low voice. As Quaresma passed by he heard the admiral say:

'You'll see. Their chaps will be here before long . . . The government's finished!'

The major stood by the window that looked out onto the garden. The sky, like fine, blue silk, was calm, peaceful and serene.

Estefânia, the doctor with the mischievous, sparkling eyes, walked by talking to Lalá, who from time to time dabbed her already dry eyes with her handkerchief. She was saying:

'If I were you I wouldn't buy there . . . They're expensive. Go to "Bonheur des Dames" . . . They say things there are good and very reasonable.'

The major once more gave his attention to the sky outside. Its peacefulness gave an appearance of indifference. Genelício appeared wearing extravagant mourning. He was all in black, his face fixed in the most tragic expression of grief. Even his blue-tinted pince-nez seemed to be affected. It had been impossible for him to get off work: some urgent business made his presence in the office indispensable.

'That's how it is, general,' he said. 'If Dr Genelício isn't there nothing gets done . . . There is no way of making the Navy send their documents in the correct manner . . . It's so disorganized . . .'

The general did not reply: he was too much overcome. Bustamente and Caldas went on muttering together. There was a sound of wheels outside in the road. Quinota came into the dining room.

'Father, the coach is here.'

The old man got to his feet with difficulty and went to the reception room. He spoke to his wife, who stood up, her face working. Her hair now had many threads of silver. She was unable to take a step, but remained motionless for a moment, and then collapsed, weeping, into her chair.

The others looked on without knowing what to do; some of them wept with her. Genelício took the first step, and began removing the candles from around the coffin. Dona Maricota got up, went to the coffin and kissed the body: 'Oh, my daughter!'

Quaresma went on ahead with his hat in his hand. In the corridor he heard Estefânia saying to someone: 'Isn't the coach pretty!'

187

He left the house. In the street it was more like a party. The children of the neighbourhood had surrounded the hearse and were making innocent remarks about the gilt and the decorations. The wreaths were brought out and hung on the pillars of the hearse: 'In memory of my beloved daughter' and 'My dearest sister'. The black and purple ribbons with their gilt lettering fluttered idly in the gentle breeze.

The coffin appeared, all of purple, with brilliant gold trimmings. All of it destined for the earth. On either side of the street the windows were crowded. A boy next door shouted from the road into the house: 'Mummy, come and see the lady's funeral.'

The coffin was finally firmly secured in the hearse, while the grey horses, covered with black netting, pawed the ground impatiently. Those who were going to the cemetery made for their coaches. They all got in and the procession moved off.

At that very moment, with a loud fluttering of wings, a number of immaculately white doves, Venus' own birds, flew into the air nearby. They circled above the hearse and then, with scarcely a movement of their wings, flew silently back to the dove-cot hidden amid those middle-class gardens . . .

IV
Boqueirão

Quaresma's farm in Curuzu slowly returned to the state of desolation in which he had found it. Weeds grew up and covered everything. His plantations had disappeared, invaded by grass, thistles, nettles and other plants. Close to the house the scene was heartbreaking: the tough old African, Anastácio, did his best, but though he was vigorous and hardworking he had no sense of initiative, and there was no method or continuity in his work.

One day he cleared here, the next day somewhere else, and so he went on jumping from one place to another so that all his labour made no impression. Consequently both the fields and the area near the house acquired an appearance of neglect quite disproportionate to the effort he made.

The ants returned too, more terrible and destructive than ever. Nothing could stop them; they devastated everything—the remains of the harvest, fruit-tree shoots, and they even stripped the guavas with an energy and boldness that made mockery of the pitiful expedients devised by the limited intelligence of the former slave, who was incapable of finding effective means to combat them or drive them away.

But despite all he went on planting. It was a mania with him, a vice, the stubbornness of a doting old man. He had a plot which he daily defended against the sauvas. As it had once been invaded by animals from the neighbourhood he patiently protected it with a fence made of the most inconceivable materials: kerosene tins beaten flat, good sound rafters, coconut-palm leaves, the sides of crates, etc., even though there were ample supplies of bamboo to hand.

His intelligence demanded the tortuous, the apparently easy; and this characteristic of his psyche affected all he did, whether it was his speech, with its lengthy circumlocutions, or the plots he designed, wide in one part, narrow in another, avoiding any regularity, any parallelism, any symmetry with the horror of an artist.

The rebellion had had a pacifying effect upon local politics. All parties became dedicated supporters of the government, so that between the two powerful contenders, Doctor Campos and Lieutenant Antonio, there was a unifying influence that brought them together in a spirit of reconciliation. There appeared a stronger claimant to the bone that they had struggled so furiously to possess, one who was a threat to the security of both; so for the moment they joined forces and played a waiting game.

The candidate was nominated by the central government, and election day arrived. Election time is most interesting in country districts. No one knows where so many exotic figures emerge from. So bizarre are they, that you almost expect to see doublets and breeches, lace-frills and swords. There are belted overcoats, bell-bottom trousers, silk hats — a whole museum of costumes donned by the yokels, and given a brief moment of life amid the pot-holed roads and dusty highways of the villages and townships. And there is no lack of dandies in knickerbockers, with long walking-sticks, out to see what is going on.

For Dona Adelaide, this procession of museum pieces past her doorway on their way to the polling station not far from the house was a welcome diversion that helped to break the monotony of her life. The days she spent in that isolation were long and miserable. For a long time now she had had with her, keeping her company, Felizardo's wife, an old mulatto, a kind of skeletal Medea who was famous throughout the municipality for her powers as a faith-healer. She had no equal in the art of relieving pains, reducing fevers and curing shingles; no one knew so much about the effects of medicinal herbs: bugloss, silvina, cipó-chumbo — all those remedies to be found growing in the fields, the woods and on the trunks of trees.

As well as possessing this knowledge which gained her general respect and admiration, she also served as a midwife. All the births among the poor of the neighbourhood, and even among the well-to-do, were entrusted to her special care.

It was a memorable sight to see her take a small kitchen knife and proceed to make the sign of the cross with it over the painful spot, or the job she had in hand, all the time muttering prayers to drive away the evil spirit that was present. There were stories of miracles she had performed, extraordinary deeds that attested to her strange, almost magical power over the occult forces that either molest or befriend us.

One of the most curious of these, and one which was always

being told everywhere, was about how she drove away the caterpillars. A field of beans had been invaded by thousands of caterpillars. They covered the leaves and the stems, and the owner, in despair, had given everything up for lost when he remembered the miraculous powers of Sinhá Chica. The old woman came. She surrounded the plantation with crosses made of brushwood, just as if these were the supports of a fence constructed of some invisible material. One side was left open; she took up her position at the opposite side and began to pray. Then the miracle took place. In a slow, winding column, and if coaxed along by a shepherd's crook, the caterpillars fled before her in their twos, their fours, their fives, their tens, their twenties until not a single one remained.

Doctor Campos felt not the slightest jealousy of his rival. Though rather contemptuous of the woman's superhuman powers, he never invoked any of the whole arsenal of laws which forbade the practice of such methods of healing. That would make him unpopular, and being a politician . . .

In the interior, and for this it is not necessary to go very far from Rio de Janeiro, these two schools of medicine coexist harmoniously, each attending to the mental and economic needs of the population. That of Sinhá Chica, being almost free, served the poor, those in whose minds, either by contact with others or by heredity, evil spirits and manitous still exist, and can be driven off by means of exorcism, conjuration and fumigation. Her clientele, however, was not limited to the poor who were born and bred in the region; there were even newcomers from distant lands—Italians, Portuguese and Spaniards. These had recourse to her supernatural power not so much on account of its cheapness or the contagious effect of local beliefs, but also because of that strange European superstition that all negroes and coloured people have the ability to discover malign influences and to practise witchcraft.

Whilst Sinhá Chica's liquid and herb therapy attended to the needs of the poor and destitute, that of Doctor Campos was required by the wealthier and better educated, who were sophisticated enough to demand the orthodox, official medicine.

Occasionally those of one group passed over to the other; this was when the more complicated and incurable diseases would not yield to Sinhá Chica's herbs and prayers, or when the doctor's pills and syrups had no effect.

Sinhá Chica was not the most agreeable of companions. She lived in a dream, submerged in the mysterious power of her charms, and would remain sitting cross-legged, her head lowered, with her staring, lifeless eyes looking like those of a mummy, so wrinkled and withered she was.

Nor did she forget the saints, The Holy Church, the Commandments and the orthodox prayers. Though she could not read she knew her catechism, and was also familiar with parts of the scriptures, to which she brought her own interpretations and colourful interpolations.

Together with Apolinário, the famous prayer-leader, she was the supreme spiritual authority in the district. The parish priest was relegated to the position of a kind of government official in charge of baptisms and marriages, for all communication with God and the Invisible was made through the intermediary of Sinhá Chica or Apolinário. Marriage had to be mentioned, but it could quite well be forgotten, for our poorer classes make little use of this sacrament, illicit liaisons everywhere taking the place of the solemn, catholic institution. Her husband, Felizardo, rarely appeared in Quaresma's house, and when he did it was at night. He spent his days in the bush for fear of being recruited, and as soon as he arrived he would ask his wife whether the rebellion was over. He lived in constant fear, sleeping in his clothes, and leaping out of the window to dive into the bush at the slightest sound.

They had two sons, miserable specimens of humanity. To the moral dejection of their parents they added a repulsive physical inertia and lethargy. The elder, José, was about twenty. They were both idle and listless, with no strength and no beliefs, not even in the sorcery, prayers and conjurations of their mother which their father so highly esteemed.

No one ever succeeded in putting anything into their heads or obliging them to do any sustained work. From time to time,

192

that is about once a fortnight, they would go and cut some firewood and sell it to the first inn-keeper for a half of its value. Then they would return home, cheerful and pleased with themselves, with a brightly coloured scarf, a bottle of eau-de-cologne, a mirror, or some such trinket that revealed their still primitive tastes.

Then they would spend a week at home, either sleeping or wandering about the streets and the stores. At night, and almost always on holidays and Sundays, they took with them their accordion. They were excellent players, and were always in demand whenever there was a party in the neighbourhood.

Although their parents lived in Quaresma's house, they rarely appeared there. If they did so it was because they had absolutely nothing to eat. They lived carefree and improvident even to the extent of having no fear of being recruited. Nevertheless, they were capable of affection, loyalty and good-heartedness, but to work continuously for a whole day was repugnant to their nature, like an imposition or a punishment.

This debility of our people, this kind of sickly despondency, or nirvana-like indifference to all about them, envelopes the countryside like a dark cloud of hopelessness, destroying the charm, the poetry and the seductive exuberance of nature. There is probably not one of the great oppressed nations — Poland, Ireland or India — that offers such a spectacle of stagnation as does the interior of Brazil. Here everything slumbers drowsily, sleeps, seems to be dead; there, there is revolt, idealism; with us . . . Oh . . . we sleep on . . .

With Quaresma's absence, this general atmosphere of the countryside descended on 'The Haven'. It fell asleep, an enchanted sleep, waiting for the prince to come and waken it.

Agricultural machinery that had never been used rusted away with the dealer's label still attached. Those steel ploughs that had arrived with their blades gleaming a pale blue were now in a sorry state, neglected, rotting in idleness, beckoning despairingly to the silent sky. In the morning there was no longer heard the clucking of the fowls in the chicken-run, nor the fluttering of the doves: — that morning hymn of life, work and abundance no longer mingled with the rosy sunrise and

193

the gay twittering of the birds. No one now could see the silk-cotton trees in blossom, with their lovely pink and white flowers that from time to time would drop to the earth like wounded birds.

Dona Adelaide had neither the wish nor the energy to superintend these affairs and enjoy the charm of country life. She missed her brother, and lived as though she were in the city. She bought her food at the store and did not bother about the farm.

She longed for her brother to come home. She wrote him pleading letters, to which he replied recommending patience, and making promises. The last one she had received, however, was written in quite another tone: no longer confident and enthusiastic, it betrayed discouragement, disillusionment and despair.

'Dear Adelaide, I am only now able to reply to the letter I received almost two weeks ago. As it happened, it reached me just after I had been wounded—a slight wound it is true, but one which has confined me to bed and will necessitate a long convalescence. What a battle, my child! The horror of it! When I think of it I put my hands over my eyes as if to shut out a horrible apparition. I have acquired a horror of war such as no one can possibly imagine . . . The turmoil, the hellish whistling of shells, the ghastly flashes, the curses—and all this in the depths of the night . . . At times we put aside our fire-arms and fought with bayonets, rifle-butts, axes and knives. My child, it was a struggle between cave-men, prehistoric creatures . . . I do not believe, I cannot believe in the justice of all this; I doubt the reason for it; it is not right, it cannot be right or necessary to awaken in us our dormant ferocity, that ferocity that was implanted in us thousands of years ago in combats with savage beasts for the possession of the land . . . I did not see men of our times; what I saw were Cro-Magnon men, Neanderthal men armed with flint axes, with no pity, love or generous thoughts, killing, solely bent on kill-ing . . . Even your own brother played his part too; he too discovered within himself such brutality, such ferocity, such cruelty . . . Oh my sister, I too have killed; I have

194

killed . . . Not content with killing, I have pulled the trigger when my enemy was gasping at my feet. Pardon me. I beg you to pardon me. I need pardon, and I do not know of whom I can ask it, of what God, of what man, but of someone . . . You cannot imagine my suffering . . . When I fell beneath a gun-carriage the pain I felt was not from the wound—it was deep in my soul, in my conscience. And when Ricardo fell wounded beside me, groaning and pleading, "Captain, my cap, my cap,"—it seemed like my own thought mocking my destiny.

'This life is absurd and illogical, and I am already afraid of living, Adelaide. I am afraid because we do not know where we are going, what we shall be doing tomorrow, or in what manner we shall contradict ourselves from sunrise to sunset . . .

'The best thing is to do nothing, Adelaide. As soon as I am free from my duties and responsibilities I intend to live in retirement, absolute retirement, so that from deep down within me, from the mysterious heart of things, no action of mine shall ever conjure forth passions that are foreign to my will, to bring me suffering and destroy the sweet joy of being alive . . .

'Added to which I feel that all my sacrifices have been in vain. None of my ideas has been realized. And the blood I have spilt and the suffering I shall endure for the rest of my life has been used, thrown away, wasted, slandered and prostituted for some pettifogging political end . . .

'No one understands what it is I want; no one seeks to know or to share my feelings. I am taken for a fool, an idiot, a lunatic, and life goes inexorably on in all its brutality and ugliness.'

As Quaresma said in the letter his wound was not serious, but it was a delicate one which would require time before it was completely healed and in no danger of complications setting in. Ricardo was in a worse way; but if Quaresma's suffering was essentially moral, Coração dos Outros' was physical, and he never ceased groaning and cursing the fate that had turned him into a soldier.

The hospitals where they were treated were on opposite sides of the bay, and as this was now impassable they had a twelve hours train journey from one side to the other. This meant that both coming and going the wounded Quaresma passed through his home station. But as the train did not stop he was only able to take a long, homesick look out of the window at 'The Haven', his farm, with its poor soil and ancient trees, where he had dreamed of spending peacefully the remaining years of his life, yet which had precipitated him into the most terrible of adventures.

He asked himself where, in this world, could real peace be found. Where was that haven for body and soul which he longed for so much after the storms he had weathered—where? In his mind's eye he saw the maps of continents, the boundariês of states and the plans of cities, but he could not find a single country, province, city or street where it might be.

What he felt was exhaustion, not so much physical, but moral and intellectual. He wanted never more to have to think, never more to have his deepest affections engaged. He wanted the pleasure of mere physical existence, to live for the sheer material sensation of being alive.

His convalescence was long, slow and joyless, without a single visitor or the sight of a single friendly face. Coleoni and his family had left town, and the general was too lazy and indifferent to bother. He spent these leisurely days of his convalescence alone, thinking about Destiny, his life, his ideas, and above all his disillusionments.

By now the revolt in the bay was drawing to a close. Everyone felt this, waiting anxiously for the relief it would bring. The admiral and Albernaz, however, viewed the approaching end with mortification. Their motives were identical: the first saw his dream of commanding a squadron, and consequently returning to active service, disappear; the general rued the loss of his commission, and with it those emoluments that had so conspicuously improved the family's financial situation.

Early one morning Dona Maricota roused her husband:

'Chico, get up. Don't forget you have to go to the mass for

Senator Clarimundo.'

Heeding his wife's summons Albernaz immediately jumped out of bed. He must not miss it. It was a self-imposed duty and meant a great deal. Clarimundo had been a famous republican of bold, revolutionary ideas at the time of the Empire; but after the advent of the Republic he had had nothing useful or constructive to offer to his fellow senators. Despite this he had retained a considerable measure of influence, and was referred to, along with several others, as the patriarch of the Republic.

Republican grandees have an unquenchable thirst for glory, and try desperately to impress their fame upon their posterity in an attempt not to be forgotten. Clarimundo was one of these, and during the recent troubles, for some unknown reason, his prestige grew to the point where they were even talking of him as successor to the marshal. Albernaz had known him only slightly, but it was practically a declaration of principles to attend his mass.

The painful memory of his daughter's death had by now largely disappeared. It had been her sickly condition, her madness and slow decline that had caused his suffering. Death has the virtue of shocking us by its suddenness, but it does not gnaw away at us as do those long, wasting diseases in our loved ones. Once the shock is over we are left with a tender memory, a pleasing image that is for ever before our eyes.

This is what happened with Albernaz, and his natural good-humour and *joie de vivre* insensibly began to return.

In obedience to his wife he got himself ready, dressed and went out. Although the rebellion was still taking its course, these memorial services continued to be held in churches in the centre of the city. The general arrived on time. There were many uniforms and top-hats, and everyone was pressing forward to sign their presence. It was not so much that they wished to make their respectful act known to the dead man's family; what principally concerned them was the prospect of getting their names in the newspapers.

Albernaz himself did not fail to make a bee-line for one of the lists that were lying about on the tables in the sacristy. As he was about to sign it someone spoke to him. It was the admiral. The mass was beginning but they both kept clear of the crowded nave and remained talking by one of the windows of the sacristy.

'So it'll soon be over, won't it?'

'They say the fleet's already left Pernambuco.'

Caldas had spoken first; the general's reply produced an ironical smile, and he said:

'At last . . .'

'They've got a circle of guns all round the bay,' went on the general after a pause, 'and the marshal is going to call on them to surrender.'

'About time,' said Caldas. 'If I'd had anything to do with it it would have been all over by now . . . taking seven months to deal with a few broken down tramp steamers! . . .'

'You're exaggerating, Caldas; it wasn't so easy as all that. What about the sea?'

'What was the fleet doing shut up so long in Recife, tell me that? Ah, if yours truly had had any say it would soon have left and gone into the attack! . . . I'm all for quick decisions.'

Inside the church the priest was still interceding with God for the repose of the soul of Senator Clarimundo. There came the mysterious smell of incense, but this perfumed offering to the God of peace and goodwill was unable to distract them from their warlike meditations.

'We've nobody left who's any good,' said Caldas. 'This country's done for; we'll end up being a British colony.'

He scratched nervously at one of his sideboards and stared down at the tiled floor for a moment.

'Not now it won't.' Albernaz put in, half sarcastically. 'The authorities have acquired prestige and support — a new era of progress is opening up for Brazil.'

'The hell it is! Where have you ever seen a government . . .'

'Not so loud, Caldas.'

'. . . where have you ever seen a government that makes no use of the country's talent, neglecting it, leaving it to rot? . . . It's the same with our natural resources: they're just lying about, going to waste.'

198

The bell tinkled and they glanced at the crowded nave. Through the door they could see a group of men all dressed in black, kneeling penitently and beating their breast as they muttered the confession: *mea culpa, mea maxima culpa* . . . A shaft of sunlight found its way through an opening high up and shone on some of the heads. The two men in the sacristy instinctively raised their hand to their breast and joined in the confession: *mea culpa, mea maxima culpa* . . .

The mass came to an end and they both moved forward to pay the customary respects. The nave, full of the heavy odour of incense, gave a comforting sense of immortality.

All bore signs of unutterable grief: friends and relations, the known and the unknown, all seemed to suffer equally. Albernaz and Caldas were seized by this deep emotion as they moved into the body of the church, and set the expression of their faces accordingly.

Genelício was there too. He was addicted to masses for important people, messages of condolence and birthday greetings. For fear that his memory might fail him he kept a little book where he noted down the dates of birthdays together with the appropriate addresses. The index was very carefully arranged. There was no mother-in-law, cousin, aunt, or sister-in-law of an important personage who failed to receive his congratulations on her birthday, or whose death did not bring him to church for the seventh day memorial mass. His mourning suit was of thick, heavy cloth, and whoever looked at him was instantly reminded of some Dantesque punishment.

In the street Genelício was brushing his top-hat with the sleeve of his overcoat and talking to his father-in-law and the admiral.

'It's nearly over . . . Soon . . .'

'And what if they resist?' asked the general.

'Not on your life! They won't resist! People are saying they've already offered to surrender . . . What's needed is a manifesto to the marshal . . .'

'I don't believe it,' said the admiral. 'I know Saldanha well, and he's too proud to give himself up like that . . .'

Genelício was a little alarmed at his relative's tone of voice. He was afraid that he might speak louder and call attention to himself so that he, Genelício, would be compromised. He kept quiet, but Albernaz went on:

'Pride's no good against a superior squadron.'

'Superior! Cockle-shells, man!'

With difficulty Caldas restrained the fury boiling inside him. Above, the sky was blue and calm. Some light, scattered clouds drifted along like white sails in a boundless sea. Genelício looked at him for a moment and then said:

'Admiral, don't talk like that . . . Consider . . .'

'What! I'm not afraid . . . Balls! . . .'

'Well,' said Genelício, 'I have to go to the Rua Primeiro de Março and . . .'

He took his leave and went off in his dark suit. He walked down the street with his short, measured step, stooping and gazing at the ground through his blue-tinted pince-nez.

Albernaz and Caldas remained for a while talking, and then parted as friendly as ever, each with his own private grievance and disappointment.

The forecasts proved right: the rebellion came to an end a few days later. The loyalist squadron arrived; the rebel officers fled in Portuguese warships, and Marshal Floriano was left master of the bay.

The day the squadron sailed in a large part of the population abandoned the city in the belief that there was going to be a bombardment. They sought refuge in the suburbs, under trees, in friends' houses or in shelters specially built by the State. It was an affecting sight to see the terror, anxiety and horror stamped on their faces. As well as bundles of clothes, baskets and small cases, they were carrying crying babies, pet dogs and parrots, and the cage birds that for so long had cheered the wretchedness of a poor man's house.

What they most dreaded was the *Niteroi*'s famous American gun, a devilish weapon that was capable of causing earthquakes and rocking the base of Rio's granite mountains. Even beyond the range of its shells the women and children were terrified of its thunderous report. And yet this phantasma, this Yankee nightmare with a force almost as strong as nature's ended its days on the quayside, abandoned, neglected and reduced to impotence.

The end of the rebellion, which was already becoming monotonous, brought general relief, while his victory elevated the marshal to almost superhuman status.

About this time Quaresma was released from hospital, and one detachment of his battalion was sent to garrison Enxadas Island. From the interior of his office at the headquarters in the condemned tenement block Bustamente continued zealously supervising his force. The accounts were up to date and recorded in perfect handwriting.

It was with extreme reluctance that Quaresma accepted the role of jailer, for Enxadas Island had been made into a camp for naval prisoners. Such a function only served to increase his inner suffering. In a mixture of annoyance and pity he tried not to look at them, feeling sure that one amongst them must know the secret of his conscience.

Moreover, his whole system of ideas—the reason for his participation in the civil war—had crumbled to pieces. He had not found a Sully, still less a Henri IV. He realised too that the ideas that had motivated him were not to be found in any of the people that he had met. They felt no nobler impulse, being activated either by puerile political theories or by self-interest. Even among the young men, of whom there were many, although their motives were not selfish they made a fetish of the republican system, exaggerating its virtues, and tending towards a despotism that his studies and reflections had convinced him was not just.

The prisoners were crowded into what had been the cadets' classrooms and living quarters. There were seamen and non-commissioned officers, clerks and shipboard workers; there were whites, negroes, mulattos, caboclos—men of every colour and description. These were men who had become involved in the venture by their habit of obedience, who had no connection whatever with the issue at stake; they were men who had been dragged by force from their homes or the street

201

corners; they were young, immature or who had enlisted out of despair; they were simple, ignorant, sometimes cruel and perverse like innocent children, sometimes gentle and docile like lambs; in short, they were men with no responsibility, no political ambitions, no will of their own—mere puppets in the hands of the leaders and officers who had abandoned them to the mercy of the conquerer.

In the evening he would go for a walk and gaze at the sea. There was a breeze blowing and the gulls were hunting for fish. Ships passed. Sometimes they were smoky launches going to the far end of the bay; sometimes they would be small boats or canoes skimming gently over the water, leaning this way and that as if their white, smoke-stained sails wished to caress the mirror-like surface. The distant Orgão mountains slowly dissolved in shades of delicate violet; the rest was blue, an immaterial blue that dizzied the senses like a heady wine.

He would stay there a long time, watching, and on his way back he would look at the dusk falling on the city, held for a moment in the crimson embrace of the setting sun.

As night came Quaresma would still be walking beside the sea, deep in meditation, tortured by the memories of hatred, bloodshed and ferocity. It seemed to him that life and society were hideous, and that they themselves provided the example for crimes that the latter punished and sought to repress. His thoughts were black and despairing; many a time he thought he was going out of his mind. He regretted his loneliness, wishing that he had a companion to talk to and so help drive away those gloomy thoughts that beset him, and which were being transformed into an obsession. Ricardo was with the garrison on Cobras Island, but even if he were with him the rigours of army discipline would not permit a more intimate conversation. Night closed in completely, covering everything with a blanket of darkness and silence.

Deep in thought, Quaresma stayed some hours longer out in the open, gazing at the far end of the bay where there were few lights to break the solid curtain of darkness. So intent was his gaze that it was as if he was trying to accustom his eyes to penetrate the obscurity, and within the blackness to guess the

202

shape of the mountains and the outline of the islands that had disappeared into the night.

He would retire to bed worn out, though he rarely enjoyed a good night's rest. He suffered from insomnia, but if he tried to read he found it impossible to fix his attention on his book, and his thoughts would go wandering far away.

One night when he was sleeping rather better he was awakened at dawn by one of his men.

'Major, sir, the man from Itamarati's here.'

'Who?'

'The officer who comes for the Boqueirão squad.'

Without knowing what it was all about, Quaresma got up and went to meet his visitor. The man was already inside one of the buildings. There was an escort at the door. He was followed by a number of soldiers, one of whom carried a lantern which threw a weak yellow light round the room.

The huge room was full of half-naked men, of every conceivable colour, lying stretched out on the ground. Some were snoring, others slept peacefully, and as Quaresma entered one groaned out loud in his sleep. He shook hands with the man from Itamarati but neither spoke. They were both afraid of speaking. The officer woke one of the prisoners and said to the soldiers, 'Take this one.'

He moved on further and woke another: 'Where were you?' 'I was on the *Guanabara*, said the sailor. 'Were you, you dog!' retorted the man from Itamarati . . . 'This one too . . . off with him!'

The soldiers led him to the door, handed him over, and returned.

The officer passed by a group of them without making any observation. Further on he noticed a small, fair boy who was not sleeping. 'Get up,' he roared. The boy stood up, trembling. 'Where were you?' he asked. 'I was a nurse,' said the boy. 'A nurse!' said the officer. 'Take this one too.' 'But lieutenant, sir, let me write to my mother,' pleaded the lad, almost in tears. 'Your mother!' answered the man from Itamarati. 'Get out there! Quick!'

Like this a dozen were picked out at random, surrounded by

the escort and put on board a barge which was immediately towed away from the island by a launch.

At first Quaresma did not realize the significance of what he had seen. It was not until the launch had drawn away that he found an explanation. Then he could not help wondering what mysterious force, what ironical destiny had caused him to become involved in such horrible concerns, and to witness the frightful means by which the régime was being consolidated . . .

The vessel was not far off. The sea murmured continuously against the stones of the jetty. The ship's wake left a phosphorescent glow on the water. Overhead the stars shone serenely in the vast blackness of the night sky.

The launch disappeared into the darkness of the bay. Where was it going? To Boqueirão . . .

V
Olga

It seemed so illogical to him to be shut up there in that narrow prison. Did he, the gentle Quaresma, the Quaresma of those ambitious, patriotic ideas deserve this tragic end? By what cunning means had Destiny brought him to this, keeping him unsuspicious of her extravagant design, so apparently out of keeping with the rest of his life? Was it he himself by his past activities, the whole sequence of them, that had caused the old god to lead him docilely to the execution of his purpose? Or had he been the victim of external circumstances, making him a slave to the will of the omnipotent divinity? He could not tell;

the more he thought about it the more confused and entangled the two ideas became so that he was unable to come to any definite conclusion.

He had not been there for many hours. He had been arrested in the morning shortly after he got up. By a rough calculation he decided it must be about eleven o'clock: he was without his watch, but even if he had had it he would not have been able to read it in the feeble light of the dungeon.

Why was he under arrest? He could not say for certain. The officer who had escorted him refused to explain, and on his way from Enxadas to Cobras Island he had neither spoken to anyone nor seen anyone he knew, not even Ricardo, who with a look or a wave would have been able to calm the doubts in his mind. But he attributed his arrest to the letter he had written to the president protesting against the scene he had witnessed the day before.

He had been unable to restrain himself. That batch of wretches chosen at random and led off in the early hours to a brutal execution had pierced him to the very depths. It had brought before his eyes all his moral principles, challenging his moral courage and common humanity, and he had written the letter with vehemence, passion and indignation. He spared nothing of his thought, but wrote clearly, frankly and directly.

This must be why he was caged up, cut off from his fellow beings like a wild beast or a criminal, locked in that dark dungeon, foul with damp and his own excrement, almost without food . . . What will they do with me? What will become of me? This was the question he asked himself amid the tumult of thoughts occasioned by his distress. There was nothing on which to base an opinion. The Government's behaviour was so variable and uncertain that he could expect anything: liberty or death, but more likely death.

It was a time of death, of executions; everyone had this lust to kill in order to assert their victory, to be sure in their hearts that the triumph and the honour belonged to them.

He was going to die; perhaps that very night. What had he done with his life? Nothing. Because of this intense love of his he had spent it all pursuing a mirage, studying his native land in the hope of contributing to its happiness and prosperity. For this he had wasted his youth and his manhood too; and now that he was an old man what recompense, what reward, what decoration did he receive? A shameful death. What had he failed to see, to experience, to enjoy in life? Everything. Simple pleasures and amusements, love — all that side of our existence that is a little removed from its essential sadness he had never seen, never known.

From the age of eighteen patriotism had been the moving force of his life; for its sake he had committed the folly of studying trivialities. What did rivers matter to him? If they were long what difference did it make? How much happier did it make him to have known the names of his country's heroes? Not a whit. The important thing is that he should have been happy. Had he been? No. He called to mind his Tupí, his folklore and his attempts at farming . . . Had they left in him any trace of satisfaction? None at all. None at all.

His Tupí had been greeted with general incredulity, laughter, mockery and scorn; it had been the cause of his madness. This was his first disillusionment. And agriculture? Again nothing. The soil was not fertile or easy to cultivate as the books said. A second disillusionment. And when his patriotism turned him into a soldier what did he find? More disillusionment. Where was the meekness of our people? Hadn't he seen them fighting like animals? Hadn't he seen them slaughtering countless prisoners? Yet more disillusionment. His life had been one long disillusionment, or rather a series, a whole chain of disillusionments.

His native country as he wished it to be was a myth, a phantasy conjured up in the silence of his study. In the sense that he had imagined it it simply did not exist, neither physically, morally, intellectually nor politically. What did exist was the Brazil of Lieutenant Antonino, of Doctor Campos, of the man from Itamarati.

And when we come to consider it, what does 'fatherland' really mean? Could it not be that his whole life had been orientated by an illusion, a false idea with no basis in reality, by some god or goddess whose dominion was passing away?

206

Did he not know that this idea originated from the belief of the Greco-Roman peoples that their dead ancestors lived on as shades, and that it was necessary to sustain them so that they would not molest their descendants? He remembered his Fustel de Coulanges . . . He remembered that this notion is meaningless to the Menenanā and to so many people . . . It seemed to him that this idea had been exploited by the conquerors, momentarily aware of our psychological weaknesses, in order to serve their own interests . . .

He considered history, examining the territorial gains and losses of all different countries, and he asked himself what conception a Frenchman, an Englishman, an Italian or a German would have of his fatherland if he had lived for four centuries.

For the Frenchman, at one time Franche-Comté was the land of his fathers, but later it wasn't; at one moment Alsace wasn't, then it was, and finally it wasn't any more.

We ourselves, didn't we once own Cisplatina and then lose it? And don't we sometimes suffer at the thought of the spirits of our forefathers that linger there?

This notion obviously had no rational basis and urgently needed to be revised. Then how was it that such a calm, clear-thinking man as he had wasted his time, devoted his life and grown old in the service of a mere chimera? How could he not have suspected, not have recognized the truth instead of allowing himself to be deceived by a false idol, worshipping it and offering it his whole life as a sacrifice? It was his solitariness, his neglect of himself. And as a result he would go to the grave leaving no trace of himself behind—no son, no love, no passionate kiss, nothing—not even an indiscretion. The world had withheld her delights from him, and he left nothing behind that would attest his passage through life.

But who knows, those who were to come after him might be happier? The answer, however, soon came. How could that be if he remained silent, left no message, failed to perpetuate his dream by giving it form and substance. And even if he had done so what would it achieve? Would this eventually bring any measure of happiness to the world? For countless years worthier lives than his had been offered up and sacrificed, yet things remained the same; the suffering, the oppression and the misery of the world were unchanged.

And he remembered that a hundred years ago, here in the same place where he was, perhaps in that very prison, illustrious noble-minded men had been confined for wanting to better the state of things in their days. Perhaps they had done no more than express a wish, but they had been punished for the thought. Had it brought any advantages? On the surface, yes; but closely considered, no.

The trial of those men, accused of a crime that was heinous by the laws of those times, had taken two years. But he, who had committed no crime whatever, was not even heard, not even judged; he was simply sent to his death.

He had been good, unselfish, honest and virtuous—he had been all this, and yet he was going to the grave without the comforting presence of a relative, a friend or companion . . . Where were they all? Would he never again set eyes on Ricardo Coração dos Outros, so simple and innocent in his enthusiasm for the guitar? Oh it would be so good if he could do so, for then he could send a last message to his sister, a good-bye to the old negro, Anastácio, and an affectionate hug to his god-daughter. He would never see them again; never. And he could not restrain his tears.

About one point, however, Quaresma was mistaken. Ricardo had learned of his arrest and was trying to secure his release. He was exactly informed about the reason for it, but even so he was not discouraged. He knew perfectly well that he was running a grave risk, for at the palace there was general indignation against Quaresma. Victory had made the conquerors merciless and arrogant, and his protest had been seen as a wish to reduce the value of those advantages they had gained. There was no longer any pity or kindness or respect for human life; what was needed was to make an example by a massacre, a furtive one though, in the true Turkish manner, so that the constituted authority should never again be attacked or even questioned. This was the social philosophy of the time which, with the strength of a religion, had its own fanatics, priests and preachers, and was productive of all the cruelty of a creed which we believe vital to the happiness of the majority.

Ricardo, however, was not deterred, and set about procuring the influence of friends. As he was going into the Largo de São Francisco he met Genelício, who was coming from the mass in memory of Deputy Castro's mother-in-law's sister. As always he was wearing his heavy, leaden-looking black overcoat. He was already assistant director, and now his main concern was to think up ways and means of becoming director. It wasn't so easy, but he was working on a book, *Audit Offices in Asiatic Countries*, which, revealing as it did erudition of the highest order, might put the coveted position within his grasp.

On seeing him Ricardo did not hesitate. He ran after him and said:

'Sir, could I have a word with you please?'

Genelício drew himself up, and affecting a bad memory for humble faces he asked solemnly and arrogantly:

'What do you want, my man?'

Coração dos Outros was wearing his 'Southern Cross' uniform, and it would not do for Genelício to show that he was acquainted with a mere soldier. The singer, believing that he had really forgotten, asked innocently:

'Don't you remember me, sir?'

Genelício closed his eyes for a moment behind his blue-tinted pince-nez, and said dryly:

'No.'

'I'm Ricardo Coração dos Outros, who sang at your wedding,' said Ricardo humbly.

'Oh yes, of course. Well, what is it you want?'

'Did you know that Major Quaresma has been arrested?'

'Who's he?'

'He used to be your father-in-law's neighbour.'

'That madman . . . Ah yes . . . What about it?'

'I was wondering if you might . . .'

'I never interfere in these matters, my friend. The government knows best. Good day to you.'

209

Genelício went on his way with the measured step of one who is trying to save the soles of his shoes, leaving Ricardo standing gazing at the square, the passers-by, the motionless statue, the ugly houses, the church . . . Everything seemed hostile, evil or indifferent; the faces of the men had the appearance of beasts, and Ricardo felt like crying with despair at not being able to save his friend.

Then he remembered Albernaz and ran off in search of him. It was not far to go but the general had not yet arrived. He appeared an hour later, and on seeing Ricardo, asked:

'What's the matter?'

In a voice shaking with emotion the singer told him what had happened. Albernaz adjusted his pince-nez, fixed the gold chain on his ear and said mildly:

'My boy, I can't . . . You know how it is; I'm for the government, and it would look bad if I were to intercede for a prisoner . . . I'm very sorry, but . . . what's to be done? Be patient.'

And he went gaily into his office, serene and self-confident in his general's uniform.

Officers went in and out, bells tinkled and attendants bustled about. Ricardo scanned every face in the hope of finding someone he could turn to, but not finding one he began to despair. Who could help him? Who? Then he remembered: the commander; and he set off once more to speak to Colonel Bustamente in the old lodge that served as headquarters for the gallant 'Southern Cross'.

The battalion was still on a war footing, for although the revolt in the port of Rio de Janeiro had been put down it was necessary to send forces to the south. As a result the battalions had not been disbanded, and among those due to leave was the 'Southern Cross'.

The lame second lieutenant was still at his post in the soap-stained yard training the new recruits: 'Should. . . er . . . arms! Abou . . . t turn!'

Ricardo went in, ran swiftly up the tottering staircase of the old tenement house, and as soon as he reached the commander's office he shouted: 'May I speak to you, colonel?'

210

Bustamente was in a bad temper. This business of leaving for Paraná was not at all to his liking. How could he supervise the accounts in the heat of battle and the confusion of marches and countermarches? It was crazy to order the commander to go; his job was to stay with the rearguard taking charge of the books. These thoughts were passing through his mind when Ricardo asked to speak to him.

'Come in,' he said.

The doughty colonel was stroking his long beard; his jacket was unbuttoned and he had just put on one of his boots so as to be more decently dressed to receive his inferior.

Ricardo explained the purpose of his visit and waited patiently for the answer, which was a long time coming. Finally Bustamente shook his head, and in a tone of awful severity said:

'Be off with you or I'll have you arrested. At once.'

And he thrust his finger in the direction of the door with a fine martial gesture. Ricardo needed no second bidding. Outside in the yard the lame instructor, veteran of the Paraguay War, was still solemnly bawling out his commands, which re-echoed round the decaying building: 'Should-
. . . er . . . arms! Abou . . . t turn!'

Ricardo was downcast and despondent. The world seemed empty of love and affection. In his modinhas he had always sung the praises of love, devotion and faithfulness, and now he saw that such feelings did not exist. He had been seeking for things that were without the pale of reality, mere chimeras. He gazed up at the sky. It was calm and peaceful. He looked at the trees. The palms stood up proudly like Titans reaching for the sky. He looked at the houses, the churches and the large buildings, and he thought of the wars, the blood and the pain that it had all cost. This was how life, history and heroism were made: with violence, oppression and suffering.

Soon, however, he remembered that he had to save his friend and that it was necessary for him to do something. Who could help? He racked his brain. Turning the various possibilities over one by one he finally remembered Quaresma's god-daughter, and set off to Real Grandeza in

211

search of her.

On arrival there he described what had happened and told her of his fears for the outcome. She was alone, for her husband was busier than ever, never wasting a minute, dogging the heels of the authorities to be sure of getting his share of the spoils of victory.

A clear image of her godfather formed in Olga's mind: she saw that eternal dream of his, his gentleness, the stubbornness with which he pursued his ideas, his innocence like that of a maiden of romance . . .

For a moment she was overcome with an immense pity which robbed her of the will to act. She felt that this pity of hers would be enough and that in some way or another it would ease her godfather's sufferings. But then she pictured him covered in blood, so kind-hearted, so good, and she resolved to save him.

'But what can we do, my dear Senhor Ricardo, what can we do? I don't know anyone . . . I've no relations . . . My friends . . . There's Alice, Doctor Brandão's wife, but she's away . . . Castriota's daughter Cassilda can't do anything . . . Oh my God, I just don't know.'

These last words were uttered in an anguished tone of desperation. Neither of them spoke. The girl, who was sitting, buried her head in her hands thrusting her long, shiny nails into her dark hair. The bewildered Ricardo stood by her.

'Oh God, what can I do?' she repeated.

For the first time she realized that there are certain things in life that are beyond hope. She had the strongest possible determination to save her godfather; she would sacrifice anything and everything; but it was impossible, utterly impossible. There was no way, no means. He must go to his execution; he must face his Calvary with no hope of a resurrection.

'What about your husband?' suggested Ricardo.

She paused for a moment, considering carefully her husband's character: but it was not long before she realized that his egoism, his ambition and his relentless self-seeking would effectively prevent him taking the slightest step.

212

'Who, that . . .'

Ricardo, not knowing what to say, looked blankly at the furniture and the high, black mountain that could be seen from the room where they were. He wanted to be able to make a suggestion, give some advice, but no ideas came.

The girl was still twisting her fingers in her dark hair, gazing down at the table where her elbows rested. The silence continued.

Suddenly Ricardo's face brightened and he said:

'If you were to go there . . .'

Olga raised her head; her face grew taut and her eyes widened with surprise. After a moment's reflection she said firmly:

'I'll go.'

She went off to get dressed, leaving Ricardo alone.

As he sat there he was filled with admiration for that girl who for the sake of mere friendship was prepared to run such a terrible risk; who was so remarkably self-possessed, and whose spirit soared so far above this our egoistic, sordid world. And he felt a great surge of gratitude towards her.

It was not long before she was ready to go out, and she was just buttoning her gloves in the dining room when her husband arrived. He was radiant, with his huge moustaches and his round face beaming with self-satisfaction. He gave no sign of having seen Ricardo and went straight up to his wife:

'Are you going out?'

She was flushed on account of her desperate anxiety to save Quaresma, and answered rather sharply:

'Yes, I am.'

Armando was surprised to hear her speak in that tone. He turned towards Ricardo as if to question him, but then addressed his wife, speaking authoritatively:

'Where are you going?'

As his wife did not answer immediately he spoke to the singer:

'What are you doing here?'

Before Coração dos Outros could pluck up courage to reply, for he foresaw a violent scene which he would have preferred to avoid, Olga intervened:

'He's going with me to Itamarati. Now you know.'

Her husband appeared to calm down. He believed that with a little persuasion he could prevent her from taking this step that would be so hazardous for his own interests and ambitions. He said lightly:

'That's most unwise.'

'Why?' she asked heatedly.

'Because you'll compromise me. You know . . .'

She did not reply immediately, but gazed at him scornfully with her large eyes; the moments passed, then she gave a little laugh and said:

'Of course. "I", and "because I"; it's only "I" here and "I" there . . . You don't think of anything else . . . Life is made just for you; everyone has to live just for you . . . It's very funny! And so I—now it's my turn to say "I"—I have no right to sacrifice myself, to show my friendship, to do anything above the ordinary in my life? It's most interesting! I am nothing, nothing at all! Am I some object like a piece of furniture, an ornament, with no friends, no interests, no character? Really!'

At one moment she spoke slowly and ironically, at another, rapidly and passionately. Her husband was dumbfounded by her words. He had always lived at such a distance from her that he never imagined her capable of such a fit of anger. Could this be that child? Could this be that 'bibelot'? Where had she learnt all this? He tried to disarm her with irony, and said with a smile:

'Do you think you're on the stage?'

She flashed back:

'If noble actions are only performed on the stage then I am.'

And she added with greater emphasis:

'I tell you I'm going: I'm going because I have to go, because I want to go, and because it is my right to go!'

She picked up her parasol, straightened her veil, and left the room, head erect, proud and dignified. Her husband was utterly at a loss what to do. He was stupefied. And in silent stupefaction he watched her walk out through the front door.

Before long they were at the palace in the Rua Larga.

214

Ricardo did not go in, but left the girl to do so and went to wait for her in the Campo de Sant'Ana.

She went in. The place was in an uproar with so many people coming and going. Everyone wanted to be seen by Floriano, to congratulate him, demonstrate their loyalty, and show by the services they had rendered that they were co-partners in his victory. To achieve this they used every means and employed every wile and stratagem. But the dictator, formerly so accessible, now held himself aloof. There were even those who wanted to kiss his hands like a pope or an emperor, but he was sickened by such servility. The caliph did not imagine himself sacred, and his irritation grew.

Olga spoke to the attendants asking for an audience with the marshal. It was useless. With great difficulty she succeeded in speaking to one of the secretaries or adjutants, but when she mentioned the purpose of her visit the man's clay-coloured features turned pale and a sudden glint flashed into his eyes:

'Who, Quaresma?' he cried. 'A traitor! A criminal!'

Then repenting of his vehemence he added more politely:

'It's impossible, madam. The marshal won't see you.'

She did not bother to wait for the end of the sentence. She drew herself up proudly and turned her back on him. She was ashamed at having asked, of having sunk her pride and tarnished the moral greatness of her godfather by her request. With such men as these it was better to have left him to a lonely, heroic death in some remote spot, carrying intact to the grave his pride, his gentleness and his moral integrity unstained by any solicitation that might diminish the injustice of his death, or make his executioners believe they had the slightest shred of justification for their deed.

She left the building, and as she walked away she gazed up at the sky and the trees on Santa Teresa hill. Here in these parts, she reflected, there once lived savage tribes, one of whose chiefs gloried in the deaths of ten thousand enemies. That was four centuries ago. She looked again at the sky, the trees, the houses and the churches; she saw the trams passing by; a locomotive whistled; a splendid coach and pair crossed in front of her as she was about to enter the square . . . So many

215

great changes had taken place. What had that park been? A bog perhaps. The land itself—its character and appearance, perhaps even its climate—was so much altered . . . Let us wait a little longer, she thought, and walked calmly on to her rendezvous with Ricardo Coração dos Outros.

Todos os Santos (Rio de Janeiro), January–March 1911